Claudia Piñeiro lives in Buenos Aires. For many years she was a journalist, playwright and television scriptwriter and in 1992 won the prestigious Pléyade journalism award. She has more recently turned to fiction and is the author the crime novel *Tuya* (finalist for the 2003 Planeta Prize), *Elena sabe* and *Un ladrón entre nosotros. Thursday Night Widows* is her first novel to be available in English and won the Clarín Prize for fiction in 2005.

T0153549

THURSDAY NIGHT

WIDOWS

Claudia Piñeiro

Translated by Miranda France

BITTER LEMON PRESS
LONDON

BITTER LEMON PRESS
First published in the United Kingdom in 2009 by
Bitter Lemon Press, 37 Arundel Gardens, London W11 2LW

www.bitterlemonpress.com
First published in Spanish as *Las viudas de los jueves*
by Clarín/Alfaguara, Buenos Aires, 2005

Bitter Lemon Press gratefully acknowledges the financial
assistance of the Arts Council of England

© Claudia Piñeiro, 2005
English translation © Miranda France, 2009
Published by arrangement with Literarische Agentur
Dr. Ray-Güde Mertin
Inh. Nicole Witt e. K., Frankfurt am Main, Germany

A CIP record for this book is available from the British Library

ISBN 978-1-904738-41-1

Typeset by Alma Books Limited
Printed and bound by CPI Group (UK) Ltd, Croydon, CR0 4YY

To Gabriel and to my children

Yes, I have tricks in my pocket. But I am the opposite of a stage magician. He gives you illusion that has the appearance of truth. I give you truth in the pleasant disguise of illusion. To begin with, I turn back time. I reverse it to that quaint period, the Thirties, when the huge middle class of America was matriculating in a school for the blind.

Tennessee Williams, *The Glass Menagerie*

Without servants there can be no tragedy, only a sordid bourgeois drama. While you are washing your own tea cup and emptying the ashtrays, passion ebbs away.

Manuel Puig, *Under a Mantle of Stars*

1

I opened the fridge and stood there for a moment with my hand still on the door, bathed in the cold light, gazing blankly at the illuminated shelves. Only the alarm going off, warning that the open door was letting out cold air, brought me back to my senses and reminded me why I was standing in front of the fridge. I looked for something to eat. I collected some of the previous day's leftovers on a plate, warmed them up in the microwave and took them to the table. I didn't put on a tablecloth, just one of those rafia place mats brought back from Brazil a couple of years ago, from one of the last holidays the three of us took together. I mean as a family. I sat down opposite the window – it wasn't my usual place at the table, but I liked to look out at the garden when I was eating alone. That night, the night in question, Ronie was having dinner at El Tano Scaglia's house. The same as every Thursday – except that this day was different. It was a Thursday in September 2001. Thursday 27th September 2001. *That* Thursday. We were all still in shock after the attack on the Twin Towers and were opening our letters wearing rubber gloves, for fear of finding white powder inside. Juani had gone out. I didn't ask him where, or with whom. Juani didn't like to be asked. But I knew anyway. Or I thought I did.

I ate almost without dirtying any plates. A few years back I had accepted that we could no longer afford full-time domestic staff, and now a woman came only twice a week to do the heavy work. Meanwhile, I had learned how to create the least possible mess: I knew how to keep my clothes crease-free and how to leave the bedclothes scarcely rumpled. It wasn't so much that the chores were a burden, but washing plates, making beds and ironing clothes reminded me of what I had once had, and lost.

I thought of going out for a walk, but I was nervous of running into Juani, in case he thought I was spying on him. It was hot; the night was star-filled and luminous. I didn't want to go to bed if it meant lying awake, worrying about some property transaction that was not yet complete. At that time, it felt as though every deal were doomed to collapse before I'd had a chance to collect my commission. We had already weathered a few months of the economic crisis. Some people were putting a better face on it than others, but one way or another all our lives had changed – or were about to change. I went to my room to look for a cigarette. I had decided to go out, regardless of Juani, and I liked to smoke as I walked. As I passed my son's room, I thought of going in to look for cigarettes there, but I knew that I wouldn't find any. It would simply be an excuse to go in and poke around, and I had already done that this morning, when I had made his bed and tidied his room – and I hadn't found what I was looking for then, either. I went on to my room, where there was a new packet on the bedside table; I opened it, took out a cigarette, lit it and went down the stairs, ready to go out. That was when Ronie came in and my plans changed. Nothing turned out as expected that night.

Ronie went straight to the bar. "Strange you're back so soon…" I said, from the foot of the stairs.

"Yes," he said, and went upstairs with a glass and a bottle of whisky. I waited for a moment, standing there, and then I followed him up. I walked past our bedroom, but he wasn't in there. Nor was he in the bathroom. He had gone out to the terrace and was settled onto a lounger, preparing to drink. I pulled up a chair, sat down next to him and waited, following his gaze but saying nothing. I wanted him to tell me something. Not anything important or funny or even particularly meaningful – but just for him to play his usual part in the scanty exchange to which our conversations had been reduced over the years. We had an unspoken agreement to string set phrases together, to let words fill the silence, with the aim of never addressing the silence itself. They were empty words, husks of words. If I ever complained, Ronie argued that we spoke little because we spent too much time together – how could there be anything new to talk about when we had not been apart for most of the day? Yet these were our circumstances ever since Ronie had lost his job six years ago and had not found any other occupation, apart from one or two "projects" that never amounted to anything. I was not anxious to discover why our relationship had gradually become stripped of words, so much as why it was that I had only recently noticed the silence that had taken up residence in our house, like a distant relative whom one has no choice but to accommodate and look after. Why did it not cause me more pain? Perhaps it was because the pain was taking hold very gradually and in silence. Like the silence itself.

"I'm going to fetch a glass," I said.

"Bring some ice, Virginia," Ronie shouted after me, when I had already gone inside.

I went to the kitchen and, while filling up the ice bucket, pondered different explanations for Ronie's early return. My hunch was that he had argued with someone. With El Tano Scaglia, or with Gustavo, surely. Not with Martín Urovich, because Martín had given up fighting with anyone, even himself, ages ago. Back on the terrace, I asked Ronie point-blank – I didn't want to find out the next day, during a tennis game, from someone else's wife. Ever since he had lost his job, Ronie had nursed a resentment that was liable to flare up at the least opportune moment. That social mechanism that prevents us making unwelcome comments had long been faulty in my husband.

"No, I didn't have a fight with anyone."

"Then why are you back so early? You never come home on Thursdays earlier than three o'clock in the morning."

"I did today," he said. Then he said nothing else, and left no room for me to say anything either. He stood up and moved his lounger closer to the balustrade, all but turning his back on me. It was less a gesture of rejection than of a spectator seeking the best spot from which to view a scene. Our house is diagonally opposite the Scaglias'. There are two or three others in between but, since ours is taller – and in spite of the Iturrías' poplars, which interfere with the view somewhat – from that vantage point you can see almost all their garden and their swimming pool. Ronie was looking towards the pool. The lights were off and there wasn't much to see other than vague shapes and outlines; one could make out the movement of water, sketching shifting shadows on the turquoise tiles.

I stood up and leaned on the back of Ronie's lounger. The silence of the night was underscored by the occasional rustle of the Iturrías' poplars as they moved in the warm air, making a sound like rain in the starry night. I wasn't sure whether to stay or go because, for all that Ronie seemed absent, he had not insinuated that I should leave – and that mattered to me. I watched him from behind, over the top of the wooden chair back. He kept moving around on the lounger without finding the right position; he seemed nervous. Later on I discovered that fear was the problem, not nerves – but I didn't know that at the time nor would I have suspected such a thing, because Ronie had never been fearful of anything. Not even of that fearful thing that had been frightening me for months, pursuing me day and night. That fear that made me forget what I was doing while standing in front of the fridge. That fear that was always with me even when I feigned otherwise, even when I was laughing, or chatting about something, or playing tennis, or signing a document. That night, in spite of Ronie's distance, the same fear prompted me to say, with false composure: "Juani's gone out."

"Who with?" he wanted to know.

"I didn't ask him."

"What time is he coming back?"

"I don't know. He went on his roller blades."

There was another silence and then I said: "There was a message from Romina on the answerphone. She said she was waiting for him so that they could go out and do the rounds. Could 'doing the rounds' be some form of code between them?"

"Rounds are rounds, Virginia."

"I shouldn't worry, then?"

"No."

"He must be with her."

"He must be with her." And we both fell silent again.

There were more words later, I think, though I don't remember. More of those pat phrases to which we had grown accustomed. Ronie poured himself another whisky and I passed him the ice. He grabbed a handful of ice cubes and some of them fell on the floor and slid towards the balustrade. His eyes followed them and it seemed as though he had forgotten about the house opposite for a moment. He looked at the ice cubes and I looked at him. And perhaps we would have stayed in these poses, but at that very moment the lights went on at the Scaglias' swimming pool and voices could be heard amid the rustling of poplar leaves. El Tano's laughter. Music; it sounded like some sort of wistful, contemporary jazz.

"Diana Krall?" I asked, but Ronie said nothing. He had gone tense again; he stood up, kicked away the ice cubes, and returned to his seat. He raised his clenched fists to his mouth, gritting his teeth. I realized that he was hiding something from me, something he dared not let out of that mouth clamped shut. It had something to do with whatever he was watching so intently. An argument, or resentment, a slight that had rankled. Humiliation disguised as a joke: that was El Tano's speciality, I thought. Ronie stood up once more and went to the balustrade to get a better view. He drained the whisky glass. Now he was blocking my view through the poplars, watching something I could not see. But I heard a splash and I guessed that someone had dived into the Scaglias' pool.

"Who jumped in?" I asked.

There was no answer and the truth was that I didn't really care who had jumped in, but I cared about the silence, which was like a wall I kept banging into every time I tried to get closer. Tired of making futile efforts, I decided to go downstairs. Not because I was annoyed, but because it was obvious that Ronie wasn't with me at all, but across the street, throwing himself into the pool with his friends. While I was still at the top of the stairs, the jazz that was wafting over from El Tano's house stopped, right in the middle of a riff, breaking it off.

I went down to the kitchen and rinsed out my glass for longer than was necessary, my head filling up again with more thoughts than it had room for. Juani was on my mind, not Ronie, no matter what distraction methods I used to avoid thinking about him. Like those people who count sheep to get to sleep, I focused on work that was pending at the estate agency: whom I was going to take to see the Gómez Pardo house; how I was going to secure finances for the Canetti sale; that deposit I had forgotten to charge the Abrevayas. Then up again popped Juani – not Ronie. Juani, in even sharper focus. I dried the glass and put it away, then took it out again and filled it with water; I was going to need something to help me sleep that night. Something to knock me out. There must be a pill in my medicine cabinet that would do the trick. Fortunately I had no time to take anything, because just then I heard hurried footsteps, a shout and the dry, hard thud of something striking the decking. I ran out and found my husband lying on the ground covered in blood and with one of his leg bones protruding through the skin. I went dizzy, as though everything around me were spinning, but I knew I must get a grip on myself because I was alone and I had to look after him, and thank goodness I hadn't taken anything because I was going to have to make a tourniquet – and I didn't know how to do that – to tie a rag somehow, a clean towel, to staunch the blood and then call an ambulance; no, not an ambulance because they take too long – better to go straight to the hospital and leave a note for Juani: "Daddy and I have gone to do something but we'll be back very soon. If you need me, call the mobile. Everything's fine. I hope you are too, love Mummy."

While I was dragging him towards the car, Ronie cried out in pain, and the cry galvanized me.

"Virginia, take me to El Tano's!" he shouted. I ignored this, believing him to be delirious, and somehow I manhandled him into the back of the car.

"Take me to El Tano's, for fuck's sake!" he shouted again before passing out (from the pain, they said later in the hospital – but that wasn't it). I drove fast and badly, ignoring the speed bumps and signs that said "Slow down. Children playing." I didn't even stop when I saw Juani bolting across a side street with no shoes on. Romina was behind him. As if they were running away from something – those two are always running away from something, I thought. And forgetting their roller blades somewhere or other. Juani is always losing his stuff. But I could not start thinking about Juani. Not that night. On the way to the entrance gate, Ronie woke up. Still woozy, he looked out of the window, trying to see where he was, but seemingly unable to make sense of things. He wasn't shouting any more. Two streets before leaving The Cascade we passed Teresa Scaglia's SUV.

"Was that Teresa?" Ronie asked.

"Yes."

Ronie clutched his head and began to cry, softly at first, a kind of lamentation which grew into stifled sobbing. I saw him in the rear-view mirror, curled up in pain. I spoke to him, trying to calm him, but this proved impossible, so I resigned myself to the litany, just as one resigns oneself to a gradually encroaching pain, or to conversations full of empty words.

By the time we arrived at the hospital, I was no longer paying attention to my husband's weeping. But it continued nonetheless.

"Why are you crying like this?" asked the duty doctor. "Is it very painful?"

"I'm scared," replied Ronie.

2

The Scaglias' house may not have been the best in Cascade Heights, but Virginia always said that it was the one that most caught the eye of her clients at the estate agency. And if anyone knew about the best and worst houses in the neighbourhood, it was her. Tano's house was unarguably one of the largest in our gated community (we liked to call it a "country club"), and therein lay the difference. Lots of us were secretly envious of it. The exterior boasted pointed brickwork, black slate roof tiles in various tones and white woodwork. Inside, arranged over two levels, were six bedrooms and eight bathrooms, not including the maid's room. Thanks to the architect's contacts, the house had been featured in two or three decor magazines. On the top floor there was a home theatre and, next to the kitchen, a family room with rattan furniture and a table made from wood and oxidized metal. The living room looked onto the swimming pool and if one sat in the sand-coloured armchairs which faced the wall-to-wall, ceiling-to-floor window, one had the impression of being outside on the wooden deck that extended from the veranda.

In the garden, each shrub had been positioned with careful regard to its colour, height, bulk and movement. "It's like my calling card," said Teresa, who had abandoned graphology shortly after she moved to Cascade Heights in order to take up landscape gardening. And, even though she did not need to work, she was always on the hunt for new clients, as if their conquest signified much more to her than simply a new garden to tend. In her own garden, there were no dried-up or diseased plants, nothing that had grown by chance because a seed blew in and landed there, no ants' nests or slugs. Her lawn was like an immaculate carpet, intensely green, with no changes in hue. An imaginary line, an exact point at which the grass changed colour, marked the end of the Scaglias' garden and the beginning of the golf course: the seventeenth hole. The view from the house was completed by a bunker to the left and to the right a "hazard" – an artificial pool of glassy water.

That night, Teresa had entered the house through the door from the garage. She didn't need to use keys: in Cascade Heights we never lock the doors. She says that she was puzzled not to hear her husband and his friends – our friends – laughing as usual. Drunken laughter. And she was pleased not to have to go and say hello; she was too tired to smile at the same old jokes, she said. Every Thursday the men got together to have dinner and play cards, and for a long time it had been traditional for the wives to go to the cinema. Except for Virginia, who had bowed out some time ago, with different sorts of excuses which no one bothered to analyse too much; quietly we all attributed her absence to money problems. The Scaglia children were not at home either, that night. Matías was spending the night at the Floríns' house, and Sofía – much against her will, but at her father's insistence – had gone to stay with her maternal grandparents. And it was the maid's day off. El Tano himself had said that she should have Thursdays free so that there would be nobody in the house to bother him and his friends, interrupting their card game for whatever reason.

Teresa went upstairs, dreading to find the men sleeping off an excess of wine and champagne in the home theatre, while pretending to watch a film or some sporting event. They were not there, however, which meant that there was no risk of running into them on the way to her room. The house felt deserted. She was intrigued, rather than worried. Her husband's friends must be somewhere nearby, she thought, unless they had left on foot; pulling into the drive, she had had to avoid Gustavo Masotta and Martín Urovich's SUVs, parked outside her house. Now she leaned over the balcony and, in the darkness, she thought she could see some towels on the wooden deck. September was barely over, but it was a pleasant night and, now that El Tano had installed a boiler to heat the water, the usual quandaries regarding swimming and weather no longer applied. No doubt they had sobered up in the pool and were getting dressed in the changing room. So, because she did not feel like thinking about it any more, she put on her night dress and got into bed.

At four o'clock in the morning she woke up alone. The left side of the bed was undisturbed. She walked to the front of the house and, through the window, saw that the SUVs were still there. The house was still silent. She went downstairs and into the living room and confirmed that what she had seen from the balcony were towels and T-shirts lying on the deck. But there were no lights on around the pool, and it was hard to make anything else out. She went to the family room; there was nothing unusual here: empty bottles, ashtrays full of butts, cards strewn across the table, as though the game had only recently ended. Next she went down to the pool house and in the changing room she found the men's clothes lying on a bench; some scrunched-up underpants were lying on the floor; one sock without its mate was hanging from a tap in the shower. Only El Tano had neatly folded his clothes and left them at one end of the bench, beside his shoes. They couldn't have gone for a walk at this time of night in their swimming trunks, she thought. Then she went towards the swimming pool. She tried to put on the lights, but they were not working in this area, as if the circuit breaker had cut in, she thought, but later she found out that it had been the thermal overload trip, not the circuit breaker. The water was calm. She felt the towels and realized that they had not been used – they were slightly damp to the touch, but otherwise dry. Three empty champagne flutes, arranged in a row at the edge of the pool, caught her off-guard. Not because the men had been drinking there – they drank all over the place – but because these were the crystal glasses from her wedding set, the ones that El Tano's father had given them and which El Tano himself reserved for very special occasions. Teresa moved to pick them up, before they could be toppled by the morning breeze or by a cat or frog. If it weren't for this sort of accident of nature, life at the Cascade would be almost free of risks. That was what we used to believe.

Teresa barely glanced at the still water as she collected the glasses. Two of them knocked together as she picked them up, and the ringing sound of crystal made her shudder. She examined them to make sure they were not broken. And she walked back to the house. She walked slowly, taking care not to let the glasses knock against each other again, and oblivious to the knowledge that the rest of us would learn about the next day: beneath the warm water, sinking to the bottom of the pool, were the bodies of her husband and his friends, and all three of them were dead.

3

Cascade Heights is the neighbourhood where we live. All us lot. Ronie and Guevara moved here first, just before the Uroviches; El Tano came a few years later; Gustavo Masotta was one of the last to arrive. As time went on, we became neighbours. Our neighbourhood is a gated community, ringed by a perimeter fence that is concealed behind different kinds of shrub. It's called The Cascade Heights Country Club. Most of us shorten the name to "The Cascade" and a few people call it "The Heights". It has a golf course, tennis courts, swimming pool and two club houses. And private security. Fifteen security guards working shifts during the day, and twenty-two at night. That's more than five hundred acres of land, accessible only to us or to people authorized by one of us.

There are three ways to enter our neighbourhood. If you're a member, you can open a barrier at the main gate by swiping a personalized magnetic card across an electronic reader. There's a side entrance, also with a barrier, for visitors who have received prior authorization and can supply certain information, such as identity card number, car registration number and other identifying numbers. For tradesmen, domestic staff, gardeners, painters, builders and all other labourers, there's a turnstile where ID cards have to be presented, and bags and car boots are checked. All along the perimeter, at fifty-yard intervals, there are cameras which can turn through one hundred and eighty degrees. There used to be cameras that could turn three hundred and sixty degrees, but they were invading the privacy of some members whose houses were close to the perimeter fence, so a few years ago they were deactivated, then replaced.

The houses are separated from one another by "living fences" – bushes, in other words. But these are not any old bushes. Privet is out of fashion, along with that erstwhile favourite, the violet campanula that grows by railway lines. There are none of those straight, trimmed hedges that look like green walls. Definitely no round ones. The hedges are cut to look uneven, just this side of messy, giving them a natural appearance that is meticulously contrived. At first glance, these plants seem to have sprung up spontaneously between the neighbours, rather than to have been placed deliberately, to demarcate properties. Such boundaries may be insinuated only with plants. Wire fencing and railings are not permitted, let alone walls. The only exception is the six foot-high perimeter fence which is the responsibility of the Club's administration and which is shortly going to be replaced by a wall, in line with new security regulations. Gardens that back onto the golf course may not be contained on that side even by a living fence; close to the boundary, you can make out where the gardens end because the type of grass changes but, from a distance, the gaze is lost in an endless green vista and it is possible to believe that everything belongs to you.

The streets are named after birds: Swallow, Mockingbird, Blackbird. The grid lay-out typical of most Argentine towns does not apply here. There are lots of cul-de-sacs, ending in little landscaped roundabouts. These dead-end streets are more popular than the others because they have less traffic and are quieter. We'd all love to live in a cul-de-sac. Outside a gated community, it would be hair-raising to have to walk down that sort of street, especially at night; you'd be afraid of being attacked, or ambushed. But not in The Cascade – that wouldn't be possible; you can walk wherever you like, at any hour, safe in the knowledge that nothing bad will happen to you.

There are no pavements. People use cars, motorbikes, quad bikes, bicycles, golf buggies, scooters and roller blades. If they walk, they walk on the road. As a general rule, if someone is walking and not carrying sports gear, it's a domestic servant or gardener. At Cascade Heights we call them "groundsmen" rather than gardeners, doubtless because not many plots are smaller than half an acre, and, at that size, a garden is more like an estate.

Look up and you won't see any cables. No electricity, telephone or television wires. Of course we have all three, but the lines run underground, to protect The Heights and its inhabitants from visual contamination. The cables run alongside the drains, both of them hidden underground.

Water tanks, which also have to be concealed from view, are camouflaged by false walls built around them. Hanging out washing isn't permitted without prior approval from the Technical Department. They look at a plan of the grounds before approving a suitable place for a washing line. If a resident proceeds to hang up washing in an area which can be seen from neighbouring houses, and if someone reports the matter, he or she can be fined.

The houses are all different; no house is expressly planned as a copy of another – although that may be the end result. It's impossible for the houses not to be similar, given that they must obey the same aesthetic norms – those dictated by the building code and fashion alike. We would all like our house to be the prettiest. Or the biggest. Or the best designed. The whole neighbourhood is divided by statute into sectors where only one sort of house may be built. There is a sector where the houses must be white. There's a brick houses sector and a black slate roofs sector. One cannot build a house of one type in a sector designated as being for another type. An aerial view of the club shows it separated into three swathes of colour: one red, one white and one black.

In the brick sector are the "dormitory" apartments, set aside for those members who only come at the weekends and don't want to maintain a house here. From far away, the dorms look like three large chalets, but in fact there are a lot of small rooms squeezed into those three blocks, with a neatly tended garden at the front.

There's another characteristic of our neighbourhood, and perhaps it's the most striking of all: the smells. They change with the season. In September everything smells of Star Jasmine. This isn't a poetic detail, but simple fact. Every garden in The Cascade has at least one star jasmine which flowers in the spring. Three hundred houses, with three hundred gardens, with three hundred jasmine plants, contained in a five-hundred-acre estate with a perimeter fence and private security: that's no poetic aside. It is the reason why the air feels heavy and sweet in spring. It's sickly for those who aren't used to it. But in some of us it engenders a kind of addiction, or attraction or nostalgia – and whenever we go beyond the gates, we're longing to return, to breathe in once more the scent of those sweet flowers. As though it were not possible to breathe well anywhere else. The air in Cascade Heights is heavy, palpable; we choose to live here because we like to breathe like this, with the bees buzzing behind some jasmine plant. And even though the perfume changes with each season, the desire to breathe that sweet air remains. In summer, The Cascade smells of freshly mown and watered grass, and of the chlorine in swimming pools. Summer is the season of noise. Splashes, the shouts of children playing, cicadas, birds complaining of the heat, the strains of music through an open window; someone playing the drums. Windows without bars, because there are no bars in The Cascade. There's no need for bars. Mosquito netting – yes, to keep the insects at bay. The autumn smells of pruned boughs, recently cut and still fresh; they never leave them to rot. There are men in green sweatshirts

25

with the Cascade Heights logo who collect the leaves and branches after every storm or gale. All traces of a storm have often disappeared by the time we've had breakfast and gone out to work, to school or for a morning walk. The first we know of it is the damp ground, the smell of wet earth. Sometimes we may wonder if the gale that woke us during the night really took place or belonged to a dream. In winter there is the smell of log fires, of smoke and eucalyptus. And then the most private and secret of all, the smell of the home itself, composed of mixed elements that are known only to each one of us.

Those of us who move to Cascade Heights say that we have come in search of "green", a healthy life, sports and security. Trotting out these reasons means not having to confess, even to ourselves, the real reasons for coming. And after a while we don't even remember them. Entrance into The Cascade induces a certain magical forgetfulness of all that went before. The past is reduced to last week, last month, last year, "when we played the Inter-Club Challenge and won it". Gradually we forget our lifelong friends, the places we once loved, certain relations, memories, mistakes. It's as though it were possible, in mid-life, to tear the pages out of your diary and begin to write something new.

4

We moved to The Cascade at the end of the 1980s. Argentina had a new president. We should not have had him until the end of December, but hyperinflation and the looting of supermarkets prompted the last one to leave office before the end of his term. At that time, the move towards gated communities on the outskirts of greater Buenos Aires had not yet gained momentum. Few people lived permanently at Cascade Heights – or at any other gated community or country club. Ronie and I were among the first to risk leaving an apartment in the capital to move in here with our family. Ronie was very doubtful at the start. Too much travelling, he said. I was the one who insisted – I was sure that living in Cascade Heights was going to change our lives, that we needed to make a break with the city. And Ronie ended up agreeing with me.

We sold a weekend cottage that we had inherited from Ronie's family (one of the few things from that inheritance left to sell), then we bought the Antieris' house. It was, as I like to say, a "sweet deal". And it was the first inkling I had that buying and selling houses was something I liked and for which I had an innate talent. Although in those days I knew much less about the business than I do now.

Antieri had committed suicide two months earlier. His widow was desperate to leave the house where her husband, and father of her four children, had blown out his brains. In the living room. A small "L" shaped living room with an incorporated dining area. In the early years at The Cascade and other country clubs, almost all the houses had small living rooms. The thing is, in those days – we're talking about the Fifties, the Sixties, even the Seventies – you wouldn't expect to have parties and entertain people in a house so far from Buenos Aires. The Pan American Highway as we know it today, with its dual carriageway and flawless asphalt, was still a pipe dream. If you invited friends or relations over it was for a proper country adventure – everyone made good use of the garden, the sports area, you took them riding or to play golf. Later came the era of showing off imported carpets and armchairs bought in the best Buenos Aires stores. We moved in at some intermediate point – after the Sixties, but before the Nineties ethos took hold. Even so, it was obvious that we were much closer to the Nineties than the Sixties, and not just chronologically. We decided to knock down a wall and make the living room a few feet bigger, at the expense of a study we knew we would never use.

The Antieri episode took place one Sunday at midday. Even from the golf course they heard his wife's screams. The house is almost opposite the tee at the fourth hole, and to this day Paco Pérez Ayerra – who was the captain of the club at the time – likes to tell the story of the long drive that he sent out of bounds because the screaming started just as his one wood hit the ball. People said that Antieri had been in the military, or the navy – something like that. Nobody knew what, exactly. But definitely in uniform. They didn't have much to do with their neighbours, didn't do sports or go to parties. Occasionally we saw their girls out and about. But the parents had no social life. They used to come at the weekend and shut themselves up in the house. Towards the end, he was also spending the weeks there, alone, with the blinds down, cleaning his collection of weapons, apparently. He never spoke to anyone. So I don't think you have to look too far for a concrete motive, nor give too much credit to the rumour that went round claiming that Antieri had threatened to blow his brains out if the result of the 1989 election went the wrong way. The same threat was made by an actor who went through with it and was on all the news bulletins afterwards; someone probably confused the two anecdotes and started the rumour.

When I first saw the house, what most impressed me was Antieri's study (the one we ended up knocking through). The order and cleanliness in there were intimidating. A fully stocked bookcase lined all the walls. The spines were perfect and intact, bound in green or burgundy leather. His guns, in all their various models and calibres, were displayed in two glass cabinets. They were polished and shining, not a speck of dust to be seen. While we were looking around the study, Juani, who was just five, took out one of the books, threw it on the floor and stood on it. The book's spine immediately gave way. Ronie grabbed him by the hair and pulled him away. He took him out of the room to chastise him without witnesses. Meanwhile I took care of the book, dusting off Juani's footprint. Returning it to the shelf, I noticed how light it was, and turned it over. It was hollow. There were no pages inside, just hard covers: a box of fake literature. On the spine I read *Faust*, by Goethe. I put it in its place, between Calderón de la Barca's *Life Is a Dream* and Dostoevsky's *Crime and Punishment*. All of them were hollow. To the right of these there were two or three other classics, then the sequence was repeated: *Life Is a Dream, Faust, Crime and Punishment*, in gold filigree letters. The same series was on every shelf.

We got the house for next to nothing. Offers from various other interested parties fell away, as people found out that a man had shot himself there. The wife didn't mention it, nor did the estate agent in charge of the sale. But somehow the story always came out. It made no difference to me, to tell the truth: I'm not

29

superstitious. To cap it all, when it came to exchange contracts, it turned out that some papers pertaining to the estate weren't in order, so the widow had to shoulder all the costs, hers and ours. I even made an extra two hundred pesos when I sold to Rita Mansilla the hollow books which the widow hadn't wanted to take and which were gathering dust in the basement.

So the house ended up costing us only about fifteen thousand dollars more than the weekend getaway we'd sold, and this new place comprised a ground area of half an acre, about an eighth of which was covered; there were three en-suite bathrooms and staff accommodation. It was full of light, now that Antieri was not there to put down the blinds. Before we moved in, we painted all the rooms white, to make it lighter still. That was a favourite trick in the Buenos Aires property market, but in The Cascade, I came to realize, such devices were not necessary. In The Cascade, the sun comes in anyway, through the open windows; there are no tall buildings to cast long shadows, no dividing walls to block out the light. Only the plots with a high number of trees are likely to have a problem with light and shade, and that wasn't the case with us.

It was the first good property deal I closed in my life, and it whetted my appetite. At first, it was almost like a game. If I found out that someone was hard up, or that a couple was separating, that some unemployed husband had found a job abroad and was leaving with his family – or perhaps they were going anyway, without an offer of work, because he was tired of having no job and a golf course and swimming pool to maintain – straight away I started thinking of people who might be interested in the house and I got in touch.

It was about two years later that I sold a plot of land to the Scaglias. This was a few days after the Minister for Foreign Affairs became the Finance Minister he had always been destined to be and persuaded Congress to pass the Convertibility Law.[1] One peso would be worth one dollar: the famous "one for one" that restored Argentines' confidence and fuelled an exodus to places like Cascade Heights.

There are some events, not many, fewer than one might suppose, that actually change the course of our lives. Selling that land to the Scaglias, in that March of 1991, was without any doubt one such event.

5

I remember it as if it were yesterday. A pair of brown crocodile shoes preceded her out of the car. Teresa Scaglia took barely a step and the stiletto heel of one of them sank into the very ground I was hoping to sell the couple. Seeing that Teresa was embarrassed, I tried to play the incident down:

"It happens to all of us city girls once," I said. "It's hard to give up your heels. Believe me, it's one of the hardest things. But if you have to choose between heels and this..." I gestured extravagantly towards the trees and landscape around us.

El Tano appeared not to have noticed his wife sinking into the soil. He was walking two or three yards ahead

_____

1   By 1990, inflation was running at 1300 per cent. President Carlos Menem appointed Domingo Cavallo to Finance Minister in 1991 and the Convertibility Law was passed, reining in inflation by pegging the national currency to the US dollar.

of her. But it would be wrong, I think, to say that he was a man in a hurry. Or, if he did seem rushed, then that was symptomatic of an impatient disposition rather than the pressures of time. It was as if he did not want to wait – for his wife, or for anyone else. El Tano walked on and I waited a moment for Teresa. To think that woman ended up being a landscape gardener! When she first arrived at Cascade Heights, the only thing she knew about the subject was that she liked plants. Teresa extracted her heel from the soft earth and tried to clean it on the grass while, inevitably, the other heel sank in. All her efforts were in vain. The heel she had cleaned was doomed to sink in again, the other one was going to come out muddy and, clean it as she might, would then get dirty again. But to point out this information, denying her capacity to absorb it for herself, would have seemed as disrespectful and impatient as her husband's haste. I was already feeling anxious: the commission on the sale of this land was earmarked for various improvements pending in my own home. I wondered which option to choose. The first time I had sunk into The Cascade I had ended up taking off my shoes and looking round the site in my stockinged feet. We were young and Ronie had laughed: we both had laughed. But Teresa and I are very different. All the women here are very different, even though some people make the mistake of believing that women who live in a place like this grow to resemble one another. They call us "country-club women". That stereotype is wrong-headed. Yes, it's true that we go through the same sorts of experience, that the same sorts of thing happen to us. Or that the same sorts of thing do *not* happen to us, and in that respect we are similar too. For example, we all find it hard, at the start, to give up certain habits: there is no room here for high heels, silk hosiery or curtains that drop to the floor. In another context, any one of those details would signal elegance, but in Cascade Heights they end up signalling dirt. Because heels sink into the lawn and emerge covered in soil and grass; because stockings ladder when they come into contact with rough-edged plants, MDF or rattan garden furniture; because much more dust blows into houses than into apartments and it gets spread around by children, dogs or long drapes – and everything looks filthy.

It took Teresa a few yards to grasp that there was nothing she could do. She opted for walking on tip-toe – a compromise solution I've seen other city women try – and settled for looking from afar, instead of walking around the plot hand in hand with her husband. Meanwhile, El Tano strode ahead, his hands in his pockets, planting his feet firmly in the ground. It was clear that he was marking his territory with every step. If he had been an animal, he'd have pissed on it. There was no doubting his body language: this was the land he had been looking for. His stance should have made me think cheerfully of the commission that was close at hand, but instead it unnerved me and I told him that I would have to check with the owner that the land was still for sale.

"If it's not for sale, why are you showing me it?"

"No, yes – it is for sale, or it was. Caviró Senior, the owner, placed it with my agency a couple of months ago but, I don't know, I'd like to be sure."

"If he placed it with your agency, that means it's for sale."

And that would be the case in many places, but not in The Cascade. In The Cascade one has to learn to operate with a certain flexibility. Sometimes people tell you they want to sell, then a son turns up, claiming a stake, or they fear selling will bring social embarrassment, or they can't agree with their wives. And the agency has to pick up the pieces. In this case, that's me, Virginia, or "Mavi Guevara", to use my business name. Some people put a house or plot up for sale to test the market, or because they want to know how much it's gone up in value since they bought it, or because a valuation is too abstract a measure for them, and they need to see in front of them someone who wants what they have and has the cash in hand to get it. And then they say no, they don't want to sell.

"I want this land," El Tano said again.

"I'll do what I can," I remember answering.

"That's not enough," he said in a calm voice that was nonetheless so steely it immobilized me as surely as his wife had been immobilized by her heels anchored in the soil. I didn't know what to say. El Tano advanced as though pushing the point of his sword towards a rival who had already fallen to the ground and was ready to relinquish the fight.

"I want this land."

I hesitated for no more than a moment then, to my own amazement, I heard myself say: "Consider it done. This land will be yours."

And this was neither a pat phrase, nor a declaration of intent. Nor did it have anything to do with my concrete ability to achieve such a thing. Quite the opposite. It was an expression of my absolute conviction that this man standing in front of me and whom I had only just met, El Tano Scaglia, was sure always to obtain everything that he wanted from life.

From death, too.

6

The car stopped in front of the barrier. Ernesto wound down his window, swiped his electronic card for the first time and the barrier was raised. The guard on duty acknowledged them with a smile. The girl watched him from her seat. The guard waved to her, but she did not respond. Mariana also wound down her window and took an exaggeratedly deep breath, as though this air were better than any other. It was not as sweet as she had noted it two years ago, when she first came to The Cascade. On that occasion she had come through the visitors' entrance. And it had been spring, not autumn, as it was now. They had asked for everything, even her ID number, before letting her in. They had made her wait fifteen minutes because no one could be found to authorize her visit. That time she had been going to a barbecue at the home of one of Ernesto's clients. It was someone who owed her husband a favour because he had made it possible for this man to enter into some business for which he would not have qualified without Ernesto's help. Those sorts of favours also count as debts, thought Ernesto, especially when they allow the debtor to make a lot of money. That day, the day of the barbecue, they decided that Cascade Heights was where they would like to live when they had children. And now they had two of them. They would have preferred one, but it was either that or keep waiting. And Mariana could not wait any longer. Before the judge had given them the children a month ago, she had reached her wit's end. They had even been on the point of buying a child in El Chaco: someone had mentioned a surrogate mother to them. Then by chance it turned out that another client of Ernesto's knew this particular judge who was able to get the ball rolling.

The Andrades' car advanced slowly along the tree-lined road that skirted the golf course. The streets of The Cascade competed in displays of red-and-white foliage. Not even the world's greatest artist could produce a painting to compare with their view from the window, thought Mariana. Red balsam, yellow ginkgo biloba, reddish-brown oaks. Pedro was sleeping in his car seat, beside his sister. The girl thought it a little cold with the window open, and tucked the baby's blanket round him. Then she crossed her legs and arranged her new skirt over them. Looking out of the window, she saw a sign that said "Children Playing. Maximum Speed 10 mph", but she made no sense of it because she did not know how to read.

Mariana turned away from the scenery and glanced in the rear-view mirror at the children, pretending to smooth down a lock of hair; she wondered how the fraternal bond was going to develop between these two children she scarcely knew. She had thought of the baby's name years ago, when she and Ernesto were still engaged. The girl had come with a name already given: Ramona. Mariana could not imagine how anyone, in this day and age, would give such a name to a girl. Ramona was a name for something else – not a child. During all those years of waiting and having treatments, she had thought of various possibilities: Camila, Victoria, Sofía, Delfina, Valentina, even Inés, after her paternal grandmother. But the girl had come with her own name, and the judge had not authorized a change. For that reason, Mariana had decided to call her "Romina" without asking for anyone's authorization, as if this change were simply the result of some confusion over vowels. Fortunately the girl had been unable to tell the judge the baby's name – if he had one – and referred to him only as "baba" instead of "baby".

Antonia was waiting for them in the doorway when they arrived; she had just been arranging the flowers sent by Virginia Guevara in a vase, which she had placed in the centre of the new pine table. She wore a blue uniform with white embroidery on the cuffs. It was also brand new – when they lived in Palermo she had not worn a uniform. She had not lived in, either. But with the move, and the arrival of the children, she had been obliged to accept the change or lose her job. The car made a sound like summer rain as it pulled onto the gravel drive, and the girl shivered. She saw through the window that it was a sunny day. "It's raining invisible stones," she thought. Mariana was the first to get out of the car. She went up to Antonia, giving her her handbag to hold and a bag containing a few items of clothes that had not been brought over in the move, the previous day. Then immediately she returned to the car, opened the back door and undid the seat belt on the baby's chair. The girl watched Mariana pick up her brother. She murmured something like "come here, little one," then lifted him out of the car. The baby's blanket fell onto the gravel.

"Isn't he looking lovely today, Antonia?"

Antonia nodded.

"Go and make him up a bottle. He must be starving."

Antonia went into the house with the clothes and the handbag. Mariana, holding Pedro in her arms, glanced back at the car, as though looking for something.

"Ernesto?" she said, and Ernesto emerged from behind the boot, pushing a pram on which he had piled up tennis rackets and a suit-carrier. They went into the house together and the little girl saw the door close behind them. She studied the house through the polarized car window, thinking it the most beautiful house in the world. It seemed to have been made from toffee and cream, like the one in the story they had told her, in the church at Caá Cati. She would have liked to get out of the car and run across the lawn that looked like a carpet – but she couldn't, because she did not know how to unfasten the seat belt. She tried and failed to release it and was scared to break something and get a beating; she didn't want anyone to hit her any more.

Time passed. The girl entertained herself by watching people go by in the street: a lady with a dog on a lead; a woman who wore the same uniform as Antonia, pushing a baby in a pram; a boy on his bicycle and a girl on roller skates. She would like to go on skates too, one day, she thought. She had never seen a pair of skates up close, and the girl went by too fast for her to get a proper look. She did see that they were pink, though, and that was her favourite colour.

The front door opened and Antonia came out and went to the car. "What are you still doing here. Come on, come on," she said, undoing the seat belt with an effort – because she, too, was unused to the mechanism. She took the girl by the hand and into the house. Her new home.

On the Monday following their move, the girl was starting school. She had never been to school before. Mariana and Ernesto had managed to get her into the first grade at Lakelands – the school to which they had always dreamed of sending their first child – even though she had no previous knowledge of the language. By "the language", they meant English. It wasn't going to be easy for the girl, because term had begun two months ago. The head mistress told them that this was a challenge they would have to face together: the school would give the girl one-to-one attention to help her acquire the same English skills as her classmates, but Mariana must organize extra tuition, to ensure that these skills were reinforced. They did not talk of a teacher, but of a "coach". Mariana agreed. They had to give it a go. Pedro was going to go to Lakelands anyway, from grade one, just like any child. And, for practical reasons, it made sense for Pedro and the girl to go to the same school.

Mariana did not have very high expectations of Romina's first steps in school. She had learned not to get her hopes up as a way to deal with frustration during the years of fertility treatments when, month after month, she would go to the bathroom fearing the worst and finding her fears confirmed: the stain that blotted out all hopes, turning the calendar back to day one. Then, in the United States they had diagnosed "irreversibly empty follicles" and she was grateful for their frankness. She wanted to adopt the same policy with the girl's schooling: banish all hopes, expect the worst and ward off future frustration by anticipating it. When the moment came, however, she could not help but feel anxious. She got everything ready the night before, ironing the uniform herself, to be sure that the pleats of the skirt were perfectly symmetrical, then she left the clothes neatly folded on a chair: the white blouse, the blue sweater with its bright red-and-green detail, the kilt. The girl was asleep. Even in the darkness of the room, her black hair shone.

Mariana went down to the family room, switched on the television and lit a cigarette. Ernesto was working on the computer. She flicked between one channel and the next without knowing what she was watching. All she wanted was for time to pass, for it to be the next day, and the one after, and another one, until the day arrived when she forgot from where, and from whom, her children had come. Especially the girl. It was different with Pedro – he was barely three months old. He would soon forget smells, a particular breath, a voice, a heartbeat, a blow. She would be able to mould him as he grew. Not so the girl. Her eyes had seen too much already. You could tell. Mariana found it hard to meet her eye – it scared her. As if those dark eyes could show her some of the things that they had once seen.

The alarm went off at half-past seven. Mariana got up, got dressed and went down to breakfast. Only then did she ask Antonia to wake Romina, take her some breakfast and get her dressed. Then she herself would go up to brush her hair. Ernesto was not going to go with them to the school. He would have liked to go: at these events one always meets someone who may end up being a useful contact, or a good client, and he wanted to get to know the community to which he now belonged. But Mariana had asked him to stay at home with Pedro. He had coughed all night, and she was worried. And Ernesto knew from experience that no business opportunity was worth having Mariana worry.

Mariana went up to the girl's room. She brushed her hair as best she could; it was black, glossy and thick as wire. A hairdresser had been waiting for them the day they brought the children home from Corrientes. At that time they still lived in the flat in Buenos Aires. In less than five minutes the baby's head was completely shaved. But Mariana could hardly do the same to the girl, much though she would have liked it. That day the girl had played with her brother's shorn locks, scattered on the kitchen floor, while Mariana, to one side, gave instructions to the hairdresser.

"Not so short," he remonstrated. "She has lovely hair."

Mariana hesitated and looked at the girl as she sat on the floor staring at the tiles. Antonia's broom scratched over the girl's hand, as she swept up her brother's dead hair.

"Well then trim the ends, but at least thin it out a bit."

But the hairdresser couldn't. Every time he approached her with the scissors the girl started screaming.

"She's crying like a baby," said Antonia.

"She's howling like a banshee," corrected the hairdresser.

The girl was afraid. So was Mariana. Even though a month had now passed since that first afternoon together, every time Mariana brushed her hair, the girl trembled.

"Keep still, or I can't brush your hair," was all she said, and the girl made such an effort not to move that she was soon tired and aching.

Mariana secured her hair with a tartan ribbon that matched her school skirt and tortoiseshell clips that were no match for the girl's gleaming tresses. She wondered where the girl had been born, and who her parents were. The fact that she and Ernesto had gone to Corrientes to get her meant nothing. She knew that the boy had been born there, at the hospital in Goya.

But people had said that their mother was not from the area. The girl might be from Corrientes, but could also be from Misiones, El Chaco or Tucumán. Mariana thought most likely Tucumán. She could imagine that in a few years she would be as sturdy and strapping as the Tucumana woman who cleaned her friend Sara's house. Pedro was also sturdy, but would gradually show it less. With any luck they had different fathers and he had got better genes, she thought. Half-siblings. Now, with his shaven head, he hardly looked like her. While he was a baby they would keep shaving it, every week if necessary. When he was grown up he could keep his hair short like Ernesto and, if he turned out to be stocky, well then he would make a good prop in the school rugby team. At any rate, he was always going to get the best and healthiest food, she thought, and that would help. And sports, loads of sports. As for the girl, no matter how much you made her diet or killed her with exercise regimes, she was always going to have thick ankles and Mariana knew that there was no solution for that.

She took out the hair clips and put them in again a little higher up. The girl watched her almost without blinking. Mariana told her about the new school, about this wonderful opportunity unfolding before her, about how you're a nobody if you don't speak English and that she was going to have to try very hard. She picked up the girl's backpack and left the room. The girl followed a few steps behind, but when she reached Pedro's room she slipped inside. "Goodbye, baba," Mariana heard her say from the passage. She went back to get her.

"Don't wake him up. He's been coughing all night," she said. When they had reached the bottom of the stairs, she added: "It's '*baby*', not 'baba'."

"Baba," the girl repeated and Mariana said nothing.

The children were to line up in the playground. Mariana found out which was the first-grade line and left the girl in it. She watched her from a distance. Romina was the tallest. The biggest. And the darkest. The morning sun ricocheted off her hair. Mariana stood to one side. Some of the parents were going to stay to watch the flag being raised. A woman beside her was talking. She was also new and, it turned out, they had also just moved into the area.

"What school have you come from?" she asked, and Mariana pretended not to hear. She counted the heads of the girls waiting in the line for 1A : six blondes, eight light-browns, two brunettes. And the girl.

"Which one is yours?" persisted the woman beside her.

"That one," said Mariana, without pointing.

"The little blonde girl with the blue bow?"

"No, the great big dark one."

The woman started looking but before her gaze could alight on the girl, Mariana added: "She's adopted."

The opening bars of the national anthem rang out.

7

The first sign that we were going to be included in the Scaglias' inner circle of friends came a few months after they had moved in. I was stepping into the shower, in a hurry, because I had an appointment to show a client around a house that was just coming up for sale, and I had over-slept. The Convertibility law had breathed new life into the market for reasons I couldn't explain: the plots were even more expensive now that they were in dollars; I never was much good at economic variables and cross-effects, but the people with money to invest were happy – and so I was too. The telephone rang. I ran from the shower to get it, thinking it was my client. My feet were so wet I nearly slipped over. It was Teresa. "We'd like to invite you over for dinner on Wednesday night, Virginia, at about nine o'clock. There'll be ten couples, friends of ours, and we'd love you to come. It's Tano's birthday."

Ronie had crossed paths with El Tano a couple of times at the tennis courts before we received that first invitation, and once they had had a drink together after a game. I had not seen them since they had signed the contract; during the building work, one only ever saw them surrounded by architects and, although I was tempted to approach them several times, their demeanour, especially El Tano's, was not encouraging. I got the impression that I was not the only one to feel put off. El Tano was obviously someone who liked to pick and choose his friends. You couldn't take the initiative and approach him unless he had given a clear signal first. And rejecting an invitation of his wasn't something you would do lightly either.

On the day they moved in, I had taken flowers round to them with a card that said: "Don't hesitate to ask me for anything you need – your neighbour, Virginia". I sent the same card with flowers to all my clients after they moved. It was a way to step away from the role of agent, once all the details were finalized, and for that reason I liked to sign as Virginia, not "Mavi", the shortened version of María Virginia which I used for professional purposes. Otherwise friends never stopped being potential clients, and clients never became anything more than potential friends. I've written about this in my red notebook. Everything's weirdly mixed up at The Cascade. It must be because the definition of the term "friendship" is too wide here, to the extent that it actually ends up being narrow.

Ronie is punctual by nature and we were the first to arrive at the Scaglias'. El Tano opened the door to us, with a welcoming smile that made us feel reassuringly expected. "So glad you came!" Ronie gave him the present. It was a tennis shirt, very classical, bought in the pro shop down by the courts. I bought it, as a matter of fact. I always give this sort of thing. As a gift, a T-shirt is both politically correct and easy to change. I find it hard – not to mention dangerously risky – to buy a present for someone I don't know well. I would never buy a book, especially not for a man, because, if men read at all, it tends to be essays on current affairs, politics and economics, rather than novels. What if you give a book proposing "A" to someone who believes in "B"? It would be like giving a Boca football shirt to someone who supports River: a nightmare. It's the same with music and, anyway, I don't really know enough about music. Juani knows, but he gets annoyed if I ask his advice and anyway, at that time he was just a boy. He's still just a boy. A T-shirt always saves the day. If the person celebrating is a golfer, I get him a polo shirt with buttons – never a round neck: they're not permitted on the links. If he runs, it's a training shirt in Dri-Fit, absorbent fabric. If he plays tennis, it's the classic white shirt, with blue edging, perhaps, but fairly plain if it's someone I've only recently met. And I get it from the pro shop at Cascade Heights, where they don't bother with receipts and you can easily change things without even taking the bag back.

One of the few things I knew about El Tano on that day he celebrated his first birthday at The Cascade was that he had a passion for tennis. In fact, most of the guests at his party were linked to the sport in some way: Roberto Cánepa, the president of the Tennis Committee and his wife, Anita; Fabián, El Tano's coach, and his girlfriend; Alfredo Insúa – who was The Cascade's number-one player until El Tano arrived and was now taking up golf, after losing three matches on the trot – and his wife Carmen. She and Teresa organized *Burako*[2] tournaments in aid of the poor children's centre, in Santa María de los Tigrecitos. The only people there who had nothing to do with tennis were Malena and Luis Cianchi, a couple who lived in a neighbouring country club, who had become friends with Teresa because their children went to the same school. Also Mariana and Ernesto Andrade, who were new to our community but known to El Tano because of some business deal Andrade had arranged for him. There was no relative or friend who did not live in Cascade Heights, or in a country club less than two exits down the highway from ours.

"It's just a mistake mixing people up," said Malena, selecting a canapé from the tray that the Scaglias' maid was holding in front of her. "Some of them end up in one corner and some of them in another; they don't mingle and you're left doing all the work – going from one corner to the other without having any fun."

"No, and you put them in an awkward position, too," said Teresa, watching how her maid performed her duty,

2 Burako is a popular game in Argentina, similar to Rummy, but played with tiles rather than cards.

"because to come all this way, in the evening, on a week-day, just for two or three hours... better to do an *asado*[3] for them at the weekend. Bring some more wine, María."

"You say that now," someone added, "when you've only just moved in. A few months down the line you won't be inviting *anyone*. You ask people over for an *asado* at lunchtime and they take over the house and stay all day – you're lucky if they don't spend the night, too. They treat your house like their own place in the country. Where did you get this china?"

By this stage in the evening, the women had already drifted to one side of the room and the men to the other. Apart from me. I've always liked to mix it up. When I'm with women, I want to know what the men are talking about, and when I'm with men I wonder what's making the women laugh. I could just as easily get stuck into a conversation about shoes and handbags as one about the rise in the stock market and the fall in interest rates provoked by the Convertibility Law, or the pros and cons of Mercosur.[4] Equally I could be bored by all these things. I was sitting on the arm of Ronie's chair – he was telling Luis Cianchi about the financing of some new project he was working on at the time – when I noticed Teresa leaving the group of women with an air of exaggerated mystery. I watched her leave by the corridor that leads to the maid's room. Five minutes later she made a triumphant re-entrance. She was followed by a clown.

"Darling, since you already have everything, my gift to you this year is a little magic." Teresa smiled and the

---

3 An elaborate barbecue.
4 Mercosur is a free-trade agreement among Argentina, Brazil, Paraguay and Uruguay, founded in 1991.

magician, behind her, smiled too. El Tano didn't smile. I felt uncomfortable, as though I were to blame for some part of what was happening, simply by being a witness to it. It may be that we are responsible only for our own actions, but to watch is an action, too (or so I wrote that night in my red notebook). There was a moment's silence that seemed to last a lifetime. Then I made the decision to applaud, as though at the end of a speech. I glanced around, looking for fellow clappers. The others followed my lead, less vigorously, but with conviction. Even El Tano ended up clapping. I felt a certain relief, in spite of the fact that my hands were hurting: the ring I had won in the latest *Burako* tournament had slid round and was biting into my palm with every clap.

The magician began his show and Teresa went to sit with her husband. I was close by, sitting opposite him, and I read his lips: "Who asked you to bring that? Next time clear it with me." He spoke calmly but firmly, looking straight ahead. I guessed at the rest of their conversation as I poured myself some wine. Even without hearing him clearly, I sensed the steel behind El Tano's calm and measured tone, just as I had that time that he had said, "I want this land." And it made me think of my own voice. And of my tendency to shout. I had known for a long time that shouting had no effect either on Ronie or Juani. But I shouted all the same. Doubtless it was more a way to let off steam than to make myself heard. "If only I could learn from El Tano," I thought, at that first birthday party. As I walked past them, with my replenished glass, El Tano smiled at me and I returned the gesture. I sat on the floor, in the front row. The show was OK although the magician wasn't up to much. His suit was shabby and he raced through his set of stock jokes with little regard for intonation or timing. I clapped anyway, and the others followed suit. This time I removed my ring and put it in my trouser pocket. Every so often I turned to look at Teresa and El Tano, who were sitting together; El Tano had put his arm around her shoulder in an ambiguous gesture that could have indicated affection or control.

"I wonder if we'll be lucky enough to have the guest of honour come up and take part in a trick," said the magician. El Tano made no move – as if he were not the person to whom this invitation was extended.

"You're the birthday boy, aren't you?"

"No," said El Tano.

The magician was disconcerted; Teresa glanced uncomfortably at her husband, but still he said nothing. El Tano, meanwhile, was riding out the situation without any sign of discomfort. The others didn't know whether they should laugh or show concern, and no one was going to risk jumping the wrong way. I thought I knew what to do, but I didn't dare do it. Ronie was braver. And it struck me then how our personalities still complemented one another even while there seemed no other obvious reasons for us to stay together. We functioned as though all that had once held us together was lost, apart from a precise and tacit distribution of roles and jobs which supported the lifestyle we had put together by force of will, rather than with passion or feeling.

Ronie stood up and said: "I am the birthday boy."

The magician pretended to believe him, although he knew otherwise. His face softened and he offered up silent thanks. Everyone else went along with the joke. "The show must go on," said the magician, more to himself than to his audience. That was what they were paying him for, after all.

I clapped again, with even greater gusto, and more than one person may have concluded that I was drunk. The magician got Ronie to cut a rope into several sections, which were then joined again, then once more cut up, with knots and without knots and so on, many more times than the remaining tension in the rope ought to have allowed. Then there was a trick with rings which prompted the inevitable joke: "Ronito sure knows his way round a ring," said Roberto Cánepa, with no subtlety whatsoever. "For God's sake," muttered his wife by way of reproach, but she laughed along with the rest of us.

Then it was time for the last trick. The magician asked for a note. Ronie put his hand in his pocket and produced only coins. "Look who got paid today!" cried Insúa, and he laughed heartily to leave no doubt that this was meant as a joke, and that no one should take offence. Someone in the audience moved to open his wallet, but El Tano motioned him to stop. Without moving from his seat, he took out a one-hundred-dollar bill and held it out towards the magician; it was rolled up lengthways, like a bill that is destined to be tucked into the cleavage of a dancing girl. To reach it, the magician had to weave his way around the spectators while El Tano made no effort other than to hold the note in the air. The magician's hands were sweating, and the note stuck to him. "Thank you, sir… that's most kind," he said, and he returned to the improvised stage, trying not to step on anyone.

The trick consisted of noting down the bill's serial number, folding it, placing it in a box and burning it by inserting a cigarette into the box. The note would then reappear, completely undamaged.

"Years ago, instead of this trick, I used to do the one where the lady assistant gets sawn in half," said the magician as he placed the note into the box. "But I've come to realize that the dollar-bill trick creates much more tension in certain audiences."

We laughed. It was the first joke that had hit the mark. Even El Tano laughed, and some of the tension dissipated. The magician went on with his work. He asked Mariana Andrade for the cigarette she was smoking. He inserted it into the little box that held the note; the smoke became darker and denser. The cigarette passed through the box and emerged on the other side, slightly crushed. A bead of sweat ran down the side of the magician's face and I feared that the trick had failed. But no. The magician returned the cigarette to its owner, then made Ronie open the box, take out the note, unfold it and show it to the audience as it should be: perfect, intact, valid. He checked the serial number: it was the same bill. This drew hearty applause, inspired less by the trick itself than by a certainty that the show was approaching its end. The magician extended the note to El Tano, who said: "You may as well keep it. I'm sure all this is costing me a pretty penny anyway." The note hovered in the air between them for an instant, then the magician folded it more neatly and carefully than he had when he was doing the trick, and put it in his pocket. He bowed and said once more: "Thank you sir, that's most kind."

We were the last to leave and they took us to the door. As they stood in the doorway, El Tano had his arm around his wife – as he had all night – and the gesture still seemed ambiguous.

"We've had a great time – thanks," I said, as one does.

"It was really nice, wasn't it?" replied Teresa.

I looked at Ronie, waiting for him to say something and, when he didn't, I quickly covered his silence. "Yes, it was really nice, thank you."

It annoyed me that Ronie could not make his own contribution – even a monosyllabic one – to the pleasantries. I looked at him again, and gave him a little kick. There was another short silence, then he said: "Do you know what your problem is going to be here, Tano?"

El Tano wavered.

"You've got no rival."

The three of us were quiet; I don't suppose any of us understood what he intended by this remark and I even felt a bit frightened.

"There's no one here to give you a good game; you're going to end up getting bored. We need new blood, people who can play tennis at your level, Tano."

El Tano smiled, then. So did I. "I expect you to bring this up with prospective buyers, Virginia. Item one on the admissions form: excellent standard in tennis. Otherwise, no deal."

And so for the last time, before the night ended, we all laughed at a joke that none of us found funny. We made our final goodbyes, then walked slowly away, barely making a sound on the dewy grass. Behind us, we heard the click of the Scaglias' door closing. A heavy door with a lock that sounded like some piece of precision clockwork.

We walked a little further in silence and, when I felt we were far enough away, I said: "I bet you he's giving her shit about that magician." Ronie looked at me and shook his head. "I bet you he's wondering who would make a good tennis partner."

8

Virginia spent her first years at Cascade Heights looking after Juani and enjoying the sports, the woodland walks and her new friendships. She was one of us. If she ever sold or rented us a house or a plot of land during that time, it would have been a one-off transaction, in which she intervened only because she knew one of the parties concerned.

Six years later, when Ronie lost his job, she became more formally involved in the property market. For years she had managed an estate on behalf of some friends of the family, and now she was due a sizeable payment which would allow them to live comfortably for a while. This might be a shorter or longer-term arrangement, depending on the rate of their outgoings from that point on. And Ronie took it in that spirit, regarding the fallow period as an open-ended sabbatical. By the time it ended, he reckoned he would be earning an income. Mavi feared otherwise, while saying nothing. She suspected that her husband would have difficulty finding a new job, and she did not want to see her savings bleed away with no source of funds to staunch the haemorrhage. At work they had told Ronie that they needed to "cut costs", and within a month of firing him they had brought in a recently-graduated agronomist and were training him to do the job that he had done himself with no degree.

Meanwhile, like some trick with mirrors, another man had assured himself of a job. He was our own leader, the President of Argentina, who, thanks to a piece of constitutional reform, need no longer step down after four years in office, but could be re-elected for another term. Ronie was not so lucky. In that death-stricken year, many people lost their jobs – but others fared even worse. A year after the bomb that devastated the Argentine Jewish Mutual Association, the President's son was killed in a helicopter accident; there was an explosion at a munitions factory in Río Tercero which killed six people. And we lost some of our idols – that boxer who had once thrown his wife out of a window, and the first Argentine Formula One champion seen off by the entire neighbourhood of Balcarce, who set fire to the engine of his car during the funeral. But at that time death had not yet come closer to us, it had not touched our circle of friends.

"Mavi Guevara" was the first estate agency to be run by someone who really knew The Cascade. Someone we knew too. María Virginia Guevara. Virginia: we neither called her by her full name nor by the shortened version, because "María Virginia" was associated with a time before we knew her and "Mavi" was a hybrid created for business purposes. Before Virginia appeared on the scene, we used to buy and sell houses through the agencies in San Isidro, Martínez or in Buenos Aires, and it felt very impersonal: nobody knew anyone and the agents talked about the houses as though they were separable from the ground on which they stood. Virginia embraced a very different style. She knew better than anyone that each house hid treasures. And flaws, too. She knew that the streets do not run in parallel lines here, as they do in the city, that their layout does not correspond to the usual format. After showing three houses, your average estate agent could easily confuse east with west and end up calling the guard as Cascade Heights dissolved into a maze from which he could not escape even by retracing his own footsteps.

Strangers to The Cascade are like the fairy-tale Hansel, whose breadcrumbs got eaten up by birds: their sense of direction gets eaten up. They're trapped in a pattern of streets where everything looks the same and different at once. Virginia, on the other hand, could find the exit with her eyes closed. Any of us could. We know from memory the spinney above which the sun rises, the house behind which it sets. In summer *and* winter – because they aren't the same. We know at what time the first bird sings and the whereabouts of bats or weasels. That was something Virginia always kept in mind when showing a house: the bats and the weasels. When they come to The Heights, potential buyers sometimes imagine they have landed in paradise and, if they haven't been warned, they can get a hell of a shock when they come across one of these creatures. Our three barriers cannot keep the bats and weasels out, nor can the perimeter fence. You get used to them and you even grow to like them, but the first encounter makes quite an impression and it's disenchanting in a way. Those of us who come from the city arrive here with lots of fantasies about country life but lots of fears, too. "And in the estate-agency business we want to feed the fantasies and banish the fears" – that's a line in Virginia's notebook from the chapter headed "Bats, Weasels and other Creatures of The Cascade". She's added in brackets "(at least until the contract's signed)". Virginia used to carry this red, spiral-bound notebook everywhere; it was like a log book charting all that she learned about the business of estate agency. If bats and weasels were bad, a hare, on the other hand, was a bonus when showing a house – especially to families with children: "that tends to be the sort of nature they like to see".

With the passing years, and her accumulated experience, Virginia's red notebook grew in value. It came to have mythic status in our community. It was part of the Mavi Guevara legend. We all knew of its existence, but nobody had read it – although some claimed to have done so. We feared that we may have been included in it, and also that we may not have been. And we hazarded (wrongly) that all of us together could build up a picture similar to the one taking shape within its pages, simply by stringing together isolated remarks we had heard from Virginia over the years, and by inventing some other plausible ones. By repeating such maxims as we remembered, we began to build up an imaginary, oral version of the red notebook, which we defended as the truth. And Virginia did not refute it. "Behave yourself, or you're going down in my red notebook," she would threaten, laughing. She claimed to jot down everything, even when she was not sure of the usefulness of some notes. The outflow of the irrigation channels. Which garden is prone to flooding. Who is the best electrician in the area. And the best locksmith. Which neighbour is impossible to deal with. Which one neglects his pet. Which one neglects her children. People say she even notes down the names of men who are cheating on their wives or who underpay their maids. But it must all be gossip because – what does any of that have to do with buying or selling a house?

As well as the red notebook, Virginia used to carry an index file containing white, lined cards. The Insúas. The Masottas. The Scaglias. The Uroviches. Every house was indexed, whether it was for sale or not. She started including the ones that were not for sale after learning that some newspapers hold on file the obituaries of certain famous people who have not yet died. "Forward planning," she used to say, "and less macabre in my case than theirs." And even though some people objected to their inclusion in her *premortem* file, time always proved her right. Crises of one kind or another meant that houses which had been bought as a lifelong investment must suddenly be sold. The kind of money that buys you into a place like this can vanish in the blink of an eye. And Mavi was neither a prophet of doom nor eaten up with envy – which is what Leticia Hurtado shouted in her face, shortly after their house was sold at auction. She simply could see, before anyone else, the way things were going – to the extent that she even kept a card on her own house.

There came a time when, outside almost all the houses sold or rented in Cascade Heights, there was a sign reading "Mavi Guevara, Estate Agency". In terms of customer service, no one could compete with her. Virginia never ended a meeting without having a coffee with her client, or chatting about something other than business or without having at least a vague sense of who this person was signing papers on the other side of her desk. "I wouldn't feel able to sell a friend's house to just anybody. In Cascade Heights all the houses either belong or have belonged to friends. And every new arrival is a potential friend." People say this is written on one of the first pages of her notebook. Apparently she showed these lines to Carmen Insúa, one afternoon, when Carmen was no longer the woman she once had been. "Every point in a property transaction has to be crystal clear. Nobody can risk getting on the wrong side of someone, because, in Cascade Heights, sooner or later, all paths meet." And after she fell out with Carlos Rodríguez Alonso – who refused to pay the stipulated commission on the sale of his house, protesting that they were friends and that he had thought she had given him certain information "as a favour" – apparently she added in the margin of the aforementioned note: "Can you ever really become friends with someone you got to know through his wallet?" And she answered the question herself in a note at the foot of the page: "All misery is routed through the wallet."

9

Romina had already set off for school. She had gone in a minicab because getting up early put Mariana in a bad mood and was a recipe for a disastrous morning. Romina was not exactly sunny first thing, either. When Mariana had to start taking Pedro, of course she would get up early, but in the meantime she thought that it was nicer for the girl – her daughter now – to go in a taxi with Antonia, rather than to suffer her morning mood.

Mariana got into the shower and stood under the jet of water until she felt herself waking up. By the time she emerged from the bathroom, wrapped in a towel, Antonia had already returned from the school, tidied her bedroom and left a breakfast tray on the bedside table; now she was picking up the clothes left scattered around the bed. These women obviously have a different biorhythm, thought Mariana; they are pack mules. And she lay down on the bed for another five minutes. Antonia bent down to pick up the diamanté spandex T-shirt that Mariana had worn the night before, and noticed a small hole in it.

"Señora, have you seen this?"

Mariana went over and inspected the shirt. "It must have been a spark," said Antonia.

"Some idiot's cigarette. That's one hundred dollars down the drain, for the sake of a pose…"

Mariana returned the shirt to the bundle of dirty washing Antonia was carrying, and began to unwind the towel from her hair. Antonia studied the little hole beneath the armpit. "Would you like me to darn it?" she asked timidly. Mariana gave her a look. "Have you ever seen me wear darned clothes?"

Antonia left the room and went down to the laundry feeling cheerful. When Mariana stopped wearing things, she passed them on to Antonia, and this shirt was much better than anything she could have dreamed of giving her daughter for her next birthday. She inspected it before washing it by hand. The diamantes were set against the material in concentric circles that almost made her feel dizzy. None of the stones was missing and a couple of stitches would see to the hole.

When the shirt had completed its cycle of washing and ironing, Antonia took it up to Mariana's walk-in wardrobe and placed it in the compartment for black T-shirts. She knew that it would soon be hers – hopefully before Paulita's birthday – but she couldn't risk taking it without her employer's say-so.

A few days later, Mariana invited three neighbours to tea. Among other concerns, the women managed a centre offering free lunches to poor children, a few blocks away from the entrance to Cascade Heights. Teresa Scaglia, Carmen Insúa and Nane Pérez called themselves "The Ladies of the Heights", and were setting up a foundation in that name. They tried to interest Mariana in joining their crusade.

"What we need more than anything is trainers," said the one who had asked for a mango-and-strawberry infusion. "Otherwise, when it rains, half the children don't come to eat because they can't get through the mud barefoot. Can you believe it?"

"How awful," said Mariana, as Antonia passed her a teapot with more hot water.

"You have to come one day, Mariana, and bring your children so that they can see it with their own eyes. Otherwise we're just bringing them up in a bubble."

And Mariana nodded, wondering how Romina would react to seeing the children, because she had once been like them, or worse; she had been "Ramona" and she still was, in the depths of those dark, frightening eyes. Pedro, on the other hand, had always been hers, right from the start.

"Thanks, Antonia, put it just there," she said to the maid, who was standing beside her with fresh water for the pot.

A few days later, Antonia went into Mariana's room one morning and found a pile of folded clothes on the trunk at the end of the bed. The second article from the bottom was the black T-shirt with diamante stones. The rest were old clothes of Mariana's or the children and two faded golf shirts of Ernesto's.

"Put those clothes in a bag and leave them aside for Nane Ayerra," said Mariana. "She'll come to pick them up later."

Antonia didn't understand: usually Mariana gave all the old clothes to her to take to Misiones and share out among her family.

"You know Nane, right? She's the pretty blonde one who came here for tea the other day."

Antonia nodded, even though she didn't know, wasn't listening and couldn't understand why that shirt, which had so nearly been hers, was going to end up in the hands of a pretty blonde. Surely a woman like that was equally unlikely to wear darned clothes. Not daring to ask about it, she found a bag and put everything inside it. As she was about to leave the room, Mariana stopped her. "Oh, and if you're interested, on Friday we're having a jumble sale after lunch at Nane's house, to raise money for the children's free meals centre. It's exclusively for maids, so don't worry, the prices will be reasonable. All of us, no matter how much or how little we have, can do more to help, don't you think?"

Antonia nodded, but she didn't really know what she thought, because she hadn't fully understood. Or rather, she hadn't paid attention, because all she could think about was the black diamante top. Perhaps she could buy it. The Señora had said "reasonable prices". She did not know, though, what price might be considered reasonable by her employer. She could manage ten. Or maybe fifteen, because the shirt was very high quality – the Señora had bought it in Miami. And with two stitches the little hole wouldn't show.

On Friday Antonia went to the jumble sale, during the siesta, after she had finished mopping the kitchen floor.

There were two or three girls there that she knew from taking the bus on Saturday lunchtimes. She said hello, but didn't want to chat to them. The pretty blonde woman – the owner of the garage where the clothes were all laid out – was there with three other women she recognized, having seen them at her employer's house. They were chatting, laughing and drinking coffee. Every now and then, one or other of them came over to give the price of an article of clothing. One of the girls from the bus chose a coral-red silk dress. It was pretty, but it had two small stains on the hem, probably caused by bleach. If it had been blue, Antonia could have fixed that; once she had accidentally stained Romina's blue gym bottoms with bleach then used a biro to colour in the mark and Mariana had never noticed. Romina herself had suggested this, when the girl found her worrying about the mark. Romina was always helping her; the girl was a bit gruff, but intelligent – not like her, she thought. That red was going to be difficult, though. They charged the girl from the bus five pesos. If that was the going rate, Antonia reckoned that she was going to be able to buy the shirt. But she couldn't see her employer's sparkly top anywhere. She checked all the piles, without finding it. She wanted it so much, she plucked up the courage to ask one of the ladies.

"A black T-shirt… I don't think there is one." The lady asked one of the others: "Have you seen a black T-shirt that would be right for her, Nane?"

"No, there's nothing in black," put in Teresa. "But why do you want black? That colour won't suit you – it's going to drain you. Wear something that picks you up a bit, that makes your face glow. Try looking in that pile."

"It's not for me, it's for my daughter," said Antonia, but once more they were chatting among themselves and did not hear her.

Antonia continued to look through the piles, but without hoping to find anything. It was the Señora's black top or nothing. That was what she wanted, to give to Paulita for her birthday. "Thank you," she said at last and left empty-handed. Over the following days, Antonia thought more than once about the shirt that was not hers. She wondered who must have taken it. At the weekend, she asked the girls on the bus, but nobody had seen it. Finally she put it out of her mind. "At the end of the day, a shirt isn't going to change anyone's life," she thought.

And then Halloween came round. Mariana had bought sweets to give to the children who came to their door that evening. She had bought Romina a witch's outfit, so that she could go trick-or-treating round the neighbours' houses. But since coming home from school, the girl had been shut up in her room and Mariana didn't feel like coaxing her down. Pedro was still too little to go out, and burst into tears when he saw people dressed up. Lots of people knocked on the Andrades' door that night. The children of friends, Romina's classmates, "Children who like good, clean fun," said Mariana to her daughter, by way of a reproach. She had bought the sweets in the supermarket a few days before and hidden them in the desk in the sitting room, which was where Mariana hid everything she did not want to be eaten. By nine o'clock, three groups of children had already come by. At a quarter past nine, the doorbell rang again. Antonia went to answer the door with an instruction to share out the remaining sweets and send the children away. Mariana didn't like interruptions at dinner time. Outside was a gaggle of girls who had emerged from the boot of a four-by-four driven by Nene Pérez Ayerra. She too got out of the car and asked Antonia to call her employer. She had to ask twice, because Antonia now stood transfixed by the sight of her daughter, a girl of about eight, who was dressed as a witch, with silver fingernails, pointed fangs and a trickle of red paint running from the side of her mouth. She was wearing a black, floor-length skirt and the top with little diamante stones that had belonged to the Señora.

"I just had to show you this," said Nane when Mariana came to the door.

"No way that's my top!"

Antonia said: "Yes, it is," but nobody heard her.

"You know what girls are like at this age. She saw it when I was laying things out for the jumble sale and she decided on a whim that she wanted it for Halloween, so I took it out of the sale. But she knows that after Halloween she has to give it back to me – right?"

The girl said nothing: she was busy filling her little basket with sweets from the bag held out by Antonia.

"I'll let her get her way this time then put it into the next sale."

"Come on – if she likes it that much, let her hang on to it. It's a present from Auntie Mariana," she said, and bent to give the girl a kiss.

"OK, but in that case you'll have to choose one of your own shirts and give it to me instead," Nane told her daughter, "because we all have to learn to do our bit, even when we're little, if we want this world to change – don't we?"

But the girl could not answer, because her mouth was engaged in the business of trying to chew a gigantic toffee. Meanwhile Antonia was still standing there, staring at the T-shirt. She counted five diamante stones missing from the concentric circles. Luckily, the gaps did not stand out very much – two were at the side, close to the seam, two close to the hem and one under the bust. It was a shame: none of them had been missing before. At any rate, with fewer diamantes, in the next jumble sale the price of the shirt would be even more "reasonable", as her employer put it. Damaged goods are always cheaper, she thought.

10

One summer, the playground at Cascade Heights was completely overhauled. That time of year was chosen to do the work, because there are fewer residents in the neighbourhood and many of the people who are here are holidaymakers, renting one of our houses while we spend the summer somewhere else. The worst choice of holiday destination that year was Pinamar, where the summer season was much affected by the murder of a photographer who had dared to take a picture of a private postal-services tycoon as he strolled on the beach.

The Children's Commission had presented to the Council of Administration a detailed report on each piece of equipment to be replaced. The principle thrust of their argument was that, with other sectors of our club evolving, the playground must not be allowed to remain frozen in time. And they closed their presentation with this observation: "Let's not be blind; children are our future."

The contract went to a pair of architects who specialized in children's play areas, having designed playgrounds for two shopping centres and for several other gated communities in the area. They drew up a project, put forward three budgets, and the most reasonable of these was approved. Finally the wood and iron equipment, which had been in place since our community's first days, was replaced with plastic installations reminiscent of Fisher Price. It was sad when the maintenance team dismantled the slide, which was the longest any child in The Cascade had ever seen. But the report made it clear that the replacements would be the safest and most up-to-date available, and that they would require less upkeep. So they changed them. They put new plants along the borders of all the paths and replaced the drinking fountains – which, although they made a lot of mess, had given the children so much fun in summer – with purified-water dispensers. That was not part of the original plan, but was incorporated after a television programme claimed that water tables in the area were contaminated – with some substance which never turned up in any analysis.

The playground was not only home to new equipment, but to new sounds as well. For the voices around the sand pit had been gradually transmuting, without anyone really noticing it, until one day a new cadence held sway. The noise of children laughing and shouting was the same, but the adult voices were different now. Up until the start of the 1990s, Paraguayan accents had been the rule, along with the sing-song inflection of some far-flung Argentine province. But in the 1990s, the Peruvian accent began to dominate – if "dominate" is the right word, because this voice was particularly sweet, calm and polite. "Put that down, now, or you'll get all dirty." "That little boy is a naughty so-and-so." "That little girl is always half-undressed." "I saw that little girl get right in the sand and cause a nuisance." But all this was said quietly, as if they did not wish to annoy anyone. And around them the usual hubbub of laughter and shouting continued, ebbing and flowing through myriad plastic circuits.

The new playground boasted yellow, red and blue slides, tunnels and walkways. There were monkey bars that you could hang from and swing your way across from one side of the sand pit to the other. There were swings in wood-effect plastic for older children, and in green plastic, with a safety bar, for the younger ones. There were basketball hoops, a see-saw and a roundabout. They put in a house, on wooden pilings, with a blue roof and yellow door, which was imported direct to Cascade Heights from the Fisher Price factory in the United States. It was a kind of tree house, with nets in the windows (so that the children could look out without risking a fall), from which you could reach the slide, via a hanging bridge. The playground, cleaner than ever, was now brilliantly decked-out in primary colours. All that was left of the old incarnation were the chains on the swings; these were thick chains of the kind that are no longer manufactured. The architects had not been able to convince anyone that the new plastic rope was tough enough to allow the twisting and vertiginous swinging that these chains did.

11

Romina and Juani first meet in the little playground at The Cascade. Even though they go to the same school, they have never crossed paths before. They meet one afternoon. Juani arrives on a bicycle, alone. He is one of the few children who go to the playground alone. Everyone else comes accompanied by the "girl who looks after us": their families' domestic servants. Juani doesn't have one of those any more; he used to, but not now. There's just a woman who comes to clean the house in the morning, when he's at school.

The children swing themselves far too high. Some of them twist the swings up, then spin madly around. Romina doesn't look at them, so as not to feel dizzy. She uses a stick to draw in the sand. She draws a house and a river. She scratches them out. A very tall boy throws the swing over the top crossbar, to lift it further off the ground. Antonia pushes Pedro in one of the baby swings, while she chats to another maid. They are speaking the same language, but they sound different. The very tall boy grows bored and leaves. Juani gets onto the swing he has left. He untwists it. He swings on his own. Two little girls fight over another swing. One of them, in embroidered jeans, pulls the hair of the other one, who's wearing a pink dress. The other one cries. Nobody looks at them, apart from Romina. The girl in the dress cries harder. She starts shouting. Then the maids who look after these two come over. "What a little devil you are," one of them says to the child who isn't crying. "Let your little friend have the swing – don't make her cry." The girl doesn't want to; she clings on to the swing. The girl in the pink dress cries even harder.

Juani gets down from his swing and holds out the chains to the girl who is crying. "Here you are," he says. Romina watches, while drawing in the sand. "I want the other one!" the girl retorts. Juani offers his swing to the girl who isn't crying. He suggests swapping it for the one favoured by the girl who is crying. The one who isn't crying refuses. Annoyed, Juani goes back to swinging, higher and higher. "I'm going to tell your mummy," says the Peruvian girl in charge of the child who isn't crying and won't give up her swing. "Bitch," retorts the child and runs off. The one who's crying stops crying then and runs after her. They tread on Romina's drawing. They climb up the yellow slide and hurl themselves down it, laughing. The maids who look after them return to their bench and resume chatting. One complains that her *patrona* won't let her have a siesta, and her legs are swelling up as a result. Juani swings higher and higher. Romina watches him. She covers her ruined picture with sand and looks at him again. From where she is sitting, it looks as though Juani is touching the sky with his brown shoes. One of his laces is missing. Romina stands up and goes over to the other swing. She swings herself. She tries to reach him. Just when she thinks she may reach him, Juani throws himself from the highest point and falls onto the sand. The swing continues to move haphazardly, now that it carries no weight. Romina would like to jump, but doesn't dare. "Go on – jump. You'll be fine," says Juani from below. She goes back and forth, undecided. "Go on, I'm waiting for you." Romina throws herself off. She lets herself fall through the air and, for the first time since she left Corrientes, she feels light. She falls onto the sand, twisting one foot. Juani gets up to help her.

"Did you hurt yourself?" he asks.

"No," she says, and laughs.

"What's your name?" he asks her. She writes it on the sand: "Ramona".

12

To stand at the tee on the first hole and let your eyes wander over a vista of never-ending green is a privilege that those of us who live in Cascade Heights sometimes take for granted. Until we lose it. People get accustomed to what they have – especially when what they have is wonderful. Many of us can go for months without playing a single hole, as if we didn't care that the course was a few yards from our house and entirely at our disposal.

You don't have to be a golfer to enjoy such natural beauty – "natural" because it comprises grass, trees and lakes, not "natural" in the sense of belonging to a landscape that was here before we arrived. This used to be a swamp. The course was designed by engineer Pérez Echeverría, who famously sketched the plan for a club in the south while aboard a helicopter, as it flew over the forest that would need to be felled. Today it's impossible to imagine that our fairways were once marshes. There are species of tree that had to be brought specially from nurseries in different parts of the country. The shrubs, planted by landscape gardeners, are tended every week and changed with the seasons. An automatic sprinkler comes on every night. And then there are fertilizers, insecticides, supplements. The river that crosses hole fifteen was here before we arrived. But we purified it. Now it's a more turquoise green, thanks to water treatment, and the introduction of certain algae which keep the ecosystem aerated. The fish that were there before the purification have died. They were undistinguished fish, a sort of bream, brownish-coloured. We put in orange perch, which reproduced and became the new masters of the stream. There are ducks and otters, too. Although recently the ducks and otters are down in numbers. Some say it's because people are killing them. For food. But that's very unlikely. Even if someone tried it – the maintenance staff, caddies, gardeners, anyone who dared – it would be impossible for them to smuggle their catch past our security guards. Once they caught a caddie throwing a dead duck over the perimeter fence to a woman on the other side. He claimed to have hit it accidentally, with a killer shot from the fourth tee. But nobody believed him. I mean, the woman on the other side had all but brought her casserole dish. The committees for Golf and for the Environment served him a joint indictment.

The lakes are, in fact, the sole true remnant of the marsh that was once here. But nobody would know that; there can't be a golf course anywhere in the world that doesn't have a lake. We use a system of pumps to drain rainwater collected in the irrigation channels around our community into the lake and thus avoid flooding; the water is pumped in and then the river itself carries it out of the club. The Municipal Government complained once that we were exporting the problem of surplus water to the neighbourhood of Santa María de los Tigrecitos, but there were a couple of meetings between their council and ours and somehow the matter was resolved. It would be like blaming the city of Córdoba for the flooding in Santa Fe. Some sort of inexpensive alteration had to be made. The last major investment was in chemical toilets, which became a requirement once the ladies took over the course. If a man's caught short, he can urinate anywhere: behind a tree, in some bushes. Even on a golf course. Not so a woman.

Our course is re-sown every year. You won't find that in every club. Most of them only re-seed the tee of each hole. Pencross on the greens and Bermuda on the fairways. The re-seeding, together with the cost of the machines, the staff involved, the irrigation and draining systems, etc., mean that maintaining the golf course accounts for one of the most congested columns in our budget. The tennis players grumble about it. There's some mutual goading between aficionados of the two sports. People complain that the club spends much more money on golf than tennis and that it all comes out of the same fees and the same pockets. But investment in the course does not benefit the golfers alone. Members of our community can stroll on the links, have a drink on the terrace at the ninth hole (with its enviable views), listen to music while watching the sun set over the fifteenth hole or even go on a photographic safari to take pictures of wild birds. The Environment Committee has provided a great outreach service by placing at each hole a wooden sign with photographs of the birds you can expect to see, showing their markings and characteristics. But, quite apart from the enjoyment that each one of us may take in it, there is an important economic benefit in having a course – as we all know. The value of our houses is directly related (whatever the percentage is, it must be significant) to their proximity to good links. The same house, in a neighbourhood without a course, would be worth much less.

Years ago, playing golf was an exclusive activity. In other countries it still is. Not so in Argentina. It's expensive, but the Convertibility Law has narrowed all manner of gaps and "expensive" no longer has to mean "exclusive". In the golf bar there are wooden shields bearing the names of the winners of the club's annual tournaments. And over the years, the engraved surnames have become progressively less grand. In 1975, one Menéndez Behety was the champion. In 1985, a McAllister. And in 1995 it was a García. Not García Moreno. Not García Lynch. Not García Nieto. Just plain old García. On Wednesdays the course fills up with Japanese players. On Thursdays it's hired out to companies. When Koreans enquire, the Starter has instructions to say that the course is full or to lie about the cost of the "greens fee", which is levied on all non-members who wish to play a round. Apparently ours is not the only course to make Koreans unwelcome. Other golfers complain that they tend to shout, fight, throw their clubs around and bet monstrous sums of money, provoking violent outbursts. But, Koreans aside, at the start of the 1990s it was already clear that golf would not much longer remain the preserve of gentlemen. Fewer and fewer men bother to don the requisite polo shirt and pleated trousers. Even some of our members shout. Some of the women think it acceptable to play in a sleeveless top. There are members who throw their clubs in disgust when they drop one too many shots on a tournament-winning hole. There are players who are slow and won't let anyone past, and players who complain vociferously about the slow ones and aren't above sending an intimidating ball in their direction. There are players who withhold score cards with more shots than expected in order to keep up a socially desirable handicap. Such golfers do not care whether they play well or not; the only thing that matters to them is keeping their handicap at ten or below. On the other hand there are players who conceal score cards with fewer strokes than expected in order to keep a high handicap that will give them an advantage in tournaments. In short, players are increasingly likely to lie on their score cards. You get all kinds. The last straw was Mariano Lepera. In the Club Cup he got a hole-in-one, then tried to deny it in order to avoid buying a round of champagne. He had teed-off at the sixth hole, and the ball, after describing a perfect arc, fell onto the green, bounced three times, rolled around, then dropped into the hole marked by a flag. It was one shot, without a doubt. No more swings were necessary. Only one. On any course, anywhere in the world, it is a courtesy and unwritten law (to which no one has ever objected) that a golfer who scores a hole-in-one must buy a drink for everyone on the course at that moment. Usually champagne. Sometimes whisky. For every player from the first to the eighteenth. Mariano Lepera asked the Starter how many people he had brought out that morning and made a quick calculation: 120 players at roughly five pesos each: 600 pesos. "Over my dead body." And off he went, before anyone could get their order in. That's just not done. Or it *wasn't* done. Nothing happens to you – it's not like there's a sanction – but it's not gentlemanly. That's why they have hole-in-one insurance policies. Any insurer will provide one. Most of us get offered it when we take out housing insurance. Fire, theft and – for a few more centavos a month – hole-in-one. You're insuring a particular kind of misfortune, which is neither fire, theft nor third-party damage. Really, you're insuring a moment of joy, because anyone who can get a ball in the hole from 150 yards should consider himself very fortunate. The fact that there's a national register in which these lucky few can have their names recorded goes to show how special it is. Although most people prefer to put their names in the United States register to get international recognition. The procedure's simple: a letter, a few forms. It's plain silly not to get the insurance and take full pleasure in your triumph. In life there may be few chances to get a hole-in-one, but there are many to prove oneself a gentleman.

13

It was a shock the first time I was called to Juani's school. To Lakelands. I opened the red folder and between two letters – one inviting me to a ceremony for National Flag Day, and another reminding me to submit fees – there was an official summons on paper with a letterhead. Lakelands' letterhead is a shield with four words in English around it. I never remember exactly what the words are. "In God We Trust" says Ronie drily. Dear parents, please come to the School Office at 9 a.m. on Monday, 15 June to talk about, a series of dots, then, written in hand: *Juan Ignacio Guevara.* Juani. I had never before been formally summoned to talk about my son. I started to worry. Juani was in fifth grade. The letter was signed by the headmistress and the school's psychologist.

I received the letter on a Friday. All weekend I worried. I couldn't imagine why they wanted to talk to me. I asked

Juani: he didn't know either. He'd never been kept in at break; he hadn't been sent to see the head, or made to sign the discipline book. I followed him around the house. "Have you hit anyone? Did you swear?" I followed him into the bathroom and kept asking questions while he was showering. "Stop it, Mum." He ended up in tears. I rang a friend to see if she had also been summoned. No, she hadn't been called in. I rang another. Nor had she. I didn't ring anyone else after that; I didn't want the whole world to know about – whatever it was. But they found out anyway, at the tennis tournament that weekend. As we were changing ends, Mariana Andrade said, "So you have to go into school on Monday?" And she added: "I bet any day they'll call me in, about the girl," referring to Romina, with whom Juani spent a lot of time.

"How did you hear about it?"

"Leticia Liporacce told me, when I ran into her at the supermarket."

And while I was wondering who might have told Leticia Liporacce, Mariana served an ace into the corner of the base line, a weak, flabby ball, soft as a balloon, but I never even saw it go by.

On Monday, I was there at nine on the dot. Lakelands is two highway exits away from Cascade Heights. There was a time when we fantasized about moving it inside our compound, as in other country clubs, where the children can go to school by bike or on skates. "It would be so lovely to recapture that neighbourhood thing we had as children," said Teresa Scaglia at the parents' meeting where the idea was proposed. But there was a lot of opposition: the school already had too many children from other gated communities and, even though none of those sent as many children as we did, their combined fees represented income that the school could not afford to lose.

The primary school and administration are housed in the main building. To one side of it is the secondary school and, behind that, the kindergarten. The school is virtually mixed. I say "virtually" because, although it takes boys and girls, they do not share classrooms or a playground. There are separate divisions for girls and boys. They're only together in the kindergarten. In the playground the areas are divided by a double yellow line (like those road markings that indicate "no overtaking") beyond which neither sex must stray into the other's patch. Juani used to sit on one side of the line and Romina on the other and they communicated using sign language. However, a watchful teacher misinterpreted one of Juani's gestures and after that he was forbidden to talk to his friend across the line, on threat of suspension. But they didn't call me in that time – there was just a note in the folder, written in English, which I had to ask Dorita Llambías to translate.

The first time I went to register Juani, I asked the headmistress if the division of sexes was based on some pedagogic theory relating to psychological development and gender differences in learning. "Something like that," she said. "In 1989 we had to start taking boys, because otherwise it was very difficult for families with lots of children to manage the school run and all the extracurricular patriotic ceremonies – and they also lost out on the sibling discount. So we went ahead and put them together, but immediately we realized that was a mistake; we had been naive. The girls started sitting with their legs apart, showing what shouldn't be shown and

77

swearing – typical male behaviour. Two months into the term we separated them and painted the yellow line. We pride ourselves on a capacity to react quickly and intelligently to this sort of thing."

The school's three buildings are brick-clad, with generous windows. A concern for security can be discerned in every detail: everything is on one level, to avoid the need for stairs and high windows; there are round door handles, security glass, air conditioning and central heating. There are three rugby pitches and two for hockey, a gym, changing area, a circular lecture theatre with seating on levels, a video room, laboratories, a big room for art and music. The library's on the small side – bits of it have been eaten up to make new classrooms, as the school's grown – but plans are afoot to expand it as soon as is feasible.

I sat and waited at the reception. The pine chairs were uncomfortably hard. The secretary brought me a coffee and apologized for the wait. Ronie had not wanted to come with me. "It'll be for something trivial, Virginia. Don't make me cancel stuff just to go and talk to a child psychologist." And by "stuff" he meant some project, or a million-dollar deal he never managed to clinch, whereas I had cancelled two viewings which could have resulted in commissions sufficient to pay our utilities bills that month. I finished my coffee and looked at my watch. At barely five minutes past nine o'clock, the head's door opened. The women smiled as they invited me in, but, for all their smiling, they didn't seem in the least relaxed – quite the contrary. There were a few pleasantries, then they came to the point. After our appointment they had to go to a teachers' meeting, and they didn't want to be late. The way they looked at me suggested, before they had even said anything, that they pitied me. "This is awkward, Virginia," said the headmistress. "I'd rather Sylvie explained, she'll put it better than I can." And so the school psychologist explained everything.

"Juani's been inventing some strange stories. We're concerned."

I didn't understand.

"Stories... with a sexual connotation, for want of a better word," the headmistress tried to elucidate. I was still confused.

"Probably as a result of some kind of overexcitement inappropriate for his age," explained the psychologist.

"Could you be more graphic?"

They could. They opened Juani's exercise book and asked me to read from it myself. It was a composition. His teacher had asked him to write on the subject of "My Neighbours". And Juani had written about the Fernández Luengos. "The ones who live by the tennis courts. The ones who have a black Pathfinder and a blue Alfa Romeo" – or so he referred to them, in a composition that was riddled with spelling mistakes. He wrote that he knew they had two children who went to his school, but that he couldn't remember their names. And that they had a dog, the name of which he did know: Kaiser. "That's what they shout at him: 'Kaiser get down! Kaiser, drop that or I'll kick your (beep)!'"

I was relieved that he had put "beep" and not "arse", but the relief didn't last long. He didn't even mention Mónica, Fernández Luengo's wife, but concentrated entirely on him. On Fernández Luengo senior. "The one I know best is the dad because he's the one I most often see. I get up and look at him through my window, which is opposite his study." In his essay, Juani related how he saw his neighbour working until late at his computer, which was always switched on, day and night. And he went on: "Sometimes Fernández Luengo takes off his clothes and sits back down in front of the computer with nothing on. He leaves his clothes lying on the floor, all scrumpled up." It was an injustice, he said, that this was possible in their house, while in his it was obligatory to place dirty clothes in a basket in the bathroom. The last paragraph delivered the *coup de grâce*: "When he's naked, he stops holding the mouse and puts his hands between his legs. I see him from the back, and from the side a bit. He goes on and on touching himself. He moves as though he were on a swing then finally he goes still. One night while he was doing that, Kaiser came in and started to bark and my neighbour threw a shoe at him. Another time, instead of the shoe, he threw himself on top of Kaiser and wouldn't let him go. The End." Below there was a drawing of a naked fat man mounting a dog.

I was struck dumb. The women looked at me. I didn't know what to say. "Does Juanito watch a lot of television on his own?" Yes, he had always watched television on his own, ever since he was little. "Is it possible that he's watched an adult channel, without your knowledge?"

"We don't have cable."

"Is he in the habit of lying about this sort of thing, or is this the first time?"

"I don't know."

"Do you check your computer's history?"

"What is the 'history'?"

They weren't too sure either, but the computing teacher had suggested they ask me. "Could he have had access to any pornographic sites?"

"I don't know. We don't have a computer at home – I use one at the estate agency."

"What about at a friend's house?"

"Does he drink a lot of Coca-Cola before bedtime?"

"Is there any family matter that could be affecting him?"

I started to feel dizzy. Low blood pressure, confusion, uncertainty – or all of these combined – clouded my vision and affected my balance.

"Would you like a glass of water?"

"No, thanks." They advised me to make an appointment with a psychologist. It sounded more like an order than advice.

"Given the delicacy of the matter, it's vital to act quickly. In cases like this, time is of the essence: we have to find a solution as soon as possible, before someone lodges a complaint."

"Who would do that? Fernández Luengo?"

"No, Fernández Luengo won't be informed. We could hardly tell him about such a thing. Him or anyone else. But some of Juani's friends saw the drawing. And we can't be sure that they won't mention it. Parents are scared by this sort of thing; they fear some sort of threat towards their children, and we have to reassure them that their little ones are not at risk."

Did she say "little ones"? "And what risk might they be running?"

"None that we cannot control – for the moment. If we thought otherwise Juani would no longer be a member of this school." The enunciation of this threat was like a sharp slap.

"Let us know as soon as you have the psychologist's report. Is there anything else you'd like to ask?"

I thanked them and got up to go. "Keep on top of him a bit more," the school psychologist advised, as I was leaving the room. And that doodle of Fernández Luengo on top of his dog sprang into my mind.

I didn't go to work that day, feeling guilty and ashamed, by turns. At times, I was also very angry. I took out the paper where Juani had done what he'd done and couldn't believe my eyes. I got hold of the name of a psychologist, but I couldn't bring myself to call her. I didn't know how to begin to explain what had happened. Even to Ronie. A few times I started to ring, then hung up. Then I was unsure if I was supposed to be consulting an educational psychologist or a plain psychologist. I ate dinner alone with Juani; Ronie was coming home late. Even when he arrived, I still could not bring up the subject. I watched him, and wondered where I had gone wrong. Or was it Ronie? What had we, together, done wrong? Many things, for sure.

Juani went to bed. "Keep on top of him more." Well, the truth was that I had not been on top of him much recently: I worked all day, until late – showing houses, singing the praises of empty plots, arranging mortgages – and the boy was growing up alone, "abandoned to God's mercy" as my mother would say. True enough, abandonment in a place like Cascade Heights differs substantially from abandonment in other parts. Here you can leave children pretty much to their own devices without worrying about those dangers that preoccupy mothers in the outside world. There's no possibility of kidnappings inside our neighbourhood, nor of burglars entering your house; a child of Juani's age can come and go from the club house by bike, on their own, at any time of day; if they're at the youth club, there's always a teacher watching them and the security guards doing their rounds. They're used to dropping in on neighbours – even ones they don't know particularly well – or getting lifts in other people's cars. The atmosphere here is very trusting. That mantra about "never talking to strangers" does not apply here. No one who lives in Cascade Heights is a stranger – or at least, they will not remain one long. Anyone visiting has been checked at the entry gate and that fosters a sense of security. Or the illusion of security. As the last decade of the century progressed, we began to protect ourselves ever more stringently behind bars. More formalities were required before a visitor could be authorized to enter; there was an increasing presence of security guards at the gate; more and bigger weapons on display. For several months now it had been standard to request – confidentially – a criminal records check on gardeners, builders, decorators and any other workers who came regularly to our country club. The measure was introduced after it was discovered that an electrician contracted by the maintenance team had served a term for rape ten years ago, and none of us had had a clue.

Plans were afoot to replace the perimeter fence with a solid wall, ten feet high. There had been talk of erecting a double fence: barbed wire on the outside, then something a little more elegant within it – but most of the members thought this inadequate. What we all wanted was a wall, so that nobody passing by could look in at us, let alone at our houses or cars. And also so that we did not have to look out. However, the wall had yet to be approved, for aesthetic reasons. For five months they had been arguing over the merits of brick versus concrete blocks.

One thing was certain, and that was that Juani watched a lot of television on his own and drank litres of Coca-Cola.

As soon as Ronie got back, I told him. I started at the beginning, but he wouldn't let me finish. I never got to tell him about the headmistress's worries, or the treatment they had advised me to seek, or the caffeine in Coca-Cola, or the dog. Especially not the dog.

"Don't tell me Fernández Luengo jerks off in front of the computer!" he said, laughing. Then he sat down to eat.

14

Carmen Insúa wrote down the names of the participants on her chart and took their ten-pesos registration fee. She made an effort to smile at each new face. But she didn't want to be there. She could hardly bear to be sitting and not moving. Her body urged her to pace up and down, to smoke, to drink coffee. This morning it had crossed her mind to invent an excuse and not show up – but she couldn't do that. Nobody missed the Cascade Heights annual *Burako* tournament, all proceeds of which went to support the children's centre in the neighbouring barrio. She certainly could not miss it, being no mere organizer, but a founder member of the "Ladies of the Heights".

In between registering two lots of partners, she tried telephoning Alfredo's mobile. It was switched off. Her legs jiggled restlessly beneath the little table that was serving as a desk. Accidentally, she kicked it, and Teresa Scaglia had to lunge for the sheets and ball-point pens before they ended up on the floor. "Please don't make me play against Rita Mansilla," one of the participants came to ask. "We said some terrible things to each other in the tennis tournament the other day."

She could barely concentrate on what they were saying. At least if she were also scheduled to play *Burako*, her mind would be occupied with something. She liked playing. Both *Burako* and Rummy. Today, though, she wouldn't have been able to put together a basic sequence. Usually she liked to make an *escalera* – a "staircase" of tiles showing consecutive numbers, preferably all red. Winning did not matter to her as much as making these sequences, the longer, the better. But she wasn't playing this time. She dialled Alfredo's number again. His phone was still switched off. She asked someone for a cigarette. She had given up smoking a few years ago, but she still felt the need of it, the same as if she had never stopped. She would also have liked a glass of wine, but that would be inappropriate here. While she waited for a couple to finish their game, she took Alfredo's credit card statement out of her bag and looked over it again, hoping to have misread the details: Hotel Sheraton, three hundred dollars, 15 August.

She felt the same void in her stomach that she had experienced the morning she discovered it, left on Alfredo's bedside table, for anyone to see. After that first time she had read it ten, twenty-five, a thousand times. And it always said the same thing: Hotel Sheraton, three hundred dollars, 15 August. The exact date that she had been in Córdoba to play in a Burako tournament, in aid of what or whom she no longer remembered. She had called him that night and no one had answered. The children had been in Pinamar with the parents of some school friends, and the nanny they had at the time had just suddenly handed in her notice. Alfredo said that he had gone to bed early with a pounding headache. Of course he hadn't said where, or with whom. She had believed him. That was the weekend of the club's most important golf tournament, and Alfredo wouldn't have missed it for the most seductive woman in the world. Or perhaps he would.

"Mark us down for one thousand, five hundred and seventy points. Who do we play next?" Carmen looked at the chart. She couldn't find the right place. The names of the different couples merged into one another. She noted down the figure. "You're with couple number nine, once they've finished playing on table ten," she said uncertainly. Teresa, who had been watching her, took the chart on which she had jotted down the score. She crossed out the "three hundred" Carmen had written in. "Did you say one thousand, five hundred and seventy?" she asked the players before they left the table. Carmen stood up. Teresa was looking at her, but she could not explain what she was doing on her feet. Then she said, "I'm going outside to have a fag," and she went out, taking her mobile and the credit card statement with her.

From the terrace opposite the ninth hole, she rang the hotel, claiming to be Mr Alfredo Insúa's secretary. "Mr Insúa says that the three hundred dollar total deducted from his card is incorrect and that he'd like a breakdown of the charges," she lied. They told her that they would fax through a copy of the bill. Carmen gave her home number, then hung up and went back to sit with Teresa. "Everything OK?" her friend asked. "Yes, everything's great," she replied.

A woman playing at the table by the window that looked onto the winter garden complained that her rivals were signalling to each other. The other pair got annoyed. There was an argument. Everybody watched, but no one intervened. Carmen rang Alfredo's mobile again. One of the women got up from the game and stormed off. This time the mobile did ring. The annoyed woman's partner tried to stop her leaving. Alfredo said "Hello," but Carmen couldn't think what to say and hung up. Both women ended up leaving – the annoyed one and her partner. Alfredo was going to know that it had been her ringing. The abandoned players now came to the table. Carmen was alone, Teresa having left the tea room in order to organize the prize-giving.

"What incredible cheek those women had – did you see them? Put down that we won by a walk-over. You can get walk-overs in this, just like in tennis, can't you?" Carmen's phone rang and she answered it without responding to the woman. It was Alfredo. "Yes, it cut out – there must be a bad signal here." Alfredo told her that he would be home late and that she shouldn't wait up for him. Carmen crossed off her chart the names of the couple who had left. "Yes, all right. I still have quite a lot to do here anyway, and then we'll have to count up the takings… Yes, it's gone really well…"

The winning ladies each went away with a necklace made of silver and zircons, donated by the Toledo jewellery shop. Everyone applauded, while Teresa and Carmen helped them to fasten the necklaces. The women posed for a photograph, one alone and one with the organizers. The tea seemed to go on for ever. Carmen called home and talked to the maid; this one had been with them for several months but, ever since

Alfredo had made her sack Gabina, who had always worked for her, she hadn't been able to find anyone as trustworthy and, for different reasons, none of them lasted long.

"Has anyone rung to ask for a fax signal?… OK… if they call and ask to send a fax, you stay beside the telephone and, as soon as the page has come through, you tear it off, fold it and put it in the drawer of my bedside table. Do you understand? OK, repeat that back to me, please." The maid repeated her instructions. Carmen couldn't hear part of it because one of the participants had come to ask for some change she was owed. She hung up. She looked for the change. She was two pesos short. "That's fine, give it to the children's centre."

Later on, the room was left empty and smelling of cigarette smoke. Two cleaning ladies were sweeping up and arranging the tables. Teresa and Carmen were counting up the money. Carmen's mobile rang. It was her maid; the fax had arrived, she had stayed beside the telephone while the paper came out – no, the children weren't there – she had torn the page off, folded it and put it in the drawer of the bedside table. Carmen hurriedly put their takings in the metal box and locked it. It was more than they had been expecting. A little more than her husband had spent that night in the hotel. "It's heartening to know that there are so many generous people around, isn't it?" said Teresa. "Yes," she replied. "There are a lot of generous people around."

They switched off the lights and went out. She was about to get into the car, then had an idea and went over to Teresa's car. "Do you want to go and get something to eat? Alfredo's back late tonight."

15

1998 was the year of suspicious suicides. There was the man who had paid bribes to the Banco Nación, the navy captain who had brokered sales of weapons to Ecuador and that private mail empresario who had been photographed by the murdered photographer. None of these events had a direct impact on our lives, or on the life of The Heights, other than to draw the eye, briefly, of someone reading about them in a newspaper or watching them on the television news.

We had our own things to talk about. Like Ronie Guevara, for example. By now we all knew what Virginia would not acknowledge – just as a cuckolded husband is always the last to hear the news: Ronie was never going to contribute anything more to the family finances than a few very expensive pipe dreams. She was the bread-winner, and keeping her estate agency secret was damaging her prospects. People were apt to confuse her work with "favours" and, on more than one occasion, someone had expressed surprise, or even taken offence, when she tried to charge a commission. "I know the owner too, so why should I have to give you a commission?" they reasoned. One man, instead of paying her, turned up with a handbag made in his own factory, which came nowhere near covering Virginia's costs and was "really ugly, too", in Teresa Scaglia's words. "When the moment comes to put money on the table, one's 'friend' enters straight away into another category, for which I have yet to find an adequate name," Virginia wrote later, in her red notebook.

The price of land was climbing in line with the economic euphoria of the 1990s, and Virginia wanted a piece of that euphoria. Everyone wanted a piece. All of us speculated on how much the value of our houses was rising each day and how much higher it might go. When we multiplied the surface area of our homes by the value of a square foot, we experienced a euphoria unequalled by almost any other: the pleasure principle of an algorithm. Because we weren't planning to sell our houses to anyone. It was the maths alone, that simple multiplication, that caused us joy.

The time had come for Virginia to establish an official estate agency. Cascade Heights regulations forbid members to carry out any sort of commercial activity on the site itself and, although many do, it is on the tacit understanding that this be discreet. In places like this, envy leads to complaints, and complaints to penalties. To put a sign outside her house saying "Mavi Guevara, Estate Agency" would have breached the tacit agreement. On the other hand, operating discreetly was no longer enough for her. The solution was to put her sign up outside the perimeter fence, close enough to be seen by people who were coming to look for property in Cascade Heights, and for her to expand the business that way.

Ronie agreed with the plan, and at that time he could often be heard talking enthusiastically at gatherings of friends about the future of estate agency in the area and the growth potential of his wife's business. But that was as far as his commitment went: he did not accompany her in the search for premises that would help her "make the leap". She got in the car and drove around the area scanning each block for the closest thing to a commercial lot she could find. All of us pass back and forth through these streets, at least once a day, but we never pay attention to them until we need something from them. Now, for the first time ever, Virginia looked closely.

The area outside Cascade Heights' perimeter fence is quite different from a commercial neighbourhood. There are vacant lots, areas of wasteland. In some cases buildings have been abandoned half-built, then left to the ravages of time and dereliction, people carting away anything that could be useful to them. Three properties, all next to each other, have been deserted because of burglaries and maintenance costs which were too high to be justified by their infrequent use. Diagonally opposite the entrance to The Cascade, there is a small house owned by a young couple who could not afford to live inside the barrier. They built their home with an eye to the development they believed would transform the area around Cascade Heights (this has yet to take place) and in the shadow of a security guard booth which faced the other way but was nonetheless reassuring.

A little further down the road that leads to the highway, the neighbourhood of Santa María de los Tigrecitos begins. This district is characterized by simple, jerry-built houses, almost all of them made by the people who live in them – or by their relations or friends. Residents in this area depend on the work that we provide for them at Cascade Heights. The reports published by our Security Committee – which recommend supporting these neighbours – refer to it as a "satellite community"; their work opportunities fluctuate in line with the growth rate of our community and that, according to reports, directly affects our own security.

The houses in Santa María de los Tigrecitos spring up in as unruly a fashion as the shrubs in Cascade Heights, but their disarray is not a matter of surreptitious design, as it is in our gardens. In Los Tigrecitos people do what they can: they throw up a house that bears no relation to the ones on either side; in some cases there is no relation even between one room and the next. You can make out the different stages of construction from outside: a window that was made after a room was finished, and which does not fit with the dividing wall; the upper floor that was built on top of what had originally been intended as a roof; the bathroom that could finally be accommodated, but without adequate ventilation. A railing might be painted violet and the wall beside it red, or bright blue. And next door there might be another house with unrendered brickwork. The more substantial houses have a parking area at the front and the humble ones make do with earth floors in every room, while their owners wait for the work that's going to pay for the cement.

There's a little market: a butcher, a baker, a bar with pool and table football. Santa María de Tigrecitos amounts to no more than six blocks on either side of a paved street which leads to the highway. We paid for this street ourselves through a supplementary charge on our expenses. On both sides of the street, the density and quality of the housing seem to evaporate the further you venture down its dirt side roads. Every so often the river, which is covered once it emerges from The Cascade, overflows, flooding the dirt roads.

On the main street leading to the highway, there are pavements, but not outside every house. They are not paid for by the municipality, but by the home-owners themselves, so some are broken and others have been repaired with slabs of different colours. Outside the butcher's – next to the blackboard offering the kind of bargain cuts of meat that we in Cascade Heights never eat – the locals sit together on wooden benches to drink maté. On the next block there are more locals, apparently waiting for something. Or nothing. And more of them sit on the other side of the road. They're watching the cars go by. Some of them can tell immediately who is driving through, just from the model and number plate. "You drive a blue BMW 367, right?" said an assistant to the carpenter working for Eduardo Andrade – who immediately reported the comment to the Council of Administration, for consideration by the Cascade Heights Security Committee.

At the heart of the neighbourhood, by way of a civic centre, are the football pitch, the school and a chapel that belongs to the same parish as the chapel inside Cascade Heights, with the same priest presiding over mass. Further on is the Health Centre, which houses a vaccination clinic and crèche. And all over the place, sprouting willy-nilly like mushrooms after a rainfall, there are houses. And more houses. A lot of houses crammed into a small area. They are home to large families, one of whose number travels the ten blocks to our security barrier every day, to work within our confines as a gardener, caddie, domestic servant, builder, decorator or cook.

It was in the block next to the Health Centre that Virginia spotted a small unit, once a video club. In its window there was a hand-made sign contrived out of an old poster for a Stallone film, on which someone had added a blue moustache and the words: "For Rent". Its size and state of repair made it a viable option for her agency. Some people say she gave it serious thought, that she came close to leaving her contact details. But Teresa Scaglia made her reconsider. "Do you really think that someone with the kind of car we drive is going to stop there and dare to get out?" Any one of us would have given similar advice. Perhaps in a more roundabout way, employing a few euphemisms, or dropping our voices, for we are less brazen than Teresa Scaglia. But it was obvious that that place wasn't going to work. It's unusual for anyone from Cascade Heights to stop off in Santa María de los Tigrecitos. Generally we get out of there as fast as the speed bumps will allow. The people who live there use the shops; not us. If we keep our distance, it is because of the dirt streets, the lack of adequate parking places and, above all, the distance from the security booth at the entrance to Cascade Heights. Every day you hear about robberies in Santa María de los Tigrecitos. Some people say that they steal from each other. They themselves say that the thieves come from outside the area. Hard to know for sure.

In the end, Virginia's problem was resolved by a stroke of luck. The husband of the woman who lived in the cottage diagonally opposite the entrance gate, with its back to the security post, walked out on her and their three small children. The woman opted to move in with her mother and Virginia rented the cottage from her at a minimal rate, on the understanding that she would quit it as soon as a buyer turned up. A buyer that she herself would procure, as soon as she found a more suitable venue for her estate agency. The cottage was habitable, with an acceptable kitchen, two rooms that she would ignore for the moment and the living/dining room in which she would install the office. A desk, three chairs, a sofa, a rattan table that Teresa Scaglia wasn't using and gave to her, and a wardrobe with drawers, which she converted into a filing cabinet. A rug that she no longer used at home and a pair of ethnic vases gave the office a "Cascade feel". Before moving in, she replaced the burned-out bulbs, got the office painted white and exchanged the old oven for a portable stove. The only thing she was unable to change before her launch day was the front door, which was wooden, heavy and so swollen from damp that it would only ever close if you kicked it.

16

Finally, just as people had given up thinking it possible, a suitable rival appeared for El Tano Scaglia: Gustavo Masotta. He pulled up outside my newly opened business, opposite the entrance to The Cascade, after hours, and found me kicking the hell out of the warped front door to make it close. My method was to aim a sharp knock at the latch and a kick at the base, almost simultaneously, and next to turn the key, which would then move smoothly in the lock, as though the difficulty had never existed. It was a daily ritual, performed automatically and so often that I now hardly cared about the carpenter not turning up to shave off the excess wood. In a way I quite enjoyed it, in the same way that it can be enjoyable to recognize a defect in oneself and to keep it secret from everyone, hoodwinking them.

Up until that afternoon, the deception had worked well – I had been careful not to kick the door in front of any clients. So I felt really peeved when I became aware of Gustavo Masotta's presence. I first saw him when he came forwards to help me pick up some things I had left on the ground, in order to dedicate myself more comfortably to the door ritual. My red notebook, a pile of folders, my mobile, some loose papers, the keys for houses that were up for sale or rent, envelopes containing my own and my clients' amenities bills, hand cream (I hate to have dry hands) and a yogurt that I hadn't had time to eat. All this clobber amounted to a fairly accurate display of my habitual disorganization. Neglecting preliminaries, I said, "It's warped," and pointed at the door. He didn't say hello either. "I need to rent a house for a year or two," he said, picking up my things from the ground.

"An estate agent's commission, no matter how small, should be so desirable, fortuitous and unforeseeable a prize that it merits working out of hours" – that's what is says in my red notebook, under the chapter heading: "Commissions and other Headaches". However, that afternoon I had an appointment at Juani's school and I had been worrying about it all day. At the end of the last term they had been reluctant to let me register him for the next academic year. Juani was going into the eighth grade, but the school psychologist felt that he was less ready than his classmates. She had been vague about this, not saying exactly in what respect he was different. I believe that that episode of the drawing showing Fernández Luengo on top of his dog (some years old now) still counted against him in the files. Although she would never have dared mention that. I should have listened to Ronie at the time. He had insisted that we ought to go to the school and tell the truth of the matter, but I hadn't wanted that. What Fernández Luengo got up to in his own house was his business and there was no justification in Juani spying on him through the window. That's what I said to Ronie. But it wasn't the whole story. I was scared. I knew that it would be no small thing to fall out with my neighbour. On the index card for his house I had written his name in red letters. He was a powerful lawyer, one of the country's top authorities on contraband. On how to avoid imprisonment for dealing in contraband. He knew everyone important at Customs and Excise and at the Federal Courts. I feared that he could do something to harm us, if he found out about what our son had done. I didn't know what that might be – I mean, I don't even shop in Duty Free – but I was scared, all the same. He could slander me and make it impossible for me to sell any more houses in The Cascade. Or he could talk down Ronie and sabotage the few business possibilities he had. Or he could invent something terrible about Juani: make a victimizer of the victim. I persuaded Ronie not to say anything. In any case, there was no fear of Juani ever repeating the incident. We had taken pains to explain the consequences. "If you ever draw anyone starkers again – I don't care who – I'll break your nose," said Ronie. And we moved him into another bedroom, smaller, but overlooking our garden. That episode aside, there were no concrete reasons not to let us enrol Juani for another year. His Spanish grades may not have been brilliant, but they didn't deserve this punishment. In English he had problems only with geography and history. I must confess that I hadn't paid much attention to that: I never realized that knowing which king succeeded which other one in England, or what the climate is like in Northern Ireland, could be so vital to his development. But exclusion from this school certainly would matter, because, for better or worse, it meant exclusion from the world that we inhabited. Technically, they could not make him retake the year because he had passed in Spanish, so, after much beating around the bush, they suggested I move him to another school "so that neither you nor he have to suffer the sacrifice of making him study during the holidays". Neither Ronie nor I agreed with that. We made him study English geography and history all summer long. He refused to have a tutor but got help from Romina – the Andrades' daughter – who, to her mother's surprise, was one of the brightest among the girls. They had become good friends since she first appeared in the neighbourhood and at school. "Birds of a feather flock together," the mother said to me one day and I wasn't bold enough to ask her to explain the comment.

The day that Gustavo Masotta appeared at the door of my office, I was on my way to a meeting to get a final answer on the re-enrolment. I had been waiting for this answer more anxiously than for the closing of any property deal. I realized that the fact I had often been late with school fees was not going to help my case. But I always had paid in the end, and with interest.

"I'll wait for you," Masotta said.

"The thing is, I don't know how long the meeting will take," I said. In fact I was not so much worried by how long it would be than by the mood I might be in when I returned. My temper is not particularly good, but it is predictable. I was not about to accept that Juani should change school; I already felt somewhat different to our friends, and I didn't want to widen the gap. Lakelands boasted that it could "guarantee the best English of any school in the area". I wanted Juani to speak English just as well as all the other children who lived around us – and they all went to Lakelands. I've often asked myself if Ronie's difficulty in re-entering the work market has something to do with his lack of fluency in English. I didn't speak a word of it either, but then it wasn't necessary for selling houses. And I did not want my son to end up selling houses. It was fine for me – I liked it – but not for Juani. For Juani I had imagined a different future – I didn't know what, but something different to mine.

Gustavo passed me the last folder. He had bitten fingernails, which did not chime with an otherwise well-groomed appearance. The side of his thumb was even bleeding, as though he had just pulled off a hangnail.

"Honestly, I can wait. I need to resolve this matter." I wondered what he meant by "this matter". It didn't sound as though he were talking merely about renting a house. But my matter mattered to me more.

"Why don't we meet at the weekend? It's practically dark now and Cascade Heights looks so much better in daytime. Artificial light doesn't do justice to this place; it's truly unique." I passed him my card, giving him no option but to postpone our meeting to a more convenient time. Then I got into the car and drove off.

I realized that I had probably lost a client, but if I didn't lose him then, I would doubtless lose him when I returned, raging that anyone should call attention to my imperfections, or those for which I was responsible: my son's imperfections. Over time the consequences of those imperfections had turned my rage to pain – not emotional pain but a real, physical pain, a stabbing sensation in the middle of my chest, as though my sternum were about to split down the middle.

As I drove off, I saw my potential client in the car's rear-view mirror. He was still there, standing outside my office, moving his hand over his face in a particular way, as if he were also enraged, and by something greater than my refusal to give him an appointment. Then the road followed a bend towards Lakelands, and I could see him no longer.

The whole thing took an hour and a half. They made me wait, then spoke for longer than I had anticipated. It turned out that Juani had passed the exams they had set him – I was about to punch the air, then I heard the word "but". Juani was an average boy, they said, and the level of the rest of the class was so high that they thought the demands on him were going to be too great, "because at this school the regime in eighth grade is arduous and the pace very demanding and there is no individual help available at this stage. They're not little any more. We look for individual effort; if you can take the pace, all well and good. If not, you're better off in a less demanding environment. It's like a form of natural selection that we allow to operate, do you understand?"

And I understood.

"We don't want to have to take into account a child's difference from the others in order for him to succeed; we're looking for parity across the board," said the headmistress, smiling.

"I'd like Juani to try it," I pressed on.

"I don't know if that's for the best…"

"Nobody can know until he does it, and I think he should have the chance."

"I disagree."

Then I got angry. "Put your disagreement and the reasons for it in writing and I won't ask for anything else. I'd like to have something formal that I can show... wherever."

The headmistress approved our re-enrolment. I hurried out of the meeting, anxious to tell Ronie that they had allowed his son to remain in the school. But I couldn't find my mobile. When I arrived at the entrance to The Cascade, a guard stopped me. "That gentleman has been waiting for you." And he pointed in the direction of Gustavo Masotta. "He says he found your mobile, but he didn't want to leave it with me. He'd prefer to give it you in person."

I parked and got out of the car. In the distance, Gustavo held up the mobile and waved it for me to see. It was mine. "Right after you'd gone I turned round and nearly stepped on it. It was on the pavement. You must have left it there while you closed the door." And he imitated my kicking ritual. "I didn't know if it was safe to leave it in the guards' room."

"If it's not safe then we can't be too clever: we pay those people a fortune. I'm sorry that you had to go to all that trouble."

There was a pause. Both of us seemed to be waiting for the other's next move. Finally he spoke: "Right, well, we'll be seeing each other at the weekend, no?"

I showed him what he wanted to see that same night. I was in a good mood, thanks to Juani's re-enrolment; besides, he had waited more than an hour and a half to give me back my mobile and I felt that the least I could do was show him around a couple of houses and take the edge off his ill-disguised urgency. I suspected that

101

he was recently separated and looking for a new place to bed down. It's rare for separated people to choose to live in The Cascade, unless they have children and don't know what to do with them at the weekend. Or if it's a separated woman who has been left to fend for herself in the house which is defined as "the former matrimonial home". Single people don't tend to choose our neighbourhood. There's no doubt that The Cascade can be an isolating place and that's not necessarily a bad thing – quite the opposite, sometimes. But one has to acknowledge its distance from other worlds: for some people that may be its greatest virtue, while for others it can become a nightmare.

Without realizing it, we had crossed a line and I found myself addressing him informally, as "*vos*".

"What sort of size property are you looking for? Have you got children?" I asked, as we delved into the streets of The Cascade.

"No, it's just two of us – my wife and me. We've been married for five years, but no kids yet."

"Maybe you'll get the urge here. This is a wonderful place to enjoy with children."

He didn't answer, but wound down the window and gazed into the street. As we drove on, I began thinking about the moment I had accepted that Juani would be my only child. Before getting married, I had dreamed of having at least three, but once Ronie had lost his job, our efforts were concentrated on maintaining what we already had, rather than taking on anything new. And what we had could be measured in square feet, holidays, comfort, private schooling, a car, sports; not in children. At least there was one to continue the family line.

"I bet your wife gets broody here. Cascade Heights is like a bubble of fertility." I don't know if he was listening to me. At various points during that drive, I had the feeling that he was not listening. He was quite determined to find a house to rent that very night; as we went up and down the streets, he kept picking out details that I would have dismissed as unimportant, and it was clear that anything I might say for or against a property would make not a blind bit of difference to his decision. "Carla doesn't like dark paintwork," "Carla hates glass-panelled doors," "My wife doesn't like lacquered floors," "If Carla saw the fittings in the main bathroom, she'd die." These were just some of the arguments he used to reject a string of potential homes.

Finally one turned up trumps. "I think she'll like this," he said, when I showed him the Garibottis' place. Built all on one level, it was smaller than the average Cascade Heights house, but with some very tasteful features: bespoke fittings, pine floors, antique ironwork. It certainly wasn't typical of a gated community. It was more like something you'd find in Boston.

"I've got another one to show you, at about the same price, but a little more modern and with a much bigger garden."

"No, this garden's ample. I'll rent this one, it's fine. How much do I have to leave as a deposit?"

"But wouldn't you like your wife to take a look at it first?"

"No," he said, and he looked at me with an ambivalence that seemed to convey strength and weakness in equal measure. He fumbled for something else to say, as though such a round "no" needed elaboration. "I don't want her to know; it's a surprise. A surprise present."

It was obvious that he was lying. "Oh, a surprise. Your wife's going to be thrilled!" I lied back. During my years at The Cascade, I had seen many surprise gifts, and lost my capacity for astonishment. There was the Mercedes Benz jeep that Insúa gave to Carmen during a dinner party for various friends at his house and which appeared as they were eating, approaching over the parkland, driven cross-country by a chauffeur, with a white bow and everything. The jeep was sporting the white bow, not the chauffeur. There was the production company Felipe Lagos set up for his second wife, at the end of a course she had been taking in cinematography. There was the shopping trip to Miami for Teresa Scaglia and a friend, funded by El Tano as a present for her last birthday, and with a cruise thrown in. But to rent a house, thirty miles away from your present home, without first consulting your wife? That seemed too far-fetched. Buy a house, maybe, but *rent* one? No way.

While I was preparing the paperwork for Gustavo Masotta's deposit, I watched him pacing the ground outside. He was breathing deeply, as though he would have liked to draw all the available air into him. A man alone, who had just chosen the house he was going to share with his wife, who did not need to confirm his decision with her, and yet was absolutely adamant that everything, to the last detail, should meet with her approval.

He came into the house and collapsed into a chair next to me. We both signed the agreement, I took his deposit and informed him how much my commission would be. He wanted to pay it straight away. I told him no, that I would not speak to the owner until that night or the following day, and that, if everything was in order, next week they could sign the rental agreement and pay the balance. "I want to move in this weekend."

"Well, we need to tidy up the paperwork and have the house thoroughly cleaned. The owner will have to remove some items."

"I'll handle the cleaning. And he can leave whatever he wants, it doesn't bother me."

"I'll see what I can do."

"I need to move in as soon as possible." This wasn't a request – his tone of voice made that clear. It reminded me of the obstinate way in which El Tano had demanded a certain plot of land for his house, and not another – no other one would do. They were both purposeful, but in other respects their bearing was very different. Gustavo did not have that same quiet confidence of getting what he wanted. There were suspicion and pain in his resolve. Not in El Tano's. And yet there was something in Gustavo Masotta that reminded me of El Tano Scaglia, something that drew them together like magnets, in spite of their being so different.

"Do you play tennis, by any chance?" I asked him, as we were leaving.

"I used to play it, a long time ago, before I got married. I was seeded."

"In that case, once you're settled in, let me know. I'd like to introduce you to El Tano Scaglia, one of our members who plays tennis spectacularly well and hasn't been able to find anyone of his level to play with."

"I hope I don't disappoint him," he said, and this sounded like false modesty. "But that would be good for me. I need to meet new people."

"Yes, when you come to live here you always need to meet new people. It's the same for all of us. Everyone else, your old friends, seem very far away." He looked at me and smiled, then his gaze was lost once more in the view through the window. Out of the corner of my eye I watched him and I wondered if I really had forgotten my mobile, or if everything had been orchestrated by Gustavo in his urgency to rent a house that very evening. And I had no doubts as to the answer.

17

It was eleven o' clock in the morning and Carmen was still in bed. She couldn't summon the energy to get up. The night before she had lain awake troubled by images from a news item which showed a plane failing to gain altitude then tacking along the coast before crashing into the Golf Association's driving range. The same driving range where Alfredo played golf every Friday, she had thought. Nearly one hundred dead, she thought that she had heard. She had finally fallen asleep, but now the prospect of facing the morning bore down on her. The maid (a new one) knocked on the frame of the door and, without stepping into the room, said, for the third time that morning: "Shall I bring your breakfast, Señora?"

Carmen gave up. She got out of bed and went to have a wash. "Bring me a glass of Rutini to the bathroom."

She was trying to give up smoking again and, rather than eating more – which was what had happened the first time – found she could not start the day without a glass of wine. Especially not this day. She turned on the shower and stepped under the hot water. The first drops stung her body. Outside the sun had already melted the morning frost in the garden. She wondered how to spend the rest of the day. No particularly tempting idea came to mind. The only thing she had learned to do during her years in The Cascade was to play Burako, which she had loved, but recently the game had lost its charm. Making *escaleras* no longer appealed. It was like knitting was for other women: something to keep your hands busy. Placing the tiles down on the table smacked of self-deception – here was uselessness disguised as productivity. For years she had been putting off various projects, persuading herself that she would come to them once her children were at school all day. Then, she told herself, she would put herself first and concentrate on her own work. But now the twins were about to leave secondary school and Carmen had still not managed to get her teeth into anything. She liked interior decorating, but Alfredo judged that the courses available at tertiary level were "not up to much, a waste of money". She liked drawing and painting. Perhaps the time had come to sign up for one of Liliana Richards's painting classes. Or maybe it would be better to leave it for a few months. She wasn't sure. She also liked psychology. She had never had analysis, but had begun to feel an interest in the subject during sessions with a psychologist after her operation. "Total hysterectomy," the doctor had said and, although she had not heard these words before, she understood their implication. Since the operation, she had not gone back to help in the children's centre at Santa María de los Tigrecitos. "Go on, it will make you feel better," said Alfredo. But she didn't go back. She would have liked to be a psychologist. Or to study counselling, a shorter course, like Sandra Levinas. Alfredo approved of that idea. Her husband liked Sandra Levinas; he said she was "cute". But any of these options would require her to take exams in the subjects still pending from secondary school and, given that nobody knew she hadn't finished school – least of all Alfredo – it was going to be very hard to do that without arousing suspicion.

At noon, she went down to the garden. She moved a lounger into the sun and lay down on it to read the decor magazine that came every month. At half-past twelve the maid appeared and asked, "Does Señora want lunch?" Carmen asked for a lettuce and watercress salad. "Bring it to me out here," she shouted, just as the woman was going into the house. Ten minutes later the maid returned with a tray. On it was a medium-sized salad bowl containing the specified greens, which were dressed with olive oil and balsamic vinegar, "the way Señora likes it", as well as cutlery, a cloth napkin, a glass, a jug of water and also a plate of chargrilled steak, "in case Señora feels like it".

Carmen sent back the steak; it struck her as impertinent that the maid should meddle with her diet. This woman was no Gabina – she did not even know how to cook. "Bring me the Rutini that I had this morning, the whole bottle," she said severely, and the maid took away the steak, then returned with the wine, making no further comment.

After lunch, she fell asleep in the sun. She dreamed. A heavy dream, as sweet and warm as the sun that sedated her. Sleep clung onto her, not allowing her to surface. She dreamed in red. But with no pictures, no story. It was the maid who woke her up, with a telephone call. "Señora, Teresa Scaglia is on the phone," she said. On the ground beside the lounger, the glass had toppled over and dregs of wine had stained the magazine.

Carmen took the phone. Teresa was inviting her to a seminar on Feng Shui in an hour's time at her children's school, "in aid of a home for needy children. Didn't you hear about it?" Carmen asked if it was for the "Los Tigrecitos" centre. "No, some other poor children, not ours." Teresa had a spare ticket. She talked her into it: "You love decoration, and I'm telling you, these tickets were one hundred pesos each, so it's got to be good, even if it is for charity."

While Carmen got changed, she tried to contact Alfredo. He was in a meeting and couldn't speak to her. Invariably, at around midday, Alfredo claimed to be in meetings, and switched off his mobile. She had found no further clues in the credit card statements, nor did she need to: it was increasingly obvious that Alfredo was cheating on her with someone, and that he didn't care if she knew about it. Perhaps he even wanted her to know, she thought. But what did he expect her to do? She was not going to look the other way.

She kept trying to get him on the phone; she was out of cheques and she needed him to bring back a new cheque book. The secretary wasn't there either. "They must be in some motel," she thought, as she put on make-up in front of the mirror.

At 3 p.m., Teresa Scaglia sounded the horn of her four-by-four. Carmen came out. "Lala's coming too, and Nane Pérez Ayerra," said Teresa with enthusiasm, as Carmen climbed into the jeep. It surprised Carmen that Nane would be interested in this sort of thing; she was very sporty and spent most of the day playing tennis or in the gym. "No, she hasn't got a clue what it's about, but she's laid up with a pulled muscle in her leg, so she thought she'd come along."

The auditorium at Lakelands School was jam-packed. Carmen counted only three men in the audience. All the rest were women. A heady confusion of imported perfumes pervaded the air and she felt herself submitting again to the torpor of her earlier siesta. But this sensation was not sweet, or red.

The speaker came onto the stage to ringing applause. Carmen applauded, too. He did not have any oriental features. He surely was not Chinese. In fact he described himself, according to the simultaneous translation feeding into Carmen's right ear, as "a Master of Feng Shui in Palo Alto, California". Looking around her, she saw that very few women were wearing the earpiece, not even Teresa, who knew only a smattering of English, gleaned on her shopping trips to Miami.

"I am not going to teach you the traditional Feng Shui practised in the East, but a westernized Feng Shui," said the speaker. He paused for dramatic effect – evoking that moment of suspense on television shows, before the commercial break – then said: "I wouldn't dare try to transform the wonderful houses I have seen around here into pagodas."

The audience laughed, appreciating his flattery. "Let us take from Feng Shui that which is useful to us, and leave the rest for others."

Carmen latched onto the word "others" and missed the next sentence. She wondered if the others referred to Chinese people, or to those who had not come here to listen to the master, or to her own father, who, after her mother left him, had lived alone in a one-roomed flat in Caballito, paid for by Alfredo, and who was buried now in a plot at the memorial cemetery, also paid for by Alfredo. The others might also be her husband's secretary, in this case "the other woman". Or her mother, to whom she had not spoken since her father's funeral, and whom she regarded as even more dead than him. The women who took part in those Burako tournaments that she had once organized with Lala or Teresa were not "others" because they were here, and they acknowledged her. The "others" were never defined, or perhaps they were lost in translation.

The second line to make her lose concentration was "the home is like a human being's second skin". Carmen shivered. Her skin pricked and she rubbed her arms. She felt hot and cold all at once, like when she was a child and had a fever. Like when she had goose pimples and her mother chided her to put on a sweatshirt. Like the first few times with Alfredo. Her eyes sought out the three men in the audience. None of them was up to much, she reckoned. If you wanted to take a lover in the neighbourhood, the best option was probably the architect in charge of improvements on your house, and the worst, the gardener. Middle ranking: tennis teachers, caddies, personal trainers, a friend's child's piano teacher – probably not outside Monday to Friday, in and around Cascade Heights. It was better to steer clear of the married men (and in Cascade Heights all the men are married). The alternative entailed complications greater than Carmen would be able to bear. The worst-case scenario, if the affair came to light, would mean one of the parties having to move. Like when Adam and Eve were cast out of Paradise, she thought, deaf now to the words of the Feng Shui master. Alfredo had, in fact, had an affair inside The Heights, but it was with a woman who was "in the process of separation", who had rented the Uroviches' house for a summer and who returned, when autumn came, to the city, relieving Carmen of the need to continue pretending she didn't know about it.

"Living in a house means: being at home, feeling happy and secure in a familiar environment which has, to a great extent, been designed by you." Carmen absorbed this observation in silence. Alfredo may have coughed up the money, but she was the one who had designed their house; she had chosen every piece of furniture and decided every colour. So whether or not she felt good about the result was her responsibility alone; she wasn't a little girl any more. She had learned long ago that complaining and crying don't bring relief, or raise the dead, or return a uterus. The Feng Shui master was finishing his spiel about feeling good inside. He meant inside a house, not that other inside, the one she felt empty within her. Alfredo had barely contributed to the design of their house. He had taken an interest only in the study and the cellar and there he was precise on every point. He personally chose the humidifiers, the thermometers and the position of the racks. It was Alfredo who had taught her to smell wine, to wait for the bouquet to be released, to reject a wine that was not yet ready. "And now he complains," she thought.

"Disturbances in sleep patterns, lack of equilibrium, marital strain and even illnesses can all be traced back to negative Feng Shui," she heard the master say, on the heels of some other observation that was now already lost in a soporific mist induced by the mingled perfumes in the auditorium.

At half-past five, her mobile rang. Several women opened their handbags, to check that it was not theirs. Carmen, tangled in the wire of the translation earphone, was slow to answer. A woman sitting in front of her turned round to give her a disapproving look. The Feng Shui master took this opportunity to tell his audience never to charge up their mobiles on the bedside table, because that attracted negative chi into the bedroom.

It was Tadeo, one of the twins, who was waiting for her to take him shopping for clothes, as they had agreed. Carmen apologized. "Something came up at the last minute. Didn't the maid tell you?" Tadeo was annoyed. "If you want, take a taxi and go with her." Tadeo slammed down the phone and she returned to the auditorium where the master was saying something in English, the only words of which she understood were "Bill Clinton". Carmen put the headphones back on in time to hear that "the furniture in the Oval Office at the White House was arranged in a negative way that brought many marital problems to the American President". It was too obvious, she thought, to look for explanations in the way her husband's office was furnished. Even so, she couldn't help it.

One of the three men stood up and left. The master watched him leave. Wanting to land a retaliatory blow on this deserter, he said, in the tone of one pronouncing a revealed truth: "Experts from Taiwan, Hong Kong and Singapore have been consulted by the leaders of great Western economic empires, to guarantee the success of their dealings." Carmen remembered her grandfather, a communist Galician who had escaped to Argentina as a stowaway, and wondered what he would have made of westernized Feng Shui. Looking around her, she realized that she had never met the grandparents or, in most cases, even the parents of any of the friends who were with her. Then again, she had not brought her father to Cascade Heights either, preferring to visit his apartment once a month, when she took him money for the rent. Rumour has it that Nane's father was imprisoned for fraud at some point. Nobody knows the exact details, but it's definitely true that her house in The Cascade is in the name of her mother. At least that's what Mavi Guevara said, in confidence.

Now Nane put up her hand to confirm to the audience that "in my husband's company, they made a tour of all the facilities with a Feng Shui consultant and they ended up building a Ta Ta Mi on the terrace to dispel the negative energy". The master was pleased by this "most opportune and illuminating interruption".

"Someone should look over the Guevaras' house, right?" said Nane, and Teresa and Lala laughed, but Lala added: "Don't be a bitch – anyway, if Martín doesn't get a job soon, I'll be the one forced to realign the chi in my house."

"Or forced to work," quipped Teresa.

"Not in a million years!" said Lala, laughing.

"In your case it's a short-term thing, but how long have the Guevaras been living off Virginia's wages? Perhaps Ronie really isn't getting work because of bad Feng Shui," Nane insisted.

"It wouldn't hurt to rearrange the furniture," agreed Teresa. "In this life you have to try everything."

Carmen thought that in this life she would like to try marijuana; as a girl, she had never dared and now she didn't know how to get hold of it. Once, on television, on a rainy afternoon she had spent in bed because she couldn't get up, she had seen a boy on a talk show explaining that he smoked joints because they produced more or less the same effect as wine, but without the hangover. And she was a bit concerned about her hangovers. A couple of times her children had seen her the worse for wear, because the new maid didn't know how to manage the situation as Gabina had and, any time Carmen was a bit wobbly, she went running to the children for help.

There was a half-hour break, during which wine and cheese were served. Carmen didn't drink anything. This was her children's school: she was frightened of what she might do. The wine was a Valmont, banned from Alfredo's cellar – "It's vinegar. Anything under twelve pesos is vinegar." Surrounded by plates of brie and Roquefort, the master was overwhelmed by women waving freehand drawings of their houses at him. It struck Carmen that, in the ranking of potential lovers, a Feng Shui expert could claim membership of an even higher category than architects. Not on the grounds of looks, but of exoticism. The organizers were handing out leaflets with events scheduled for the rest of the year: "How to Grow Orchids" in September; "The Art of Wine-Tasting" in October; "Understanding Nietzsche" in November; "Boundaries and Children" to close the year, in the first week of December, with the same psychologist who presented that talk show on which Carmen had seen the boy who smoked marijuana. She looked around her: people were moving about, holding glasses that were still almost full. The burgundy-coloured liquid swayed to the rhythm of laughter and chatter. And she wondered if she might perhaps just wet her lips… but she didn't dare.

Five minutes before the second half of the lecture, waiters began to collect the glasses. Some wine remained in almost all of them; a few of them had not even been touched. Carmen made up her mind to wait until everyone had gone in, then to drink half a glass in the lavatories. She was determined to do it. But Teresa grabbed her arm and led her back inside the auditorium. "It's interesting, isn't it?" said Teresa, nibbling a piece of Gruyere. "Very interesting," said Carmen, whose mind was still on the half-empty glasses left on the table.

The Feng Shui master spent the rest of the seminar analysing some sample houses. Different views were presented on state-of-the-art slides, each of which bore the words "Pa Kua Orientation". This same phrase had been repeated various times during the talk, but Carmen could not begin to remember what it meant. The master was explaining the significance of different corners in a house, while indicating air flow with a wooden pointer. He spoke of the place reserved for Career or Profession; the corner of Knowledge; the corner of Children. When he explained about the area reserved for Wealth, Nane said: "I always thought my architect was a halfwit – and he's still complaining that we never paid him for the extras. Right in the Wealth corner, he put a closet that's always locked! Can you believe it?"

"You'll have to pull it down or make a Ta Ta Mi on the terrace," suggested Lala.

"Why don't you try leaving the door open first?" said Teresa. "It would be a real shame to start making alterations to your house now that you've got it so pretty and everything's perfect. Did I tell you that they're going to photograph ours for La Nación's architecture supplement?"

"Seriously?"

The Californian master used his last slide to illustrate, in detail, the corner attributed by Feng Shui to the Couple and Marriage. It was in the back part of the house, at the right. Just where Alfredo had built his wine cellar. He explained how important it was that the energy in this area should be positive – ying and yang, but positive – that it should flow unobstructed, that negative effects be neutralized with mirrors, crystals and bamboo. One must avoid, on all accounts, the presence of blocked chi or vital energy – that is, chi that cannot flow, areas where movement and access are difficult, areas that are damp, or cluttered, airless, dusty, dark and lifeless. Like a wine cellar.

It was nearly ten o'clock by the time Teresa Scaglia dropped Carmen off at home. Alfredo's car wasn't there; it was too early for him to be back. Carmen knew that her children would be holed up in their respective rooms, on the Internet, and the maid would be in the servant's room, reading the Bible. "You know, the best thing about evangelical maids is that they don't steal – their religion forbids it," Teresa had told her, when she recommended this girl a few months back. But she still preferred Gabina. She went to the kitchen, grabbed a glass and a corkscrew and continued to the cellar. She opened the door. Inside it was even damper and colder than the night outside. She looked at the bottles: not just any one would do. Her eyes passed over the Rutini, then stopped on the Finca la Anita. She took out the bottle. A 1995 vintage. She hesitated, then returned it to its place. Six bottles further on she settled on one of the three Vega Sicilias that Alfredo had brought back from his last trip to Madrid. That trip that he had wanted to make alone, because he had a very important deal to close and didn't want any distractions. It still had the price tag: two hundred and seventy euros. Almost as much as that night in the Sheraton, the one that was recorded for evermore on her husband's credit card statement. The one that he had spent with someone, perhaps with the same woman with whom he had bought this wine in Spain. Perhaps with some other woman. She opened the bottle. She was about to pour some wine into the glass, then thought better of it. Instead, she raised the bottle, toasted the health of Feng Shui and of Chinese people everywhere, then drank deeply from it, pausing only to draw breath.

18

El Tano glanced up before hitting the ball. He saw his rival flit to the left, like a shadow. Only in the split-second that the ball succumbed to inertia and began to fall, when for a tiny instant it seemed to hang in the air, did he hit it. It was a slam directed at the right corner of the court, almost touching the base line. Where there was nobody. A precise shot, not forced, but swift and effective, rendering useless all his opponent's efforts to cover the back of the court in time to reach the ball. Gustavo celebrated the point. He always applauded the same way, clapping against his racket. All of us loved to see El Tano and Gustavo Masotta play doubles – it was like watching choreography. There was always a crowd to watch their matches, always one of us to tell the others about their latest feat. "Nice one, Tanito, your house speciality," said Gustavo. El Tano's tributes to his partner were much more restrained: they were barely perceptible gestures, visible only to those who knew him.

El Tano and Gustavo played together every Saturday at ten o'clock in the morning. Physically, they made an odd couple: El Tano was short and stocky, with almost transparent skin and curly hair that had once been blond; Gustavo was tall, slender and dark. Virginia Guevara had introduced them and on that same day they played a singles match. Having practically killed each other, afterwards neither of them would say who had won. Legend has it that they deliberately halted the game in the third set, when they were drawn on five games apiece, so that there would be no clear winner. It had been Gustavo's turn to serve, and when Gustavo served, he won. Delivered from height and strength, the power of his service was frightening. But there must have been a reason why he agreed to be a bit vague about who was the better player.

From that day on they became an inseparable doubles pair. El Tano would get up early and reserve a court. Gustavo would come later, on the hour, or a few minutes late. Over time, partners usually rotated, but not them: they always played together. None of us would ever have dared ask one of them to form a pair; it would be like voicing a desire for the most beautiful woman in the club to her jealous husband. They got on well; their mutual respect took the edge off any differences and it was not obvious that El Tano was nearly ten years older than Gustavo, either on the court or off it. Each, in his own way, brought to the partnership elements that made them a tough pair to beat. El Tano was all precision, cold blood, wealth of experience, flawless technique, untiring legs; his tactic relied less on his own game than on making capital from an opponent's error. It was pure strategy: he played a game of tennis as though it were a game of chess. Gustavo's style was more impetuous, yet more magnificent; some people, if they were bold enough (or quite sure that El Tano would not get to hear of it), said that Gustavo was the best player in Cascade Heights. He had a physique that lent itself naturally to the sport, he put everything into it and was capable of turning around the most unpromising score. His speciality was to serve, run to the net, then smash the ball straight at his rival's feet, leaving him unable to respond. The violence of these shots was frightening, and yet the harm they did his opponents was kept in check. You could tell, though, that this exaggerated care was studied, controlled and imposed on his own desire. As the game went on, he managed his own violence less effectively, and then, if Gustavo hit a ball when you were close to the net, all you could do to avoid getting hurt was to shield yourself with the racket.

The performance continued, after each game, on the terrace overlooking the tennis courts. Invariably the two men had a drink with their opponents and a chat. El Tano always paid, in spite of the losing party's protests that "he who loses buys the drinks". The waiter who brought the drinks knew not to accept money from anyone other than El Tano Scaglia, who had given orders to that effect. An order from El Tano could not be disobeyed without consequences. While they waited for the drinks, El Tano exchanged his sweaty shirt for a dry one, and stretched against the wooden rail. Gustavo neither stretched nor changed his shirt but remained in a collapsed state in his chair, enjoying his victorious exhaustion. El Tano drank mineral water, and Gustavo, lemonade. And they talked about business: the sale of YPF to Repsol, cars to be bought and sold, the extravagances of their wives, which they criticized, even though these served to demonstrate their own standing as high-end consumers. They talked about some tennis championship that might be taking place somewhere in the world, or about the ATP ranking. But El Tano always seemed more involved in the conversation than his partner. While Gustavo was physically present, it was clear that his mind was often elsewhere. Every now and then his eyes glazed over and, if someone pointed this out, he put it down to tiredness. But it wasn't that. It seemed that something was troubling Gustavo, that he was assailed by thoughts leading him to a dark place. At that time, none of us knew where. Nor did we even suspect that there was anything wrong. In The Cascade it's not unusual to know nothing about your neighbour, the person he was before coming to live here, or even the person he is now, in private, behind closed doors. Not even El Tano really knew about Gustavo. Nor Gustavo about El Tano.

Martín Urovich nearly always joined them on the terrace for a chat. Martín had been El Tano's partner before Gustavo arrived at Cascade Heights, and had taken his displacement in good part; he just wasn't on their level. It wasn't a question of playing style, but of the need to win. El Tano and Gustavo needed to win, and so they won – they were programmed for it. Martín Urovich was "programmed to fail", as his wife once yelled at him, in front of some of us. But that was quite a lot later, when time had gone by and Martín was still without work, when Lala had convinced herself that he would never get any, and it was very close to that Thursday in September that we never talk about, unless someone asks us about it.

19

The Uroviches come from one of the founding families of Cascade Heights. Martín Urovich is the son of Julio Urovich and, in his day, when this was no more than a chunk of land divided up among friends, nobody ever asked about anyone else's religion. It was "Julio Urovich", full stop. But as time went on, although no one ever acknowledged the fact, religion became another factor to take into account when considering the application of new members to The Cascade. This must be one of the few things I have never dared to write down in my red notebook: some of my neighbours do not welcome Jews. I've never written it down, but I have always been aware of it, which makes me complicit. It's not that they openly denigrate them, but if someone makes a joke, even quite a harsh one, they laugh and applaud the humour. For a long time perhaps I, too, failed to see the serious side. I'm not Jewish. Nor am I Korean. Only when Juani started to have problems did I get an inkling of what it might be like to look different in other people's eyes.

After so many years here, the Uroviches have come to occupy a fundamental role in our gated community: they are those Jewish friends that prove our liberal credentials. Anyway, Martín had married Lala Montes Ávila, a country-club girl all her life, from a Catholic family – so Catholic, in fact, that several of their friends in the community, on discovering that she was marrying the Uroviches' son, commiserated with her parents instead of congratulating them. "Don't go against her wishes, or it will be worse." "If you let her have her way, they'll probably fall out in a couple of months and this will all be water under the bridge." "Send her to study in the United States." "Come down on her like a ton of bricks."

But Lala and Martín got married and nobody said anything else on the matter, at least not in public.

The very afternoon that I closed the deal with the Ferreres, I knew the thing was doomed. I had left them in the clubhouse; they looked happy and they wanted to have a drink and spend a bit more time in Cascade Heights, the place they had chosen to make their home. I went home, also feeling happy, mentally calculating the exact sum that was owing to me in commission. I had just sold them a half-acre corner plot, which had been put on the market by the Espadiñeiros when they decided to get divorced. Beside the Laforgues' house. As I stepped into the house, the telephone rang. It was Lila Laforgue, a woman of about sixty who lived permanently in Cascade Heights, a "life member" as she liked to style herself (somewhat pretentiously, given that we all knew that their house and club shares were in her name because her husband was disqualified and suspected of bankruptcy fraud). "Tell me, are they from the *old country*?"

This term threw me. In a free association of ideas my mind raced from "old country" to "gauchos" and from "gauchos" to "peasants", "ranchers", "cows", "bulls", "The Argentine Rural Society", "tractor", "horses"…

"Russians, Virginia, are they Russians?"

Then "Russians" brought me sharply back down to earth.

"You mean from the Russian community?" I asked her.

"Because, it's not that I have anything in particular against them – after all, we're great friends of the

Uroviches – but it's the *density* that worries us. In a few years this is going to look like a kibbutz. And right next to our house."

"I don't think so – they're called Ferrere."

"Sephardics. I knew a Paz who was one, a Varela who was one. They trick you with those surnames and they end up making you look a fool."

I risked an interruption. "They seem like lovely people – a young couple with a little boy."

"Yes, I saw them. She looks like one of those Russians who've come down in the world. Tell me, does that percentage rule no longer apply?"

Years ago, in Cascade Heights, when the place still functioned more as a weekend country club than as a permanent residence, there was a ruling that limited the representation of any one ethnic group to ten per cent of our total community. Any ethnic group. Apparently Julio Urovich himself was on the Council when the ruling was passed, though I never dared ask him about it. In other words, if the numbers corresponding to one specific group exceeded ten per cent, the next person from that community who wanted to join Cascade Heights would have to be rejected. The explicit objective of the ruling was to prevent the club being converted into the "exclusive domain" of one predominant group. In practice, the only applicants rejected at the time were Jewish. Representatives of the black, Japanese and Chinese communities (to name distinctive racial groups) had never reached their ten per cent, or anywhere near it. And I don't think anyone had ever been asked if they were Muslim, Buddhist or Anglican. I certainly wasn't. But, for whatever reason, at some point in the history of Cascade Heights, the decision had been revoked.

"Are you *sure* it was revoked?" persisted Lilita. "Why does no one tell us about these things? Isn't there a selection committee, or something? There should be. I don't mean just for the Jews. I don't like discrimination, generally speaking, but it would be good to be able to have a bit of choice about who comes in. These aren't vertical properties, where one only ever meets someone in the lift. Here one shares many things, there's more integration and I don't want to integrate with people I would not naturally consider as friends. Do you understand? I'm not saying they're good or bad, but they aren't people I would choose. And I have a right to choose, don't I? This is a free country."

She waited for me to say something and, when I didn't, she carried on: "I'm sure that in other clubs there is some sort of mechanism for selection. Even if they pretend otherwise. They'll tell you it's natural selection, but it's not. Go and look on the registers to see if you can find an Isaac or a Judith."

"An Isaac or a Judith". Here we have a Julio Urovich and his descendents; Paladinn's wife, who I think is called Silberberg, the Libermans and the Feigelmans. But not in other clubs, it's true. I have friends, colleagues from other estate agencies, who work in some of the other private neighbourhoods Lilita mentioned, and they tell me what goes on. When someone with a Jewish surname arrives in the office, the first thing they do is discourage them, to save everyone – buyers and sellers alike – from embarrassment later on. They walk them past the community's chapel, even if it's not en route, and they tell them that all the local children go to some or other Catholic school. They show them houses that are either unsuitable or beyond their budget. If necessary, they resort to using phrases such as "this is a secular club, of course, but the great majority of the families here are Catholic". It gets complicated when the clients have a mixed marriage and it's the woman who's Jewish. The thing tends to go unnoticed until the time comes to sign contracts. By then my colleagues have been busy spending their commissions, partying and bragging, and it's only when they're finishing up the paperwork that they spot the woman's name and realize they've lost something they never really had. Then they have to decide whether to carry on, and see the sale rejected at the last moment with various excuses, or to tell their clients the ugly truth upfront. Almost nobody opts for the truth; instead they allow events to take their own course after the official version of the rejection, which is always ambiguous, acknowledging no blame. But you can never be one hundred per cent sure beforehand. Who would dare to ask a potential client, "Excuse me, sir, is your wife a Jew?" Sometimes there are indications one way or another: silver crosses, Basque rosaries, the choice of children's names, the number of children, the schools at which they're planning to register them. And there are always people with a sixth sense for these things – predators, like Lila Laforgue.

"It's Litman, not Pitman… it's with 'l' for… for Laura," Señora Ferrere explained to me on contract day. "Laura Judith Litman," she clarified.

I wrote down Litman without looking up. I felt heat rising in my face while the words ran through my mind: "Neither an Isaac, nor a Judith". It was shame that prompted my embarrassment. "I'm really happy to be coming to live at Cascade Heights," she said, obliging me to meet her eye. She smiled at me.

Some months later Lila Laforgue rang me again. "I told you they were from the old country."

"Oh really?" I pretended not to understand.

"I saw the boy playing in the pool, naked. He's got a cut-off willy."

20

They call her for dinner a hundred times, but she doesn't go down. *Ramona* doesn't go down, because that's what she calls herself, even if they have changed it to "Romina". Not on her identity card – they couldn't change that. But they registered her for school as Romina Andrade. Everyone calls her Romina. Except for Juani, because she asked him not to. She told him that, when she was born, she was given the name Ramona by her mother, whose face she can scarcely remember now. Juani has dubbed her "Rama", a hybrid that can go unheeded by the woman who insists on being called "mummy". She obviously likes calling things by the wrong name, thinks Romina. I am not Romina, and Mariana is not my mother. Both of them know as much, even though Mariana obliges her to answer "yes, Mummy" and "no, Mummy". She won't allow her simply to answer "yes" or "no", like other children, or to shake her head. Mariana finally elicited her complete answer by dint of a physical blow. But the beating is not what hurts her most. It pains her more to think that they have stolen Pedro from her. Pedro no longer knows who "Ramona" is. Nor does he want her to tell him anything about what she remembers – it even annoys him. "Don't lie to me any more, sis," he says, and runs out kicking his rugby ball. And she loves him all the same, more than anything in the world, even if he does not know who he really is.

If Romina kept a diary, she would not write in it every day, she's sure of that. A daily diary would be deathly boring because, in this place, there are days when nothing whatsoever happens: "I got up, I had breakfast with the woman who adopted me, who was going to a tennis tournament, she told me that she was taking two rackets in case her powerful passing shot broke one of the strings, I had two tests then a free period, I felt ill in the third break, I went home with Valeria's mum, who had also played in the same tournament with my 'mother' (whose racket string had, in fact, broken immediately), but who came home earlier because she was knocked out in the quarter finals, I watched television, my little brother pissed me off, I had supper alone in my room, I went to bed, end."

Nobody wastes time writing about nothing. That is what Romina does not want. Nothingness. She isn't sure what she wants, but she knows it's not that. "Let someone else write about nothing." And at fourteen, or fifteen (the judge could not establish her actual date of birth), she already knows that telling is not the same as living. It is harder to tell. Life gets lived, full stop. To tell, you must be able to order things and that is what she lacks, the ability to order internally her ideas, the things that happen to her. Fortunately she has Antonia to order her room. But she feels that the rest of her life is a mess. She feels that she is sitting on a time bomb. And a time bomb must, one day, explode.

It almost went off last night. She was at party in the country club where Natalia Wolf lives. Two exits on the highway from Cascade Heights. She drank beer, a lot of beer, all the beer. At four o'clock in the morning, she threw up. A few people were sick, not just her. Not Juani; he'd gone home early. She called Carlos, the "trusted" minicab driver, the only one "mummy" lets her call. Carlos had to carry her into the car. Not for the first time. Romina travelled in the back seat; it was hot and the smell of vomit overcame her. She asked Carlos to put on the air conditioning, but it didn't work, so she took off her shirt. "A bra is like a bikini, anyway," she reasoned. She threw the shirt out of the window, to get rid of the smell. She looked down at herself. "Bigger than a bikini, in this case," she thought. "And the guy's looking straight ahead, and who cares if I've got two non-existent tits." She fell asleep. When they got to the entrance gates, the guard was alarmed and called her father. He warned him to be prepared, "Señorita Andrade has just entered the Club and is proceeding to your address, naked and apparently on drugs."

"I didn't take drugs," Romina said, when Mariana and Ernesto confronted her.

"The guard said you came home on drugs and naked."

"In my bra, and not on drugs."

"The guard says you were."

"The guard is an idiot who's never gone anywhere near a joint."

Ernesto slapped her across the face. She stumbled. But she was not drugged. She had drunk a lot of beer, for sure. But she doesn't do drugs. She has smoked marijuana two or three times, but the last time it affected her badly and she hasn't tried it again. Beer hits the spot, she doesn't need anything more. She likes gin, too. Not as much, but she does like it. Especially the one Ernesto hides in the dresser in the living room. Vodka occasionally, rarely. Nothing else.

They're calling her to dinner again. Antonia says to come down, that "mummy is furious". And "mummy" furious is a fearsome sight.

21

Some time after moving into Cascade Heights, Carla followed Gustavo's suggestion and signed up for the Fine Arts course which took place in the clubhouse, on Wednesdays, at 2 o'clock in the afternoon. Gustavo had been pressing her to do this for a long time. He was not concerned that his wife should develop any special talent for art – indications were that she had none – but that she should try to fit in and, as he put it, "make friends as a springboard to a new social life". A social life that was different from the one they had come here to leave behind. El Tano had passed him the information about the course. Carla would have preferred to go back to Buenos Aires and finish her degree in architecture, but Gustavo was not in favour of this. "You'd have to make a gigantic sacrifice – you always found it hard studying for a degree. And when we have our first child, you'll drop out, I know you." She knew that he could not promise her a child. And equally, finishing her degree was a promise she could not be sure of keeping.

While Carla scarcely knew two or three people, wives of Gustavo's friends, he was already totally integrated into the new community. It was easier for Gustavo: he liked sport, and in Cascade Heights that smoothes the path to friendships. Children also open doors. But they had no children. Carla was very different to Gustavo – shy, withdrawn, almost frightened of people. On several occasions, acquaintances of Gustavo had tried to get her involved, inviting her to different events, but she always found an excuse to stay away. She only had two friends now, both from her school days. One of them lived in Bariloche, and the other, she didn't know where, because they had not seen each other since Gustavo argued violently with her husband – about what she no longer remembered. All the others were Gustavo's relations. Carla's reclusive tendencies had increased after a miscarriage ended her pregnancy at five months, the longest a baby had ever survived within her body and something neither of them wanted to talk about.

On Wednesday, at 2 o'clock in the afternoon, Carla set off for her first painting lesson. The teacher, Liliana Richards, also a resident of Cascade Heights, introduced her to the rest of the group. They appeared to have known each other all their lives, although Carla later found out that most of them had not been in The Cascade longer than two or three years. She knew some of the women by sight. She must have crossed paths with them in the store or in the restaurant at the clubhouse, because she didn't go anywhere else in the neighbourhood. She believed she may have had dinner with some of them, one night at the Scaglias' house. Liliana gave Carla a brief explanation of the methods they were using, emphasizing that in her workshop "these do not include patinas, découpage, or stencils, or any of those lesser techniques". In her workshop they made "paintings". And it surprised Carla to hear the word used. Carmen Insúa interrupted: "Oh, speaking of paintings, you have to come and see the Labaké I bought, Lili."

At the end of the class, one of the women offered her a lift home. Carla was the only one who had arrived on foot. Her house was just a few blocks away, and she would have liked to walk them, but it seemed impolite to turn down the offer. Her companion apologized for the state of the car, explaining that she had three children and might, any time now, decide to have a fourth. "What about you? How many do you have?"

"No, we don't have any yet," said Carla.

"Better not leave it too late," came the pronouncement, "because you never know how hard it may be to get pregnant."

The following Wednesday, Carla began to draw on the canvas. She was finally beginning to feel some enthusiasm; in a few days it would be Gustavo's birthday and she thought that her first painting would make a very meaningful present for him. The teacher said that in the first instance she should let whatever she wanted flow out. And Carla could draw only stripes. The following Wednesday it was also only stripes, black ones in varying widths, that her classmates observed without making any comment. Beside her, Mariana Andrade was painting a still life. It was an illuminated table, covered with a tablecloth on which there were some apples, a bottle, grapes and a jar which was lying on its side but not spilling any liquid. It amazed Carla that someone could paint an apple that so closely resembled an apple.

Dorita Llambías, who had been working until that moment on her own canvas, apparently oblivious to her neighbour's progress, asked, "What are you copying today, Mariana, a Lascano?" Mariana looked up with irritation and only then did Carla see the colour plate that was on her lap, from which she was working. Liliana looked closely at the plate. "That's not a Lascano. It's a bad copy."

Now Carla felt ashamed to have judged Mariana's apple as being so perfect, when for the teacher not even the one in the original was good. Dorita called over from her easel, "Carla, since you don't know any of my previous paintings – come and tell me what you think of this."

Carla went over and saw a kind of plain, on which the brush strokes were rather too apparent for her taste. Among the clouds one could make out the shapes of hands and feet, in different sizes. "I know, it's hellish: the same things keep appearing to me. Everything comes out with a surrealist slant. Because I don't feel the need to copy, do you understand?"

Carla understood and returned to her stripes. She stood staring at them. She wondered what they represented and why that was what came out of her, rather than feet and hands wrapped in clouds. She did not even know if what she was painting had any aesthetic value. Liliana had told her not to worry about that for the moment. But it began to dawn on her that this was in fact important and she was being patronized as a beginner. As Carla was mulling this over, Mariana said: "If I were you, I'd try a still life, an arrangement of fruit, or something like that. I don't know your house, but I doubt that's going to go with your living room." She came closer and added in a low voice: "Look at Dorita, surrealism coming out of her ears but you wouldn't want to hang the result even in the lavatory."

The following Wednesday was the day of the "painting girls'" monthly tea. It was Carmen Insúa's turn to host, and everyone was there. The class ended five minutes early, so that they could leave everything clean and tidy. Carla travelled in Mariana's car and they were joined by Dorita, whose SUV was having its three-thousand-mile service. They covered the six blocks almost in silence. Carla remembers only that one of the women said, "I hope that the tea *will* be tea." And that the other said nothing, but made a reproachful gesture.

They parked behind Liliana's car, and the others parked behind them. Six cars and nine women, parking as close to the kerb as possible, hoping to avoid having their tea interrupted by security staff on account of one of them blocking the road.

The table was set and looked impeccable. A Villeroy Bosch service graced the white linen tablecloth. Sandwiches, nibbles and, on a hostess table to one side, lemon pie and a cheesecake. Beyond that there was a tray with glasses and two bottles of champagne in silver ice buckets full of crushed ice, which Mariana took pains to point out to Carla, with a disapproving sigh, as if she had guessed as much.

"Wouldn't you prefer something cold to tea?" asked Carmen, serving herself a glass of champagne. Dorita and Liliana exchanged glances.

"Hey, I love the painting. Very sober," said Mariana, indicating the Labaké. And under her breath, Liliana said to Dorita: "Did the silly cow say 'sober'? Can you believe it!"

"What do you think of it, Liliana?" Carmen asked anxiously. Liliana paused for a moment then said: "As a piece of work, it's fine. It's fine."

134

Carmen seemed relieved and said, "Do you know the dealer told me it's already worth twenty per cent more than when I bought it?"

"Yes, that could be. There are some people who do inexplicably well out of very little. Perhaps he has a knack for striking rich seams, do you think?" said Liliana, inserting a canapé into her mouth.

"But didn't Labaké win the last National Painting Prize?" asked Carmen with some concern. "That's what they told me when I bought it."

"And you think that's not fixed?" said Liliana. "Please pass the tea."

Carmen appeared confused, as if there were something she would like to say, but the champagne prevented her processing the words. She opted to say nothing and pour herself another glass. Carla stood up and went to look at the painting. It was dominated by the colour ochre (identical in tone to that of Carmen's armchairs) which had been given an unusual texture and worked with hessian and other reliefs. Carla liked it, very much. It seemed to show three trees, bare but not dried-up, the roots of which plunged into the sand, where they met ears of corn and a very small canoe, and inside the canoe was a woman who was completely still, but alive. A completely still woman. And on the sand, two open ears of ripened corn. The woman in the canoe looked even harder to draw than the apple and, faced with the certainty that there were things she would never be able to do, Carla felt an urge to weep.

"Thank you very much for the tea. Next time let's do it at my place. And I loved the painting," Carla said as she left. As Mariana started the car, Carla saw Carmen, through the window, pouring the remains of the other glasses into hers and knocking them back.

"She's getting worse," said Dorita. And Mariana heaved a sigh. "Do you know that she paid for that painting by selling all the jewellery Alfredo had given her?" Dorita added.

"No, seriously?" said Mariana. "What was she thinking of?"

"I don't know, I heard Alfredo nearly killed her."

"Hardly surprising."

"I liked the painting," Carla felt emboldened to say.

"I don't know," one of the others said. "I don't know anything about paintings. But I do know about jewellery. Did I tell you I sell jewellery at my house? You'll have to come round."

Carmen wasn't present at the next class. Liliana asked if anyone knew where she was. Nobody answered, but everyone exchanged glances. Even Carla, so as not to be left out. Liliana judged her stripes canvas to be finished. Carla had started driving to the course. After this class, she loaded the painting into the car and drove the five blocks to her house, feeling tense, as though afflicted by a worry she didn't fully understand. Gustavo was not home yet. She took the picture to the storage room and found a chair to serve as an easel for it. She studied it. Gustavo's birthday was in a couple of days and Carla was not sure that this canvas was what he would have wanted to receive from her. And she didn't want Gustavo to be annoyed. Not any more. She tried adding one or two more stripes and thought of adding a touch of colour, but nothing convinced her. She cried. She went back into the house and looked up Liliana's telephone number in her diary. She asked if they could meet the

136

following morning. "Right then, come to the house at about nine o'clock, after you've dropped the children at school."

"I don't have any children."

"Oh – really?"

Carla drove to Liliana's house. She rang the bell and the Richards' maid invited her in. She took her to the living room and served her coffee. Liliana appeared a few minutes later. "My husband's birthday's coming up. I don't want to give him the same thing as usual – clothes he doesn't wear, books he won't read; this year I want to give him a painting. One of yours."

Liliana looked surprised: in all her life, no one had ever bought one of her paintings. Not even a relative.

"He's been very supportive of this whole workshop thing, and I thought it would be a way to thank him for that. But I don't know if I'll be able to pay what it's worth."

Liliana made a reassuring gesture which allowed her to conceal a certain vanity. "Let me show you my work, then afterwards we'll see what you can pay."

She led Carla to an outdoor room, all glass – an old greenhouse that had been converted into Liliana's atelier. Heavy drapes protected the paintings from the sun, hindering the growth of those few plants that remained. She showed her about twenty paintings, most of them made many years ago. On some of them the signature had clearly been altered. Carla's eye was drawn to one of these alterations and Liliana pre-empted the question that she would never have dared to ask. "Before I married I was Liliana Sícari. Now I'm Liliana Richards. I changed the LS into an LR. Richards sounds better for an artist, don't you think?"

There was an easel propped against the back wall bearing a half-finished canvas. Carla approached it, lifted the cloth that covered it, and found herself looking at an ochre painting, with sand, and a long narrow canoe, inside which there were three women, with some ears of corn growing out of the canoe and towards a sky that was also ochre, and two trees, small but with long roots plunging into ochre sand. And pieces of hessian, here and there, stuck on with oil paint. It was a recent work, signed LR, with no alterations. "I like this one," said Carla.

Liliana hurriedly covered it with the cloth again. "That one's not finished," she said. Carla had lied: she wouldn't have picked it out. It would be like buying the same dress or swimsuit as Carmen, but in a seconds shop, and she would never do that. She looked at the others again and chose a still life that wasn't an original, but seemed validated by having been copied so much. She realized now that there were Liliana's still lifes, Mariana's, Lascano's, the plates that Mariana copied, and surely many more that she didn't know about, copied ad infinitum by women she also did not know. Moreover, she was certain that Gustavo would agree with them that a still life looks good on any wall. "I don't know, if it's for Gustavo, let's say three hundred dollars and leave it at that. Does that sound reasonable?" Carla paid, put the canvas in the car and left.

At home, Carla carried the painting to the storage room, removed her stripes canvas from the chair and substituted Liliana's. She took a brush and, with great care and a little black ink, transformed the LR into a CL, for Carla Lamas. But then she felt a pang and changed it again, to CM, for Carla Masotta; she didn't want the use of her maiden name to spark a row with Gustavo. She was proud of the alteration: it was neatly done. She was always neat.

On the evening of Gustavo's birthday, she had dinner ready for him in the dining room that they used only for entertaining people when Gustavo insisted and Carla had no choice but to receive his guests. They dined by the light of a candelabra, with music and the painting hanging on the end wall.

"I love it!" he said, and he kissed her. "And how is the workshop going?"

"There's your evidence."

"I mean the people – what are they like? Any potential friends?"

"Yes, I think I'm fitting in."

Gustavo raised his glass for a toast. She raised hers, they clinked glasses and made a toast, to Gustavo's birthday, and to friendship.

22

Every year on the 8th of December, the day of the Immaculate Conception, all the houses in Cascade Heights are decorated for Christmas. White lights are trailed around trees, pergolas and front doors. Through open-curtained windows, the lit-up Christmas trees wink on and off. People favour different kinds of pine, all of them big. The colours of Christmas baubles are never mixed: they are either all yellow or all red, silver or blue. Some people prefer red bows. Or apples. The Administration puts up a crib in the wood, complete with figures that are close to life-size. And every year a gardener, caddie or workman forgoes his family dinner in exchange for a tip collected by the neighbours, dresses up as Father Christmas and drives around the houses on this private estate delivering presents from the back of the maintenance truck. Truth be told, the only thing missing is snow.

That year, even though it was the last Christmas of the century, the decorations were no different from usual. The thing is, when one is used to making a huge effort, to make just a little bit more effort is almost impossible. The end of the century manifested itself, not so much in the trees and cribs, but in a feeling that floated through conversations at The Heights. There was talk of all kinds of computing catastrophes; someone was making back-ups and copies of all his cards, codes and bank account details, while someone else was withdrawing everything from the bank to bring it home for the holiday, fearful that his statement would appear blank on the 1st of January 2000.

On the morning of Christmas Eve, Teresa made sure, as she did each year, that the Club's administration had taken delivery of the fireworks they would let off after midnight, at the ninth hole. Every year El Tano donated quantities of fireworks for the enjoyment of his friends in Cascade Heights. It wasn't that he was a particular fan of pyrotechnics, nor did he do it for the joy of the display itself, but his pursuit of perfection had made him an expert. One year he had hit on the idea of presenting this gift to his friends in The Heights – to fill the Christmas sky with fireworks – and from then on, each year, he raised the bar. He researched which ones were the best to buy, the safety procedures that must be met, the places where you could see the best fireworks in the world. The displays in Sydney and Tokyo were his favourites. And he endeavoured to imitate them. He used the best fireworks available in Argentina, and one year he even imported some from Miami and eventually had to retrieve them from Customs by bribing an official Fernández Luengo knew because "people are getting ready to pop open bottles, and we still haven't got clearance!"

Teresa returned home. The marquee had been ready since the day before. The Scaglias always put up a marquee for gatherings of more than thirty people, ever since the first communion of their younger daughter on a day of torrential rain, which had ended with mud all over their pine floors and the deep-pile carpet upstairs. They had hired crockery, as well tables and chairs decked in white – each table with a centrepiece of jasmines – and a false wooden floor, to protect the lawn. The food was contracted out to a catering company Teresa had used for previous birthdays and parties. The maid had been told she was free to go after 5 p.m. Teresa would have liked her to clean her bedroom's en-suite bathroom before leaving. She still hadn't had a chance to shower, and wouldn't until after she had wrapped the presents. But she was not in the mood to listen to the maid complaining about how busy the buses are on holidays, and how last Christmas she had not got home until everyone was drinking the midnight toast. The catering company was bringing its own serving staff. And the crockery could be returned dirty. In truth, apart from the bathroom – which only she would see – there was nothing much to worry about at this stage.

The maid came upstairs, changed and ready to leave. Teresa was in her room, wrapping up presents. "Señora, do you need anything else?"

"On your way out, drop in at Paula Limorgui's house and tell Sofi to come home by seven at the latest, to get changed."

"Yes, Señora... and happy Christmas..."

"Thank you, Marta; don't forget to take the authorization I left on the table, or Security won't let you take out the *pan dulce*."

As soon as she had finished wrapping up everything, Teresa hurriedly rang Administration, to ask them to come and pick up the parcels. Sofía had just turned seven and still believed in Father Christmas. Matías, who was fifteen, said it was because she didn't want to miss out on any presents, but Teresa assured him that was not the case – she had been equally innocent at Sofía's age and even older. Presently the bell rang; it was Luisito, the boy who watered the tennis courts. It was his turn to be Father Christmas this year. He was not all that keen, but his wife had insisted – they needed the money and, if they couldn't raise a glass at midnight, they'd raise it some other time. Teresa told him to come upstairs and help her bring down the Barbie house for Sofía. Luisito asked permission to leave his shoes, which were covered in brick dust, at the foot of the stairs. She had bought Matías a sandboard, but it wasn't necessary for Father Christmas to hand that over in person. In fact, Matías would kill her if that happened, given his mood these days.

The guests arrived punctually at nine o'clock. Except for El Tano; he came twenty minutes later, having stayed on at the golf club making sure that the fireworks were properly spaced and ready for midnight. The only family members invited were El Tano's father, with his new wife, and Teresa's brother, with her husband and children.

142

The rest were people from Cascade Heights, neighbours who, like them, had opted to spend the holiday among friends. Gustavo Masotta and his wife, the Insúas and a few others. The Guevaras had been invited, but they wanted to spend the evening with Ronie's parents. And the Uroviches celebrated Christmas with the Catholic branch of their family. The waiters circulated with trays of savouries, ham and champagne. On every table there was a little menu detailing each dish. Starter: *vittel toné* – a traditional cold meat dish. Main Course: duck *à l'orange*. Dessert: ice cream with blueberry sauce. And to finish: an arrangement of dried fruits, preserves and *pan dulce*.

The first course had already been served, when Teresa realized that Matías had not yet come downstairs. She looked up at his bedroom window and, seeing that the light was on, asked Sofía to call him down. Sofía scampered off to carry out her mission. She found her brother's door closed and banged on it. She hammered it with her fists. "Mummy says come down now!" There was no reply. She banged on the door again. "Mummy says come down or…" Matías opened the door.

"Stop it, are you crazy?"

"What's that smell?" Sofía asked.

"What smell?" he said, and went to open the window. Then he came out of the room, pushing her ahead. "Come on, girl, get a move on."

Every now and then, above the chatter of the dinner party, the noise of a rocket made itself heard. "Don't these people realize that the fireworks are supposed to be at midnight?" asked El Tano.

"There's all sorts of simple things people don't understand, Tanito, don't go worrying yourself about it," replied Alfredo Insúa, staring at his wife, who was chatting to Carla, clutching a bottle of wine and laughing about something.

At half-past eleven, Luisito rang the bell. Teresa started, then peered around the acacia and saw the red suit. She began to shout: "Santa's here! Come on everyone!" Sofía ran after her mother, but the other young people present, all of them older than her, got to their feet grudgingly. Matías was the first to come closer. "All right, old chum?" he said, slapping Luisito on the back.

Teresa frowned at him. "Off you go, Mati, Sofía wants to see Santa." Matías stepped aside and Sofía, who was standing a few steps back, was left face to face with the Father Christmas that had been provided for her. She fixed him with a stare. Luisito felt uncomfortable: he thought perhaps the people in Administration had been right and that he should have agreed to say "Ho, ho, ho", but he already felt like enough of a dickhead dressed up in red, without adding sound effects. He looked at the little girl who kept staring at him and knew that he had failed. For all that, he got on with the job in hand, bringing Sofía's present down from the truck and carrying it towards the house. Determined to get Sofía caught up in the spectacle, Teresa kept asking questions in a too-high voice. "Have you come from far away, Santa?" "Are you tired?" Luisito did not feel like going along with the game, and said nothing. Matías pretended that he was going to look at the presents that were still in the trailer. Teresa's nieces and nephews returned to their table and the Insúas started to kick around a football that had been forgotten under the acacia tree. Luisito looked at Sofía again and felt an urge to say sorry. But she was already too excited about the Barbie house to take any notice of him.

"Aren't you going to give Santa a kiss?" asked Teresa, as Luisito was climbing back into the truck. Sofía left her present for a moment and came over to him. She waited for him to rearrange his hat and beard and then she kissed him. When Luisito had gone, Sofía confided in Matías, "Father Christmas smelled like your bedroom."

"Really?" her brother said with surprise.

"What is that smell?"

"Forget it, silly, mind your own business."

"Is it the fireworks?"

"Mind your own business."

At midnight everyone made a toast. Everyone except El Tano. He had left ten minutes earlier to be there as soon as the fireworks started. He was responsible for making sure that everything went well. At five minutes past twelve, the rest of the retinue made its way to the golf club. Teresa and the children walked, so that they could come back with El Tano in the Land Rover. On the way, they saw the colours of the first fireworks erupting in the sky, which meant, Teresa realized, that she had once again missed her husband's speech. When they arrived at the golf club, everyone came up to greet them. In a way, the Scaglias were the hosts, because they paid for the fireworks. They sat down with the others to watch. Teresa chose the front row, next to El Tano and his father. Matías walked off to the side, towards a eucalyptus that stood some distance away, almost on the road. It was somewhere he could be as sure of being on his own as he was in his room; no one selects a leafy tree under which to sit and look at fireworks in the sky. He put his hand in his pocket and groped for the joint. He lay back on the grass and closed his eyes. Between the leaves, he could see the sky covered in lights that changed colour and shape with every new explosion. Everyone was clapping. First came a blue flower encompassing nearly all the sky. Three pink flowers followed, smaller, but more elegant. Later there was a seemingly endless golden waterfall. Almost no one remembers what came after that.

Luisito had changed out of his red suit and was going home, when the coloured lights caught his eye, and he stopped for a moment to watch; by the time he got home, his children were going to be asleep, anyway. He nearly stumbled over Matías, who was sitting under the eucalyptus. For a moment they remained like this, one standing and the other on the ground.

"Do you want some?" Matías asked, offering him the joint. Luisito said nothing, but accepted the lit cigarette and took a deep drag on it.

23

He had finished arranging the boxes full of papers in the trunk of his Land Rover. Now it really was "his" Land Rover. When his friends in Cascade Heights said, "That's a nice Land Rover you've got there, Tano," he did not correct them, but he had always known it was not his. Teresa's station wagon was, but not the Land Rover.

Now finally it was. El Tano was keeping the car as part of his severance deal with Troost, the Dutch insurance company for which he had worked since 1991 until this very day, at the end of the summer of 2000, until about five minutes ago, in fact, when he had finished emptying the drawers of the desk that would no longer be his. The owners of the company, Dutch shareholders with whom he met once or twice a year, had decided to reduce the level of their investment in Argentina and to increase it in Brazil, where they saw more chances of profitability in the short and medium term. El Tano had neither been consulted nor given any notice of the decision, even though he was General Manager of the company. He found out only once the decision had been made and communicated, not to him, but to the lawyers who would handle his dismissal. The Dutch, three of them who spoke for the majority shareholders, explained the circumstances to him on a conference call. In Argentina, they planned to leave only an administrative base, with medium and low-ranking staff, and the whole operation would be managed from Sao Paulo. El Tano's conduct had been irreproachable; he had always met their expectations and those of the shareholders they represented and they thanked him for his service and dedication, but they had no job to offer him. In the new structure, everything would be beneath him. They used words like "over-skilled", "downsizing" and "deserve more challenges". They spoke a Dutch-accented English that El Tano perfectly understood. It was easy to understand, because the words were universal. El Tano spoke little. When they had nothing left to say to him, he said: "I think it's the right decision. I would have done the same." And that same day he began to arrange his departure with the lawyers who had been waiting for his call.

There was no leaving party. El Tano didn't want one. In any case, he was going to continue to be associated with the company as an external consultant for a couple of months. He could use the telephone, get new cards printed, substituting "General Manager" with "Consultant" or "Chief of Staff" – whichever he preferred; he could ask his former secretary to perform small jobs and work part-time in one of the offices. Not in his old one, in another one, smaller but perfectly acceptable (to avoid sending out mixed messages to the staff who were staying on, so they told him). From this perch, he could plot his reintegration into the market. That was also part of the negotiated settlement. "It's easier to get a job if you already have one," said the lawyer. He himself, when he had to choose someone for the firm, distrusted people who didn't have work; he speculated about the real reasons for their resignation or dismissal that lay behind the official version. His father, an immigrant, who had risen to own a sizeable metallurgical factory, always said: "If people can't get work it's either because they don't want it or they haven't got the capacity for it." And El Tano was capable, and he had studied very hard, and he liked his work. He was an industrial engineer. His father had wept in front of him for the first and only time, the day he was awarded his diploma. And this was the first time in El Tano's life that he had left one job without having another lined up. And the first time that he had felt like weeping himself. But he did not weep.

He drove the Land Rover out of the garage and along the road towards the ramp, just as he had for the last eight years. When he arrived at the exit barrier, the attendant waved him through. "Good afternoon, Señor Scaglia," he said. It was the same friendly wave as always. And yet El Tano felt it to be different. Perhaps it was the way he looked at him. Or the tone of voice. Perhaps merely a different way of breathing. He didn't know. But he did know that something had changed. How could it not have done? The attendant had something that he no longer had. And both of them knew it.

He drove, as he did every evening, down Lugones, General Paz and the Pan-American highway, and only there did he feel the air begin to change. He tried all the FM stations, but couldn't get into the music. He switched to AM. "The president has expressed his deep concern about the floods in Santiago del Estero and Catamarca." El Tano fiddled with the dial and tuned into the observations of a political analyst on the looming elections for leader of the government in the City of Buenos Aires. He remembered that he would have to vote in a few days; even though he had lived in The Cascade for years, he had never changed his address on the electoral roll. He still voted in Caballito, as he had all his life. He listened to the words of an ex-economy minister who was in the running for leadership. El Tano thought that he would vote for him. Foreign capital has faith in this man, he thought, and that was good for him, because perhaps then his company – as of this afternoon, his *ex*-company – would throw their hat back into the ring. And if not this company, perhaps it would be another – the important thing was for the outside world to keep believing in this country, to keep investing. He was sure that it would not take him long to find another job. Things weren't easy, but he had a lot of contacts, a Masters from abroad, an impeccable CV – and, at forty-one, he wasn't over the hill yet. He pushed a button and it was the political analyst again, this time interviewing a candidate that all the polls showed to be a certain loser. El Tano began to think about this man. Someone sure of his failure, acting otherwise. He

149

pictured him with a wife and children (if he had them), he imagined him trying to sleep and not being able to, he thought of him going to vote, of him speaking on some programme that had not managed to find a more promising candidate, pretending to be unaware of the certainty of his defeat.

He would not say anything yet to Teresa. There was no need, since he was in fact going to continue going to the company, almost like before. If he waited for a while, perhaps he could tell her once he had a concrete offer of work, or even a new job. Teresa gets worked up about the slightest thing, he thought. The compensation would allow them to maintain the lifestyle they had led up until now, without touching their savings. It would not be good for the children to find out either. And Teresa didn't know how to keep this sort of secret. He moved the dial again. "The president said that the situation in the flooded areas is of great concern." He looked for any sort of music on FM.

The entrance to The Cascade was close now, a hundred yards ahead. He placed his card against the electronic reader and the barrier was raised to let him through. He waved to the security guard who was stationed at the entrance. And once inside, he felt relaxed for the first time that afternoon. For the first time since he had heard the words: "I'm so sorry but… business is business." The trees were still intensely green, even though it was autumn. In a few days, this grove through which his Land Rover was slowly passing would become burnished and spotted with yellow. He lowered the windows and took off his seat belt, to make the most of these last blocks before his house. It was a calm and warm evening. Before dinner he would go for a run, as usual. And he would say nothing to Teresa. It was better that way. Now he was driving along the main road bordering the golf course, on which dusk was starting to fall; some adolescents were out on their bikes; a maid tussled with a little boy who didn't want to ride his tricycle. He passed Carla Masotta, who was coming out of the clubhouse. He wouldn't tell Gustavo yet either. Not anyone. Perhaps in a few days he might chuck a couple of CVs Gustavo's way – he had dealings with a few headhunters and could be a good contact. But not for the moment. He let his eyes drink in the greenery that was all around him on both sides of the road. He knew that there were no changes there. The Cascade was just as he had left it this morning, when he had set off to be General Manager of Troost SA for the last time.

There was definitely no need to tell anyone anything.

24

In autumn Bermuda grass goes yellow. It doesn't dry up, it doesn't die, it simply remains dormant until the summer, when the grass returns to green, and the cycle begins again. In the meantime there are two options. At least, we have two options in Cascade Heights. The first of these is to look for colour elsewhere: in the red and golden Liquidambar trees, the brownish oaks, the yellow Ginkgo bilobas, the firey Rhus typhina. But this effort has to be made with determination, and if the eye is continually drawn back to the colourless grass, disconcerting, annoying or even depressing the person contemplating it – then the first option has failed. The second option is to plant ryegrass, which lasts only for a season and boasts a colour as false as it is vivid, like cold-storage apples or battery hens. But it looks perfect; it's not so much a lawn as a carpet.

This was not a ryegrass year in the Uroviches' house. The year 2000 was well underway; we had a new president. In December 1999, during his inaugural speech – the first of many speeches, so rumour has it, to be written by his son – he had emphasized the need to control the fiscal deficit and promised that this would bring down unemployment through new investment. But autumn arrived, bringing neither investments nor work, and Martín still had not managed to get a job. Lala, practically in tears, told Teresa about it one afternoon, when the latter had gone with her workmen to dig up dead plants from the flower beds.

"I can't stand it any more. Do you know what it's like having him stuck in the house all day?"

Teresa understood, but she knew that matters would be even worse if the lawn went yellow. She took Lala to one side, far enough away not to be overheard by one of the workmen, who was kneeling on the earth pulling out weeds. "Do whatever you think best, Lala, but in three weeks the Bermuda's going to dry up and ruin the look of your park." And she returned to the workman.

"No! My God! José, that's not a weed! It's a *pennisetum!*" Teresa pushed him out of the way and combed the plant's foliage with her fingers. Lala came over to have a look at the pennisetum. Teresa smiled at her and said under her breath: "It's a battle. You explain it twenty-five times and he still doesn't get it."

The women walked around the flower bed. The worker stayed a few feet behind, weeding. Teresa made some calculations. "Look, you must have nearly half an acre of land."

"About a third of an acre," Lala corrected her.

"Exactly, so one pound per one hundred and fifty square feet, with seed costing, let's see, about one dollar or one dollar fifty the pound, with all the fluctuations, how much is that?"

"I don't know, not without a calculator..."

"No, neither do I... I was always dire with numbers, but we're talking in the region of one hundred... one hundred and fifty dollars... because that's what Virginia's just paid me, and her grounds are more or less the same size as yours."

"Virginia's re-sown?" asked Lala.

"Yes, she must have made a good commission recently." Teresa squatted down, pulled up a clod of earth and examined it. "Honey, this border really needs water," she said, showing her the dry and dusty earth.

Teresa went to get the hosepipe. Lala waited for her. Teresa had been looking after her garden for years and knew very well where all the gardening tools and materials were. The Uroviches had been among her first clients when she finished the three-year landscape-gardening course at a nursery in San Isidro. Until she and a few other women began to study and dedicate themselves to the subject of plants, all you could get in this area would be some unemployed man from Santa María de los Tigrecitos, an odd-job merchant parading as a gardener or a groundsman. The "grass-cutters", as they are known in The Cascade, came on bicycles, pulling a mower, at best electric, a strimmer, secateurs and chlorine to keep the swimming pool clear all year round – or else they'd lose their jobs. Teresa was offering something quite different. To change the flowers with every season; to combine colours harmoniously, let different shapes complement one another, make sure the vegetation was sufficient; to look out for dead plants or anything rotten; to place the plants with the best perfume in areas close to the house, the ones that dropped leaves and needles further from the pool. "You need an artistic streak for this sort of work," she liked to say of herself. And all this for a price that was slightly above what the grass-cutters charged. "When everybody else's grounds are looking perfect, with that spectacular green ryegrass, you'll want to kill yourself, won't you? You'll be driving along... green... green... green... yellow, ugh! We've come to the Uroviches! No – that would be too horrible."

Teresa left the hosepipe to one side and tried to straighten a papyrus that had inclined too much towards the sun, upsetting the symmetry of the border. Lala bent down to help her.

"Listen, honey, I know your old man's got no job, and everything's grim, but this is about more than that. Don't let yourself get pulled down by his depression." Teresa let the papyrus go and stood up. "This will have to be tied, because otherwise it's not going to stay. It's trying to rebel. I mean, it's why we have savings, isn't it? For emergencies like this." Teresa took out of her pocket a little reel of ochre-coloured twine and, with Lala's help, secured the plant. "Recycled sisal thread – never have anything non-biodegradable in your garden." Lala helped her to attach the plant's tie. "Think about it: the centuries go by, we are gone, and the plastic's still there. Speaking of plastic, weren't you going to get your tits done this year?"

154

"Yes, but now I'm going to wait a bit until Martín's stopped stressing about money. He gets so wound up."

"The silicone can wait, but not the grass. In a couple of months he'll have a new job and your lawn will be a disgrace." Teresa uncoiled the hosepipe from its automatic cart, attached the correct nozzle, to produce a gentle, consistent shower and gestured to her workman to turn on the tap; when the water started to flow, she sprayed the borders. "I know that you're thinking 'Why spend all that money every year, when the ryegrass dies in November anyway?' and it's true, it does, but, well… it comes down to priorities… we are always having to make choices in life."

"You know me, I'm going to do it, it's just a question of getting it past Martín."

"And why does he have to know?"

"Ever since losing his job, he's become very obsessive. Don't tell anyone, please, but he keeps a record of our outgoings on the computer and it drives me round the bend."

"Why don't you get him some therapy?"

"Martín go to a therapist? Knowing what they charge? There's no way he'd go, I swear, he's so stingy these days. He's even banned me from having Twinings tea, can you believe it?"

"There's only one way to deal with men like that, and that's to lie. And don't feel guilty, because it's for his own good. Don't you think it will put a spring in his step to see the grass all green when he looks out of the window?"

Teresa passed the hose to Lala. "Here, you do a bit of watering, I'm just going to get a bit of iron from the jeep for that jasmine. It looks a bit withered, don't you think?" Teresa went, and Lala kept watering. And as the water rained evenly down on green leaves, Lala convinced herself that yellow grass would definitively do nothing to improve her husband's state of mind.

25

Romina and Juani arrive in the playground one night. They're not little any more, but they still go to the playground. It is where they first met. They remove their roller blades. They take beer out of the rucksack. Two half-litre bottles each. Or three. Sometimes a litre bottle. Whatever they can get. They drink. They laugh. A guard goes by. They wave to him. They wait for him to walk on. They drink more beer. They laugh.

"Shall we start?" she asks.

"Go on then," says Juani. Romina looks for a thick stick to use as a pencil. In the sand she draws a line that curves this way and that.

"A viper," says Juani.

"I'm not that obvious."

"A spiralling noodle," he says. She laughs. "No, moron."

"The branch of an electric weeping willow."

"No."

"A spring."

"No, something way cooler than that."

Juani thinks, looking at her. He keeps looking at her. "It's not your hair, because your hair's straight." He touches it. He leaves his hand on her hair. "I give in," he says. "What is it?"

"What I have inside my stomach; I don't know what it's called, but it's like that," says Romina and she draws the twisting line on the sand again. They look at each other. They drink some beer. They look at each other while drinking beer. Juani moves closer and kisses her. Romina's mouth still tastes of the drink. She strokes his face. "We are friends," she says.

"Friends," he repeats.

"I don't want to be like them," says Romina.

"You're not like them."

"I'm scared of us stopping being friends – do you understand?"

"Yes," he says.

"Now it's your turn," she says, and passes him the stick. He draws a circle and inside it two dots.

"A button."

"No."

"A pig's snout!" she shouts, sure that she is right.

"Wrong again." Romina studies the drawing from different angles.

"A socket?"

"You've lost." She waits for an explanation.

"It's us two," says Juani, pointing to the two dots, "behind the wall."

"Behind the wall, or in front of it?" she asks.

"It comes to the same thing."

"No, it's not the same. You know that picture they show you, and you have to say whether you see an old woman or a young one?"

"Yes, I saw a young one," he says.

"The wall of The Cascade is the same," says Romina, and she traces the circle with her stick. "You can look at what the circumference encloses or at what it leaves outside, right?"

"No."

"Which is the inside, and which is the outside?" Juani listens, but says nothing. "Are we shutting ourselves in, or are we shutting out other people so that they can't come in?"

"What are you on about? Are you pissed?" Juani prods her with his bottle, which is nearly empty. Romina laughs. She drinks more beer.

"You're being really thick, Juano. What about a spoon – you've seen a spoon?" she asks and she demonstrates the shape of a spoon with her hand, in the air. "Is a spoon concave or convex?"

Juani laughs; beer spills out of his mouth. "I haven't got a fucking clue."

"It depends which side you look at it from," she clarifies. And pointing at the palm and back of her hand she says, "Concave… convex."

Juani says, "Ah…" and he laughs because he didn't get it. She laughs too, empties a bottle into her mouth and then tosses it to one side. She scrubs out the circle with the palm of one hand, then stands up and goes to the swings. Juani follows her and takes the swing next to her. Their bare feet tip above their heads. Each time they come to the top, they look at each other. They see who can swing higher. And a little higher still. Juani says, "I'm going," and throws himself off. He falls and then gets up, waiting for her on the sand. Romina swings once more. She throws herself off, too. She falls onto the sand on her knees, beside him. She lands on top of the empty beer bottle. The bottle shatters. Romina screams. Blood begins to flow and to mix with the sand. Juani doesn't know what to do. Both of them are scared. He lifts her onto his shoulder. He squeezes her thighs tight and feels Romina's blood on his chest. Romina screams and cries.

She clings on to Juani's neck, her head hanging over his back, her black hair swishing from one side to the other as he runs, carrying her. He goes for help as quickly as he can. He feels his shirt warm and wet, sticking to his chest. He keeps running. He starts to run out of breath. He panics. He slows down and realizes that he has no idea where he is going.

26

They went in two cars. Lala had suggested going together, so that they could chat, but Carla preferred to make her own way. She was in a hurry: she had to go to the supermarket, a chore that increasingly depressed her, but the fridge was empty and Gustavo was going to start complaining again. She didn't like it when he complained; she was scared that he would not be able to stop. And she knew what he was like when he could not stop himself. Each time he had not been able to stop himself, they ended up moving house. Also, she needed to preserve Gustavo's current mood, because there were some important things she had to tell him, things he wasn't going to like. She needed to tell him that she had decided to get a job, anything, to get her out of the house. She had already started making calls and sending emails, but she had not yet told him. She would tell him soon. But it wouldn't help if he started getting annoyed about something that was nothing to do with her. And she suspected that this business with Lala was going to take more time than she could spare. On the way to the vet's, Carla heard on the radio that the nation's vice-president had just resigned. She felt sorry; she liked him, but she knew that many people in Cascade Heights did not, so she kept that quiet. She found his difficulty in pronouncing "r" endearing. He had resigned over the failure to investigate bribery in the Senate. Or so it seemed. It isn't easy to single out one reason for a person's resignation, she thought.

They arrived at the pet shop almost at the same time. Lala had come with her eldest son, Ariel, who was seventeen. The boy seemed disgruntled. Perhaps he didn't like his mother borrowing a credit card in order to buy a dog in instalments, Carla thought. She certainly wouldn't like it. But she had been without a mother for so long that she would forgive such a lapse of judgement, if she could have her back. Just as she would forgive the way her mother had abandoned Carla with a father who took his grief out on her, in the absence of the wife who had left him. Or the fact that she had felt obliged to marry Gustavo when she was still so young, almost without knowing him, just to escape from the man her mother had escaped years before.

She still did not understand why she had said "yes" so quickly when Lala had called her. "You can't imagine how sweet it is! Ariana loved it, and I want to give her it for her birthday," Lala had told Carla, before asking to borrow her card. "I said to Martín, we can't pay it all at once, but in six instalments we won't even notice it. And he agreed but he said that there had just been some problem with the card and the bank and they've suspended the account. Martín says they'll sort it out any minute, but the days go by and nothing happens. Bank employees are like that. Of course they're in no hurry, so what do they care?"

Carla didn't care either, and yet here she was. When she had told Gustavo he practically killed her. "If it was for medicines or food, but for a dog... Carla, is it so difficult to say no?" And he knew that it was. Because he had often heard her say no and enough and I can't go on, but she did go on. "Don't you know that Martín's gone bust?" Gustavo had said to her, and she had not known, and she was sure that Lala did not know either. "She can't not know, she's his wife," said Gustavo. And she thought, what's that got to do with it, but she didn't say this.

Gustavo told her that for months the Uroviches had been paying only for essentials – day-to-day shopping, utilities that could be cut off if they went unpaid: electricity, gas, telephone. That El Tano Scaglia had been paying their health insurance ever since he had insisted on footing the bill for Ariana's appendix operation. "It's cheaper for him to pay the instalments every month." Martín had not been paying The Cascade's service charge for some time now. School fees, yes, though El Tano had advised him not to pay them, "because they can't chuck your kids out halfway through the year – it's against some law passed by the Ministry of Education. So long as you pay the registration fee and perhaps the first month, you can send them for the rest of the year without worrying; nothing will happen. That's what Pérez Ayerra did one year when he was short of cash and he ended up negotiating to pay half."

But Martín didn't want to do that. "Or Lala would find out," said Carla.

"If she hasn't found out already, it's because she doesn't want to know."

"Give me a break – she must have some idea where the money comes from."

"It's not deliberate – just ditziness. When girls want to behave like airheads..." And Carla decided not to listen any more. She had already said "yes" and, on this occasion, it was much easier to take out her card and pay than to go back on the agreement.

The pet shop occupied a large area at the entrance to a shopping mall. It looked like a supermarket, with long shelves from which you could serve yourself anything from healthy food to little, jangling balls, leather bones, leads in different materials and colours, tartan blankets and bronze plaques on which the name of a pet could be engraved.

Carla and Ariel waited to one side while Lala went straight to the cage where the Labrador and Golden Retriever puppies were kept. There was a black and a gold one.

"Mine is the gold one, isn't she dreamy?" said Lala excitedly, motioning them over. "Ariana's going to be over the moon!" And then, indicating Ariel, whose face registered no emotion. "Just look at this one. He's as unfeeling as they come, definitely not an animal-lover like me..."

The assistant took the dog out for her and she lifted it up in her arms. "Do you know what he said to me?" she went on, in front of the assistant. "He said, why couldn't we spend the money on a skiing trip for him. Can you believe it?"

"So what?" said the boy and sulked off to examine an iguana, confined in a fish tank.

"He's just a boy..." said Carla.

"Yes, but it makes you angry when someone's values are so skewed, because that's not the way we've brought him up."

"I would have said the same thing, at his age."

"Well, you're not an animal-lover either. It would do you the world of good to have a kitten or something. They give you company. I'm not saying it because of your pregnancy problems, mind. Animals make everyone feel good."

The women went on to the till. Ariel followed them. Lala was holding the puppy in her arms, as though it were a baby. "OK, I just have to get a health record for her. Her parents are pure-breds, but the puppy doesn't come with any papers, did you know that?"

"Yes, or rather, I'm not the sort of person who pays nine hundred dollars for a dog's family tree," Carla laughed.

"Leave that to people who have more money than sense, right?" said Lala and she shot Carla a complicitous glance. The vet was preparing to fill in the health record and to give some instructions about vaccinations.

"Do you mind if we do the card first, because I'm in a bit of a hurry?" Carla managed to intervene.

"No, of course not. Can you swipe the card, please."

"In how many instalments would you like to pay this? Three?" the vet asked.

"We agreed on six the other day," Lala replied. When the vet had nearly finished filling in the credit-card slip, Lala interrupted him. "No, wait a minute. What food should I be taking for this little darling?" The vet emerged from behind the counter, approached one of the shelves and pointed out the food recommended for the dog's breed and size. Lala followed him, while Carla waited at the counter. "And how long will one of these bags last me?"

"About three weeks."

163

"Right, put two bags on the card too." She went back to stand beside Carla. "You don't know how much these animals can eat."

"No, I don't know," Carla answered, thinking that Gustavo had better not find out that he was also financing the animal's food. Ariel plunged back among the shelves, surfacing by the tropical fish tank.

"Right, now we're ready," said Lala to the vet, who tallied up the sums on his pocket calculator.

"Altogether, that's five hundred and eighty – could you sign here, please." The man gave Lala the slip and she passed it to Carla. Carla signed.

"I can't wait to see Ariana's face when she gets home from school today!" Carla smiled and put her card away. The vet continued: "So, for forty-five days, no going outside, to avoid distemper." Lala listened, all ears.

Carla interrupted: "I can go now, right?"

"Yes, you've already signed, haven't you?" Carla nodded. "Off you go then, Carli. See you soon." Just as Carla was leaving the shop, Lala shouted from the counter: "And thanks, eh?" Carla made an effort to smile again. She looked for Ariel, to wave goodbye. But the boy didn't see her; he was standing, hand in pockets, in a corner, watching a hamster endlessly running on its wheel.

27

The day that Carla Masotta turned up at the agency happened to coincide with one of the worst days of my life. I had just come from an exchange of contracts, which should have made me happy, given that I had not been able to finalize a deal for months now, and that commission was going to be a lifeline in the stormy waters to come. It was the autumn of 2001. Paco Pérez Ayerra had sold his house and rented another through my agency. He had financial problems or, rather, his company had financial problems. The economy minister had resigned and the new one appointed by the president had lasted only fifteen days. He made a speech, he asked for belt-tightening, he made a trip to Chile and, when he came back – no more job. The president had replaced him with the bald guy who had been the previous president's economy minister. This guy was now the leader of a rebellious breakaway party, making his affiliations as a minister rather unclear. I remember Paco saying that baldy's return would probably bring about change, because people abroad trusted him. All the same he preferred to have no registered assets against which claims could be made if it came to that. Citing "*force majeure*", he insisted that only the buyer, not he, should pay a commission on the sale of his house – an argument which, of course, I could not accept. "This is how I make a living, Paco," to which he answered, "that's not my problem." Finally, grudgingly, we both agreed that he pay half the usual rate. But what really annoyed me wasn't that loss, but the fact that, while he was counting out the notes and writing down the serial numbers of the dollars as he received them from Nane, Paco put to one side all the oldest, most torn and dirty notes, until he had enough to meet my fee. Then he used those notes to pay me. "Right, is that all sorted then?" said Nane. "We can't let money cause any bad blood between us, can we?"

And I answered: "Everything's sorted, Nane," while I put her husband's dirty notes away in my wallet.

Carla came into the office looking determined, but you could tell she was nervous. She sat down opposite me while I finished a phone conversation, without removing her dark glasses. I was talking to Teresa Scaglia, not yet knowing why she had called, because she kept going round in circles without saying anything.

"Yes, someone's just come in, but that's OK – carry on."

Teresa thought it better to postpone the conversation. "I'll speak to you when you aren't so busy," she said. Carla fidgeted in her chair. Her legs were crossed and she kept swinging the top one, involuntarily jogging the table. "If you like," I said and hung up. I looked at Carla and smiled.

"I'm almost an architect," she said. And I foolishly said "Well done, you," because I didn't know what was intended by her visit or her observation, and I didn't want her to feel more uncomfortable than she was already.

"I need to work, I need to get out of the house, to have a project." I said nothing. "I need you to give me a hand," she managed to finish, before her voice broke. The telephone rang. I answered it: it was Teresa again.

"No, I'm still with the... client... but go ahead and tell me – if it's something important." She didn't want to, repeating that she would ring later. Apologizing, I returned my attention to Carla. "And how can I help you?"

"I thought perhaps I could work with you in the agency."

For her to propose this in a year when property sales had all but ground to a halt – notwithstanding a few deals of the Pérez Ayerra variety – made me think that Carla might be even more cut off from the outside world than she herself suspected.

"Look, things are very hard. I don't know if you've been following developments in this market."

"I don't have much to offer, which is why I'm not offering, I'm begging..." – she was crying behind the dark glasses – "I'm begging, and it's hard, but someone has to help me."

I didn't know what to say; the truth was that I could not afford to take anyone on.

"It could be without a salary; I don't mind when you pay me, how much you pay me or even if you pay me at all. We can make whatever sort of agreement you like. But I need to work."

Carla took off her dark glasses and showed me her black eye. "Gustavo..." she didn't finish the sentence because her voice faltered once more. Before I could think of something to say, the telephone rang. Yet again, it was Teresa and, yet again, the day's course was altered. "Yes, yes, tell me what it is, Teresa." This time I lied that I was alone: it was better to listen and get her out of the way once and for all than to have the telephone ringing every five minutes.

"I know it's not really something to talk about on the phone, but I've had a knot in my stomach ever since I found out..."

"About what?" I said, but she didn't hear me.

"...and today I'm out of The Heights all day and tomorrow... did you know that tomorrow they're playing the Challenger Cup in..."

"Never mind, Teresa, don't worry. Tell me what's up."

"Promise me you won't take it badly."

"Just tell me."

"Juani's name is on the Children At Risk list."

"The what list?"

"Children At Risk."

"I don't follow you."

"It's a list made by some sort of Commission with information that is given to them by carers."

"Who do these carers give information to?"

"To them, and they give it to the Council – that's how I know, because someone at the Council – and please don't ask me who it was – told El Tano in confidence and I just had to tell you, Vir, because otherwise how will I ever look you in the eye again?"

The more she explained, the less I understood. Opposite me, Carla blew her nose noisily on a paper handkerchief. "If it had been the other way around, I would have wanted you to tell me."

"To tell you what?"

"That one of my children was on the list."

"Teresa, can you tell me once and for all what this list is, and who these children at risk are?"

"Drug addicts, Vir, Juani is on a list of drug addicts."

I felt my body stiffen. "Hello, hello... are you there? I knew I should have waited and told you in person. Speak to me, Vir, don't leave me like this, when I'm miles away from The Cascade... Vir..."

I cut her off. I sat opposite Carla Masotta in silence, without making any move, petrified. The telephone rang. I picked up the handset and crashed it down on the base. It rang again. I let it keep ringing until it stopped. It rang again. Then Carla stood up and pulled out the cable at the socket. "What's happened?"

"My son... is on a list..."

"What sort of list?"

"A list," I repeated. She waited until I was able to articulate a complete sentence. "A Commission draws up a list of all the children who take drugs," I heard myself say, without even knowing why I was telling her. A woman I barely knew, a woman who was not one of my friends, whose husband hit her hard enough to give her a black eye. Someone who had happened to come into my office on the day that Teresa rang to say that my son's name was on a list I knew nothing about.

"And does your son take drugs?" she asked.

"I don't know."

"Ask him."

"What's he going to say?"

"Can't you believe him?"

"I'm confused." We were both silent for a moment.

"And is it legal?" she asked.

"What, taking drugs?"

"No, making lists like that," she said and stood up to pour me a glass of water. "Would this Commission have a List of Husbands who Hit their Wives?" she asked.

"I don't think so," I answered and, in the midst of our own tears, we burst out laughing.

28

Finally, the Insúas separated. Carmen Insúa was one of the few women to remain living in Cascade Heights after a separation. It wasn't easy to stay on. The first obvious source of unease after the separation was that feeling of being out of place at parties and on excursions where the rest of us were couples. Her deeper discomfort did not manifest itself until later. Because, when she had moved to Cascade Heights, Carmen, like other women, had distanced herself from a world that continued to function elsewhere and to which she was linked only by the daily tale spun for her by her husband, on his return from the office. That isn't to say that she never went back to the city, but that now she went there as a tourist, visiting a place that did not belong to her, as though peeping at it from behind a curtain. When there is no husband to arrive home, trailing victories and failures from the other place, the illusion of his wife also being a citizen of that territory is ended. Then the abandoned wife has two options: to go out once more and claim her place in that oblique world, or to renounce it. And Carmen Insúa, we all believed, had opted for renunciation.

Our initial fear, when we heard that Alfredo had left her, was that Carmen's drink problem would worsen but, just as we began to find justifications for her compulsive drinking and to feel sorry for her, Carmen became mysteriously teetotal. People say the first thing that Alfredo took away from the house was his collection of wines, and perhaps this was less to protect his wife than his bottles, which could otherwise have ended up smashed against a wall.

At the beginning, most of the inhabitants of The Cascade took her side. We visited her; we invited her to our houses and we tried, perhaps too hard, to include her in rather silly diversions. Such as the fancy-dress party at the Andrades' house, at which Carmen ended up crying in a corner, behind her Cleopatra mask, while the rest of us danced to The Ketchup Song. Or that long weekend when the Pérez Ayerras insisted on taking her to Uruguay on their boat, knowing full well that she suffered from seasickness.

Alfredo Insúa had left her after twenty years of marriage – several of them marked by infidelities that she bore with stoicism – alone, with two sons who would also leave her, once they had finished school. He left her for his business partner's secretary – just to be different. We all began by saying "What a bastard Alfredo is". But the first weeks passed and some of the husbands who were still seeing him, through work, began to observe that "there are two sides to every story". "It's no fun living with a drunk." "She probably drank to help her cope with all the crap Alfredo threw at her." "What crap?"

Soon Alfredo was to be seen back at The Heights, playing golf or tennis with one or other of us, or at an event in someone's house to which Carmen was deliberately not invited. Two or three months after the separation, only the women said "what a bastard Alfredo is", while the men kept quiet. Until, one day, nobody said it any more. And then there was a day when the men were knocking about a golf ball, or having a drink after a tennis game, that people began to say: "Alfredo really had no choice."

A little while after that, he presented his new wife in society, a girl of less than thirty who was pleasant, pretty, nice and endowed with "a pair of tits that could take your eye out", one of us joked. One weekend he took her to Uruguay in the same friends' boat on which Carmen had vomited a few months earlier. And the new one didn't vomit. After that trip, Alfredo and his new partner appeared with increasing regularity at parties in The Cascade, while Carmen became a recluse in her house. Until she was hardly ever seen.

That was when we all started to talk about Carmen's depression. "I don't know, but maybe she was better when she drank." And Alfredo contrived, with very little effort and the excuse of her depression, to get the children to live with him. Carmen stayed in that house alone. A house as big as ever it was, but now with no furniture, nothing in the freezer, no chatter or clamour. She gave away the crockery, cutlery and some pieces of furniture. The few people who went into her house reported that the only object in the sitting room was a yellow painting of a naked woman in a canoe. Some of us feared that, if Carmen did something foolish, we might be alerted only when a putrid smell began to seep out of the house. Because her maids also left her. Their turnover was faster than ever. Alfredo – who was now "poor Alfredo" – always sent a replacement, as a guarantee against receiving inopportune news.

And then one day Gabina appeared. Gabina had worked for them in the early years of their marriage; she was a Paraguayan, broad, robust and efficient. Carmen would never have sacked her but, after their move to Cascade Heights, Alfredo had begun to find her appearance jarring. "She doesn't go with this house," he complained. And since Carmen refused to fire her after so many years of loyal service, Alfredo demanded that, when they were entertaining guests, they hire someone "with a better look" to wait at table. No explanation was given to Gabina, nor did she need any. The enmity between master and servant grew to such a point that relations became unsustainable. Gabina resigned without being sacked, but she took a final liberty before leaving; she looked at Alfredo and said: "You are a little turd, Señor, and one day you'll get covered in shit." Alfredo barred "that Paraguayan from ever coming into The Cascade to work in anyone's house, I don't care whose", so Gabina had to seek work elsewhere. And they did not hear of her again, apart from the telephone call she made every Christmas to the "Señora".

When Gabina tried to return to the house, after the first Christmas Carmen had spent there alone, the security guard consulted Alfredo, in spite of knowing full well that he was no longer in residence. He rang him on the mobile. "*Noblesse oblige*," answered the guard, when Alfredo thanked him for the call. But the weariness provoked in him by his ex-wife was greater than his annoyance with Gabina, so he authorized the Paraguayan's return, in the hope that someone "can take this millstone off my neck".

The first thing Gabina did was to open the windows. And when she opened them, light shone in, exposing the grime, the dust and other imperfections which she set herself to correct, one by one. We all felt more relaxed, knowing that someone was looking after Carmen. And liberated from guilt, we pushed her even further to the back of our minds.

The day that she started to go out again found Carmen back in our conversations. She was seen strolling around the streets of Cascade Heights with Gabina; she went to the supermarket with Gabina; Gabina accompanied her to the pharmacy, to the hairdresser. And we all continued to be pleased about it. "She looks better, poor thing" was all we could think of to say about her.

But one afternoon, Carmen sat down with Gabina to have a coffee in the bar by the tennis courts. And Gabina was not wearing uniform, but her own clothes,

clothes the like of which no member of Cascade Heights would ever wear. And one Saturday they were seen having lunch together in the golf club restaurant. They were laughing. Paco Pérez Ayerra was annoyed by Gabina's guffaws, and complained to the waiter. "Look, are domestic servants allowed to eat here?" And nobody could find any written regulation forbidding it, prompting the matter to be taken up in meetings of the Council of Administration.

It was around that time that you began to hear people say: "What are those two doing together all the time? Could they be?..." "Oh stop it, don't be disgusting," Teresa Scaglia said to someone who had whispered this in her ear, when Gabina and Carmen jogged past them one morning. "If we don't do something, next thing we'll find ourselves at the gym sharing a sauna with that Indian," said Roque Lauría in a Council meeting.

The night that Carmen and Gabina went to see a film in the auditorium, Ernesto Andrade finally called Alfredo. Someone swore that when Carmen started crying, Gabina held her hand. "We didn't want to bother you, but this just can't go on, old friend." Then Alfredo once more forbade Gabina to enter Cascade Heights. The problem was that this time Carmen already *was inside.* The Chief of Security came to speak to Carmen. "What law states that she has to leave my house? Do you have a judge's order, or something?"

"I have an order from your husband."

"My husband is the one banned from entering this house," she replied, and closed the door.

"She's lost her mind," everyone started to say. "No doubt Alfredo, with his contacts, will be able to arrange a court order, an injunction or something. Poor Alfredo."

174

Alfredo swung into action. The first thing he did was to cut off Carmen's money and stop paying her bills. He did not tell the children, because they were on a trip to the United States at the time, and "a piece of news like that would knock them sideways". He would tell them about it once the matter was resolved. He asked the president of the Council of Administration to go and speak personally to Carmen, with the threat that she could be declared "persona non grata" in the neighbourhood. "Think of the children," he said. She told him to go to hell.

The women no longer went out. They spent a month closeted in there. Two months. Three. All of us who walked by their house looked inside, trying to understand. To start with, they were still receiving deliveries from the supermarket, or the pharmacy. "The money's going to run out soon," one of us said.

"But if Alfredo has closed down all the accounts, how come they can still shop in the supermarket?"

"They must be paying with a Paraguayan Express card."

"Give me a break!"

And then one morning somebody noticed that Carmen's car wasn't there. Nor was it there the following day. Nor the one after that. In fact, the women had left before dawn one morning, driving together through the Club's automatic barrier. "Your instruction was that Señora Gabina Vera Cristaldo could not enter Cascade Heights, but never that she could not leave," the guard who had been on duty that night explained to his superior. It wasn't enough to save him his job.

Alfredo came at the weekend to open the house. In the days between the discovery of the women's flight and Alfredo's arrival, we had felt a growing trepidation about what he was going to find inside. Dirt at the very least; evidence of what those women had been doing there, on their own so long; damage in what had once been his home. For that reason, several people offered to go with him. They broke down the front door. Alfredo had a key but it didn't work: Carmen had had the lock changed. The Chief of Security confirmed that "in the guard's register there is a record of a locksmith entering the Club two weeks ago".

"She never gave a thought to her children," someone said. Inside the house there was not enough light to see the interior. Alfredo pressed the light switch, pointlessly, as he himself had allowed the electricity to be cut off through non-payment of bills. Someone went over to draw the curtains and, as the panels were folded back, the light filtered in and the group was frozen in their advance, immobilized by the sight before them.

The painting of the woman lying in the canoe was no longer there. Instead all the walls of the house had been covered with photographs. The biggest of these was of Alfredo, an enlargement of a wedding shot. Then there were smaller ones: one of Paco Pérez Ayerra; another of Teresa Scaglia torn out of Country Woman magazine; the Andrades in a snap from the last club party; the president of Cascade Heights; various women in a photo from the last Burako tournament Carmen had organized; her fellow members of the painting group (apart from Carla Masotta, who had been carefully cut out of the picture) and some of other neighbours. On every photograph, pins had been stuck into the person's eyes. On some, such as Alfredo's, into the heart, too. And beneath each photo was an altar. "This is a real piece of work," said one of the guards, and Nane Pérez Ayerra grasped the gold cross dangling over her chest. Everywhere there were little pieces of knotted cloth, images, heads of garlic, feathers, stones, seeds. Alfredo approached his own "altar". It was a Villeroy Boch plate, covered in dry shit, on which a red candle had melted away.

29

"I'm not a junkie – what are you saying, Mum?" says Juani.

"I'm not the one saying it, the Security Commission lists say it."

"Those idiots think that smoking a joint makes you a drug addict."

"You smoke marijuana?" Virginia asks, crying. Juani doesn't answer. "Did you smoke marijuana, for fuck's sake?"

"Yes... once."

"Don't you realize that leads to cocaine and cocaine takes you to heroin and heroin..."

"Stop it, Virginia," Ronie intervenes.

"Where did we go wrong?" she weeps.

"Oh, Mum..."

"We don't want you to smoke, Juani," his father tells him.

"I smoked once, that's all."

"Don't do it again."

"Everyone smokes, Dad."

"But not everyone's on the list – you are!" his mother yells.

"Stop, Virginia."

Virginia sobs, banging the table with her fist. "Tomorrow he's starting therapy and if that fails we'll send him into rehab."

"What do you mean 'therapy', Mum? I smoked a joint, that's all."

"That's all? That's all, you bastard, and you're on a list of drug addicts?"

"But what is it you're worried about – that I smoked a joint or that I'm on that list?" She slaps him hard across the face. Ronie pulls her away.

"Calm down, you won't solve anything like that, Virginia."

"And how in God's name do you plan to solve it?"

"Everyone my age smokes, Mum."

"I don't believe you."

"Why do you think they call us the 'potheads'?"

"They call you *what*?"

"Not just me – all of us."

"I don't believe you."

"Who sold it to you?" Ronie asks. Juani says nothing. "Who sold it to you, for Christ's sake, so that I can go and smash his face in?"

"Nobody, Dad."

"So where did you get it?"

"I was offered it."

"By?"

"Anyone, I don't know – someone goes out, buys it, brings it back and we all smoke it."

"I don't care if everyone smokes it, I don't want *you* to smoke it."

"Dad, I smoked two or three times at the most."

"Don't smoke it again."

"Why not?"

178

"Because you'll end up in hospital with an overdose!" screams his mother.

"Because I don't want you to," says Ronie. Juani says nothing, stares at his trainers, puts his hands in his pockets. "You've tried it. You know what it's like. Do you need to keep smoking it?"

"No, I haven't smoked it for a long time."

"Well, don't smoke it again."

"OK."

"'Don't smoke again' – is that how you sort things out?" says Virginia.

"And how would you like to sort them out – by screaming like a madwoman?"

"I suppose now you're going to say my shouting's to blame for him taking drugs!"

"I don't take drugs, Mum."

"Smoking marijuana is taking drugs."

"So is taking Trapax." Virginia throws another blow, which Juani dodges, then she runs sobbing upstairs. Ronie pours himself a whisky. Juani gets his roller blades and puts them on.

"Where are you going?" his father asks.

"Over to Romina's." They look at each other. "Can I?"

Ronie doesn't answer. Juani leaves. Ronie goes upstairs to talk to Virginia. He finds her searching Juani's room: checking every drawer, all pockets, backpacks, under the bed, inside magazines, books, CD cases, behind the computer. Ronie watches, but lets her get on with it. She searches everything that day and the next, and the one after that. "When will you stop searching?" he asks her.

"Never," his wife replies.

30

El Tano was checking his emails. There was a note inviting him to a course on "Business management in the new millennium"; an email from an old university friend, attaching a CV "in case you hear of anything"; a chain letter that must not be broken and which he broke by hitting "delete"; a bulletin from an economic service explaining how Standard & Poor calculated a country's risk index, and two or three other bits of junk. No responses to any of the searches put out on his behalf by the headhunters. Actually, there was one: "This search has been momentarily suspended. We'll keep in touch. Thank you."

He had some time in hand, so he scanned the headlines on the main newspapers, looking for a piece of news, or anything to make him feel – emotionally rather than rationally – that things might be starting to change. And if they did change, if confidence could be restored, the Dutch might return with new faith. And if that happened, they would probably take him on again, because there wasn't really anything against him, he had not been fired for incompetence. On the contrary, the Dutch were more than satisfied with his performance in the company. He was not to blame. Nobody is to blame for ceasing to be necessary. And if things changed, and if the Dutch were confident again and if he were necessary again and they asked him to take charge once more of Troost in Argentina, and if everything could be as it had been before, he would have no reason to refuse. That was not to say that he had no pride. Quite the opposite: he felt pride in his job, not in just any job, in *that* one. Or another, better one. Not another one the same, because, as his father had taught him, no one exchanges one job for something at the same level. One changes in order to better oneself, to progress, to keep advancing. That was the way it had always been. And so it should be. For his father and for him, too.

At ten minutes to eight, he turned off the computer and went to have breakfast. Teresa, in her dressing gown, was serving *café con leche* to the children. She always took charge of breakfast, while the maid hovered nearby, in case she was needed. "Anyone want more toast?" Nobody answered, but Teresa put two more slices in the toaster anyway. El Tano walked over to the kitchen counter and picked up a brochure. It was an offer to travel to Maui, with a five-star hotel, all inclusive, and an optional night in Honolulu. El Tano stared at the brochure. He didn't read it, just looked. Blue and green. "Ask your secretary to look into that."

"OK." He put the brochure into his briefcase.

"It would be nice... don't you think? The alternative would be to go back to Bal Harbour or Sarasota, but I'd like to see somewhere different. I mean, how many times have we been to Miami already?"

The children climbed into the Land Rover. El Tano dropped them off at school, then continued to the office. The same as every morning. A lorry had overturned in the opposite lane, the one heading away from the city. There was an ambulance, a breakdown van, two cars which had crashed into the lorry, police, someone with his head in his hands. The curiosity of those who were travelling, like him, towards the capital, forced him to slow down and it took him twenty minutes longer than usual to get to the office.

He left his car in the street. He no longer took it into the garage: it was too much of a palaver for the couple of hours he spent at work there. Besides, they had changed his parking place to one on the side, beside the furnace. Getting the car into that space was a tight fit – scrape marks on the wall commemorated many others who had made the attempt. Not El Tano. And then there was the Troost guard, who raised the barrier for cars going in and out and who still looked at him in a funny way, as he had not done before. El Tano preferred not to find a word for that way of looking. He favoured the courtesy parking on the pavement. Even though it was for visitors. He locked the car and went inside. He walked the fifty-eight steps that it took to cover the distance from the front door to his new office. The one that was smaller, but acceptable. The one that had been assigned to him after his redundancy. Fifty-eight steps, give or take an inch. He had started counting them shortly after losing his job as General Manager of Troost. Never before in his adult life had he counted his own steps. When he was a child, yes, he knew exactly how many steps separated his bedroom from any other area in the house. But not as an adult, never. Before, there had been too much to think about as he walked: company finances; due diligence with the headquarters; the royalties that were owed to the Dutch; the bonuses with which the Dutch would reward the royalties. And then in the corridor he was always waylaid by someone with papers for him to sign, some query demanding an instant response, a waiting telephone call.

After his redundancy, everything changed: not on the first day, or the second – some changes are subtle and very gradual. But there was a particular moment when El Tano opened the door, looked around him and started to take those steps – not yet counting them – and something was different. Desperately he searched his mind, as though it were a card index file, for something – some pending business matter, a grievance, an appointment that must be cancelled, an appointment that must be kept: any concrete concern. The cards were blank. The people around him did their own thing; some greeted him as they passed; there was the odd smile, the odd glance. He looked down and discovered his shoes. Fifty-eight steps and four inches exactly, including the stairs. During the last few months, as he sat in his new office, waiting for the phone to ring or for someone to come in and interrupt his patient vigil, or for an email to say that he was once more necessary to someone, anyone, he often asked himself how many steps he must have taken every day in the last years, from the building's entrance to the desk of his old office (the one that was no longer his), the General Manager's office. He estimated them to be more than sixty-five and fewer than seventy-one. A few days ago, he had drawn a scaled-down plan of the office on a piece of paper and calculated the approximate number of steps. But he had not paced them out. Because nowadays his route (the one he was taking this morning) led somewhere else.

The forty-sixth step took him to the desk of Andrea, his ex-secretary, who was talking on the phone to someone who was evidently very insistent. El Tano waved at her and, eager not to interrupt her or himself, returned his gaze to his shoes – forty-seven, forty-eight, forty-nine – not noticing that Andrea, still talking into the handset, was trying to detain him with gestures that were lost in the air. Fifty-seven, fifty-eight. At the door of his new office, El Tano opened his briefcase and looked for his key. He searched among his papers; it was one of those tiny little keys that are intended to provide privacy rather than security. Andrea had a copy of it. He felt something metal – the key perhaps – but he didn't have a chance to take it out, because the door was suddenly opened from inside, striking him on the forehead. His briefcase fell to the floor, scattering papers. "Oh sorry!" said someone in an accented English. Through the open door, El Tano saw three men sitting in his office. The desk was covered with spread-out papers. Espresso cups. Calculators. A laptop. The men were working. One of them said something in Dutch and the others laughed. They weren't talking about him, though: they had not even seen him. Only the one who had struck him had noticed him.

"I'm so sorry."

El Tano crouched down to collect the papers and bumped into Andrea, who was already picking them up behind him.

"I didn't get a chance to warn you." The Dutch man also crouched down to help them. The three of them squatted together. "They're the new auditors from Troost in Holland. Central Office asked me to allocate them a room."

"Nice place!" said the man who had banged him with the door, as he picked up the Maui brochure and passed it to El Tano.

"I told them that none of the rooms were free, but they insisted, then the lawyer called and he said that your agreement was for a few months and that was more than a year ago… I've got your papers in a box… If you need to make any calls, I can lend you my desk for a while. Seriously, look – it's really not a problem."

"Nice place," said the Dutch man again, with the Maui brochure still in his hand.

31

The first formal invitation from the Llambías to the Uroviches came soon after Beto discovered that Martín was unemployed and with serious money problems. They invited them round to eat *chivito*, a kid goat that Beto himself had brought from the country for the occasion. And the Uroviches were punctual: at half-past nine they were ringing the bell of one of Cascade Heights' grandest and showiest houses, with its two great columns at the entrance, the marble staircase which could be glimpsed through the glazed front door and a balustrade at every window. An *asador*[5] had been brought in to roast the kid and two maids were on hand, all evening, serving at table and clearing things away with the insouciance of actors who must repeat the same performance season after season.

"Mario's a phenomenon," said Beto that night, gesturing towards the man who was labouring at the grill. "For fifty pesos he'll make you the best mixed grill you've

---

5 The *asado* is at the heart of Argentine cuisine. Essentially it is a meal of grilled meats, including steak, sweetbreads and offal, which may be cooked in a rudimentary fire pit, in the country, or on a grill at home and in restaurants. The meal often lasts several hours and the "*asador*" – who cooks the meat – is regarded both as an artist and as a kind of folkloric hero. These qualities are recognized with an invariable invitation to "toast the *asador*", and a round of applause.

ever tasted and you don't even have to worry about getting the coals to light. Isn't that right, *Marito*?" And Llambías raised his glass towards the grill, proposing a toast. "May each person do what he does best. Isn't that right?" And this time he raised his glass to Martín.

That first invitation was followed by many others, of all kinds and budgets – anything you could imagine. Seats in the official box at the Davis Cup; a flight in the Llambías's ultralight; concert tickets for some foreign singer, whoever was coming; a weekend in Punta del Este. Martín did not like accepting so many invitations that they would never be able to reciprocate, but Lala insisted: "There's nothing wrong with being liked," she said, and these outings put her in such a good mood that he ended up accepting them with barely a murmur. Thus the Uroviches were able to indulge for a time the fantasy that not only had nothing changed, but that their circumstances were in fact better than ever.

After a few months the two couples seemed more like family than mere friends. The Llambías no longer had small children living with them, but they never minded incorporating the Urovich children in their plans when appropriate. There was always a spare maid available to look after them. They had even fitted out a room in their house with a television and video to keep the children entertained.

For three or four months the two couples had dinner together every Tuesday, went to the cinema every Friday and got together on Saturday nights at the Llambías's house to watch a film in their home theatre. Only Thursdays were sacrosanct, when Martín always went to El Tano's house and Lala went out to the cinema with the "Thursday Widows".

On one of those Saturdays, Lala arrived bringing a video that Beto had asked her to get – *Last Tango in Paris*. She had heard of it, but never seen it. It had been hard to find: they didn't have it in Blockbuster or in any other video shops in the area. She had had to go all the way to San Isidro. She didn't know who the director or actors were – nothing beyond the title. Judging by the box on the shelf, it was quite old-fashioned. But Beto had asked for it. He had called her on the mobile. "You'll be saving my life, Lala, I need to see that film today." And the Llambías were always so kind to them that she did not dare let them down.

Dorita came into the room while Beto was setting up the film. She went over to him and kissed him. It was a more effusive kiss than Lala was used to witnessing and that made her uncomfortable. She and Martín didn't kiss in public, and they were ten years younger and had been married much less time. None of her friends kissed like that in public. They watched the film sitting on the big sofa, Lala at one end and Beto beside her, too close, leaving an empty space on the other side of him. Martín was behind them, dozing in a reclining armchair. Meanwhile, Dorita went back and forth, bringing things from the kitchen. Coffee, cakes, more coffee, liqueurs. It was obvious that she was either uninterested in the film or knew it too well. On the screen, meanwhile, Brando pleasured his companion. And she him. Lala had not been wrong when she guessed that this was an old film: the picture was a bit grainy and difficult to watch. Beto sank into the sofa, lying ever further back. When he wanted to say something to her about the film, he sat up a little, leaning on her leg and looking into her face. And she did not know exactly what he was saying, but she felt his pressure. On one of those occasions, Beto left his hand on Lala's thigh and did not take it away. Lala kept still, waiting, and the heat of Beto's hand warmed her leg. When he began to stroke her, she tensed up and moved his hand; he stopped then, and looked at her. Lala held his gaze, simply because she didn't know what to say. She did not want to make a scene in front of her husband and she thought that her expression would make her feelings sufficiently clear. But that must not have been the case, because Beto continued to look at her, smiled and, without taking his eyes off her face, reached once more for her leg and began moving his hand up her thigh. Now Dorita, who had seemed all this while to be somewhere else, drew up a chair in front of them, blocking the screen. She smiled at them, came closer and put her hand over her husband's.

Lala sprang to her feet and rushed over to the window. She did not dare to look at them, to scream or to run out of the room. It was as much as she could do to look out of the window. When she felt able, she turned very slightly and watched them from the corner of her eye. Dorita and Beto were kissing with a frenzy on the sofa where she had been sitting. Martín, meanwhile, was still asleep in the reclining armchair.

32

Romina doesn't know what job Ernesto does. At school they asked her to write an essay on her father's work or profession. But she doesn't know. She knows what they tell her, but that isn't the truth. She calls Juani. He doesn't know either. He laughs: it would be very simple for him to write about his father's work. Four words would do it: "My father doesn't work." But they haven't asked him to do this essay. They asked Romina, and he tries to find out. However his mother, who knows everything about everyone, dodges the question.

"Go on, Mum, isn't it written in your red notebook?" She says it isn't, but Juani doesn't believe her.

"You'd be amazed by all the things that happen that I don't write down," she says. "I haven't written a single line about drugs, for example."

Juani's annoyed. "God, you're really screwed up." He goes out, slamming the door, and heads for Romina's. He's let her down. He had promised to find out about her father, but he could not. So she asks Antonia.

"Your daddy works very hard," she says. "He leaves very early, you know, and comes home very late." But she doesn't say what he works at. "Your daddy works very hard," she repeats and leaves the room.

Romina already knows what Mariana will say: "Daddy's a lawyer." So she doesn't even bother asking her. Everyone in Cascade Heights believes that he is a lawyer, but she knows that he isn't. Mariana must also know – she's his wife. But Mariana tells lies. You can't lie in an essay. At least, you can't use other people's lies – you invent your own. Her father styles himself "Doctor". But he is no more a doctor than he is her father. If someone goes to him with a legal query, he tosses out one or two generalities, then he explains that he does not specialize in that particular area but that he will find out the answer. And he does find it out. So no one is any the wiser. His cards say: Doctor Ernesto J. Andrade. To think that he scarcely even finished secondary school! That much she does know, because once her grandmother, Ernesto's mother, let it slip. "He's doing so well, he looks so refined, and to think that he couldn't finish high school."

Romina knows that he has an office in the centre of town – she's been there once. There's a bronze plaque on the door. And a secretary and two lawyers who work for him, although she isn't sure that they're really lawyers either. The plaque reads "Andrade and Associates", which is also what the secretary says when she answers the telephone. Ernesto's phones are always ringing: his mobile, his home telephone and the line he reserves for "private business". One day Romina answers the private line and someone on the other end says, "Tell that bastard Andrade to watch his arse, because when we get inside the barrier we're going to kick it." She doesn't tell him – it would mean owning up to having answered the phone which is off-limits. But she doesn't think Ernesto's arse is at any real risk. However hard they try, they won't be able to get past the barrier. Nobody can, thinks Romina. For a time she didn't answer that phone. Then she got over it, or there were no more calls. She can't remember which.

Romina confronts the blank page. Juani suggests she lie. She's not sure. She draws little pink arses. On some of them, she draws a little flower emerging from the crack, on others little hearts adorn the buttocks. Juani is very amused. He asks if he can keep the drawing. Romina gives it to him. "Would you like me to lie for you?" Juani asks her. Romina says she would. To spare Romina from trouble at school, he tells the lie that everyone would like to hear. In English, he writes: "My father is a prestigious lawyer, specializing in criminal, civil and commercial law. His offices have taken on some very high-profile cases."

And so it goes on. One, two, three more paragraphs. It doesn't matter much what he says, who he names, what titles he uses, or which words. The whole thing is a fabrication. Except for those little arses which Romina gave him and which he has tucked away in his pocket.

33

The problem of the "cimarron" dogs came to light at the beginning of 2001. The first notice appeared in March of that year, in the local bulletin that is handed out on weekends at the entry gate. The notice came from the office of the Environment Committee. "Given the undesirable presence of packs of stray dogs in our neighbourhood, we would ask the residents of Cascade Heights to be extra diligent in the disposal of their rubbish and to use lidded containers to prevent animal foraging."

By this time, almost everyone in Cascade Heights knew about dogs. And then some. But we knew about pure-breeds. Not strays. We had a lot to learn. Some people did not even know exactly what "cimarron" meant. "It sounds like something out of *Martín Fierro*,"[6] said Lala in the Tuesday painting class. Even now there is confusion over whether this was in fact the correct choice of word: these were dogs without owners, raised in the wild, who came into our compound looking for food. Feral dogs. Not like our dogs, our Golden Retrievers, Short-haired Labradors, Beagles, Border Collies, Chow Chows,

---

6 *Martín Fierro*, by José Hernandez, is an epic poem and a classic of nineteenth-century Argentine literature, extolling the rough life of the pampas, and of the gauchos who worked on the land.

Schnauzers, Bichon Frisés, Basset Hounds, Weimaraners. For those were the breeds most often to be seen out for a walk in Cascade Heights, wearing collars and identity discs engraved with a name and telephone number, lest they stray. There was the odd Dalmatian, bought at the insistence of a child who had seen the Disney film. But very few. It's well known that Dalmatians are eternal puppies, breaking everything in their path. That Beagles howl at night, as though they were barking at the moon in the English countryside and that you have to cut their vocal chords if you don't want problems with the neighbours (apparently it doesn't hurt at all – a little snip, and no more barking). Chow Chows will fill your house with hairs. Bichon Frisés need their teeth cleaned every so often or their breath can kill you. Schnauzers have a nasty temperament. As for the Weimaraner: lovely blue eyes, but it's not easy to live with something that size. There are other breeds – but not at Cascade Heights. There are the dogs that we had as children and forgot about, the dogs that went out of fashion. In this area, it's unlikely that you would see Poodles, Bulldogs, Boxers. Nor Collies, like the one in *Lassie*, nor police dogs. Especially not sausage dogs, Chihuahuas or Pekinese. Alberti's wife used to have a Chihuahua that she took everywhere inside her Fendi bag. It probably wasn't a genuine Fendi, but one of those perfect imitations that Mariana Andrade gets from a catalogue. She took it to teas, Burako tournaments, tennis matches. One day she even went with it to mass. But she took umbrage if you called it a Chihuahua. "He's a Miniature Pinscher," she would correct you, as the dog peeped out of her unzipped bag. "Look at his eyes – can't you see that he's much prettier than a Chihuahua?"

We knew about all these breeds of dog, and how to look after them. A balanced, nutritious diet, guaranteeing faeces that were firm, small, round and much easier to pick up with a spade than any other sort. A health record with vaccinations all up to date. Sprays to control ticks and fleas. A leather bone for them to chew. A bath at the veterinary clinic every two weeks. Nails cut regularly to stop them clawing doors and upholstery. A trainer, at least at the beginning, to teach them to understand basic commands in English. *Sit* and *Stop*. "He won't sit because you're pronouncing it wrong, Granny," Rita Mansilla's granddaughter told her one day. "It's not 'siiiiit', it's '*sit*', do you understand? *Sit* – nice and short – *sit*." And Dorita was amazed to observe "how well children learn English in those private schools". A walk two or three times a day keeps them fit and tired-out. Professional dog-walkers are a much rarer sight in Cascade Heights than they are in the public squares of Buenos Aires. Here, we walk our own dogs, or get our maids to walk them. But usually the owners go out themselves. Just as, years ago, people used to put on their best clothes to walk around the square on Sundays, to see and be seen, so on afternoons in Cascade Heights, the neighbours come out to walk their dogs in fitness gear, with air-cushioned running shoes or designer trainers.

Years ago, when almost nobody lived permanently at Cascade Heights, people who had dogs and brought them at the weekends behaved as if they had brought them to the country: they let them off the lead. The dogs ran free and nobody complained about it. These were families who were used to dogs. People who, for better or worse, had spent time on their own country holdings, or those of friends, who knew what to do if approached by an animal. And there were fewer of us then.

The massive affluence of the 1990s brought about a rule change: now you had to take other people into account. Because the "other people" were not the same as they had been. Now the maxim was: if my dog annoys a neighbour, I must take responsibility. And the moral: because if I don't, my neighbour may report me and I'll be fined. Today, if a dog is seen wandering without an owner in The Cascade, anyone who feels menaced or offended, or merely irritated, lodges a complaint and Security sends someone to catch the animal and take it to the pound. If he can, that is: no security guard has been trained to catch dogs and nearly all the dogs know instinctively how to shake off their pursuers. But if he manages it, if that man on a bicycle creeping up on an animal armed with nothing more than a rope attached to a pole (with which he means to lasso it) catches it, then the dog is taken to the neighbourhood pound. There it stays until such a time as the owner comes to collect it. Close to the Club's riding centre, the pound contains enormous cages where the animals are given the same food they would receive at home. Before he can take his dog away, the owner must pay an eighty-peso fine, plus fifty additional pesos per day to cover kennelling and food. That's a strong incentive not to let your dog escape.

But no one comes to live thirty miles outside Buenos Aires in order to keep their dog shut up as though it were still in a city apartment, or attached to a chain, however long. In Cascade Heights it is against the regulations to enclose a property with anything other than plants, but plants are no match for canine exuberance, so some time ago invisible fencing started to catch on. This is a system similar to that used on the pampas to stop cattle escaping. A cable is buried all the way around the property. That cable transmits a signal, causing a battery inside the dog's collar to give off a six-volt charge. The animal is trained for a time, with coloured flags – generally white or orange – which are staked along the perimeter. Every time the dog gets close to the flags wearing its shock collar, the system emits first a sound and then, if the dog keeps going in spite of the sound, it delivers a bolt of electricity to the neck. The flag has no specific function other than to create in the animal a conditioned reflex about how far it can stray. Later, even when the flags are removed on aesthetic grounds (because no one wants their land bordered by little flags), the animal has absorbed the lesson and it is very rare for it to try to get out, at the risk of getting another shock. It's an ingenious system, a life-saver, and all for seven hundred dollars.

So we had also learned about invisible fencing. But we still had not learned about wild cimarron dogs. In one of the bulletins for May, the Environment Committee was even more explicit: their warning was once more entitled "Cimarron Dogs", but this time in capital letters. "In spite of all efforts on the part of security personnel, the cimarron dogs are proving almost impossible to catch. They move in a pack and, when confronted with the presence of an agent, they escape at great speed. It has not yet been possible to establish how they are entering our communal property. Given that no evidence of digging or broken wire has been found along the perimeter fence, it is estimated that the dogs have been entering via the public access gate, under the barriers. Although they are looking only for food and have not yet attacked any resident, approaching them is not recommended. At present, the only solution to the problem is to keep rubbish adequately protected, because this is what attracts them. They come in to look for the food that they can no longer find in their natural habitat around The Heights. Therefore, all residents are requested NOT to leave rubbish bags containing household waste in an area accessible to these animals. We recommend the use of iron, lidded containers into which the bags can be placed. If the design of the container is such than an animal can claw at the rubbish and spill it or insert its snout to that end, we recommend it be lined with close-weave mesh in the same colour, as far as possible, as the container. Let us take care of our rubbish and banish the cimarrons. It is up to us."

And we knuckled down to the task. If the cimarron dogs were coming in to look for the food they could not find outside, well, they would not find it in here either. Those who did not have an adequate rubbish container acquired one. Square ones, cylindrical ones. Some smaller and others larger. Built in to the same column that housed the gas meter. Hidden in the shrubbery. Green, black or grey. Nearly all of them in metallic weave, though some were wooden and others resembled funerary urns. People got tall ones, to keep animals at bay, or short ones, for ease of lifting heavy bags. The Llambías's house had two: one in metal mesh for general rubbish and another in sheet metal for the rubbish that they did not want anyone to see. In the neighbourhood store, there was a variety of models and sizes available. At the end of June, a directive was issued about "Appropriate positioning of rubbish containers, and characteristics of the same".

And now that we had bins with lids for our rubbish, we could all rest easy.

34

Gustavo got up at half-past nine, the same as every Saturday. At ten o' clock he had a tennis game with El Tano. Glancing out of the window, he saw that Carla's four-by-four had already gone. He looked in his wardrobe for his tennis clothes. There they were, washed, ironed and neatly folded on the corresponding shelf. Carla left them there every Saturday, so that he didn't have to search around for them and get annoyed about being late for the game.

He got dressed. He laced his trainers tighter than usual. Why did she have to go so early if the agency opened at ten? He went down to have breakfast. Waiting for him on the table were his napkin, a clean cup, a thermos of coffee, the newspaper, the sugar bowl, the peach jam that he ate every morning and slices of toast in a rattan bread basket, wrapped in a white napkin. He unfolded the napkin: the toast was still warm. With one hand resting on the warm bread, he calculated that Carla must have left not more than ten minutes earlier. He was sorry not to have heard her getting up. He flicked through the newspaper without giving it his attention. He looked at his watch: a quarter to ten. He called her mobile. It was switched off.

He was a few minutes late arriving at the court and El Tano scolded him. Why did she need to work weekends, too? Why did she need to work? He brought home enough to maintain their lifestyle – more than enough. He started a doubles match with El Tano, the same as every Saturday. But he missed too many balls. El Tano got irritated; after the first set he made a comment about finding another partner. They started a new set. Yes, he understood that an estate agency, especially one dealing with gated communities, works more at the weekend than during the week. He would be the first to understand that, having invented that story about Virginia's lost mobile just to get her to see him on a weekday. It had been a matter of urgency to find a house into which they could move straight away, and urgency does not distinguish between working days and holidays. He had not wanted to keep seeing people who criticized him or pitied his inability to control himself. They put all kinds of ideas into Carla's head, and that was no way to solve anything. He and she would find a solution together, without anyone else sticking their nose in. He had promised her. She had promised him. But was it wrong to want one's wife to stay at home on Saturdays and Sundays? he asked himself as his opponent served a ball he failed to return. She must understand that. A telephone rang in the middle of a rally. It was Gustavo's mobile. He ran to the bench to answer it. It wasn't Carla, so he rang off immediately. He started to return to the court, then decided to go back and check his messages. El Tano began practising serves, venting his fury at the interruption. Gustavo lost the next set and the one after that. He alone lost them, even though it was a doubles match. El Tano could barely bring himself to speak. Gustavo didn't stay on to have a Coke after the match. "I'm very worried – there are some problems at work."

"Evidently," said El Tano testily.

He went back to the house and straight to the kitchen. He poured himself some cold water: two glasses. He drank one after the other, almost without drawing a breath. He called Carla again. Her mobile was still switched off. He called Virginia's office. "Carla's gone out to show a house to a client." Carla in a client's car. A man's. "Yes, I'll tell her you called."

He showered. The water, hotter than perhaps was advisable, hurt his back. He had lunch. Alone. Without getting dressed, his towel wrapped around his waist, his feet bare. He put the plates in the sink. He went upstairs to get dressed. He left another message: "Call me". He opened the door of Carla's dressing room, but he didn't go in. He switched on the television. He turned it off. He went downstairs. He watered the plants. He cleaned out the swimming pool. Carla should be back by five o'clock at the latest. They had agreed that she would not work later than that. At half-past five he called her mobile again. It was still switched off. This time he left no message. He went up to the bedroom. He turned on the television again. He watched a film that had already started. He thought that he had seen it before. He had seen it before. He entered Carla's dressing room. He ran his fingers through her clothes, hanger by hanger. He smelled them. He caressed them. He stopped at the brown silk skirt which she had worn on his last birthday. It was soft, it smelled of her and he buried his face in the fabric. With which other client would she be now? He breathed into the brown silk. He let it go. He played at guessing what she might have put on that morning. The high-heeled black shoes he had given her for their last anniversary were missing. Shoes that were far too fancy for getting in and out of cars showing houses.

And the white cotton shirt, the one through which her bra showed. He ran through the hangers again. Surely she had not put on that shirt. Violently, he pushed the hangers aside. Another shirt slipped from its perch and fell onto the floor. He trod it underfoot, still searching for the white cotton shirt. He couldn't find it. On the last shelf, beside the window, Carla's mobile was charging up.

He went downstairs and made a coffee. Black, very strong. He filled it with sugar. The coffee went cold in its cup. She can't have put on that shirt and those shoes to show houses and plots of land. He called the agency, then rang off. If Virginia knew and was covering for her, the last thing he needed was to be taken for an idiot. The telephone rang. He ran to answer it. He had been standing near it, but he ran anyway. It was El Tano. "Do you want to play tomorrow? Today's game left me wanting more."

"Well, OK."

"Is something up?"

"No…"

"Sure?"

"Sure. I'll see you tomorrow at ten."

"We're seeing each other tonight at Ernesto Andrade's – had you forgotten?"

"No, I didn't forget."

He hung up and went back upstairs. He went into the dressing room. He switched on Carla's telephone and checked the calls she had made that day and the one before. The agency. His own mobile. Her voicemail. A Cascade Heights guard. The agency again. A number he did not recognize. He rang it and waited for an answer. "Cine Village, good afternoon…" He rang off.

Another unfamiliar number. He dialled and a man's voice answered. He let him say "hello" several times, but didn't recognize the voice. It could be a client of the agency, or not. Perhaps it was one of those men Carla met in chat rooms, in the early morning when she couldn't sleep, although she had denied she visited chat rooms, even when he had grabbed her hand on the mouse, twisted it, and bent her arm up behind her back until she cried out in pain. He went out to the garden. He watered the grass. He cleaned the pool again; the wind had scattered a few leaves into it. He had never liked Virginia Guevara. Ronie, yes – but she struck him as untrustworthy. She had asked too many questions that day that she leased him the house. She made stupid comments. She had lied – he didn't remember in what way – but she definitely had lied. Just as she might be lying now. "I told her you called, hasn't she rung? The thing is, oddly, we have a lot of work on today. The sun's out and everyone wants to move to our country club."

He took the car out to drive around The Cascade. Systematically, he swept down each road, the verticals, then the horizontals, the cul-de-sacs, then back to the horizontals. He didn't see her. Any of those cars parked in front of any of those houses could belong to the man to whom his smiling wife, with her black high heels and transparent cotton shirt, was now showing a bedroom. He returned to the house. On one corner he almost bumped into Martín Urovich, but he raised his hand and continued. Seven o'clock. He went into the kitchen. To the bar. He poured himself a whisky. What if, instead of showing houses in The Cascade, she had gone to the cinema with someone? He went back out to the garden. He kicked away a branch that had fallen beside the quebracho wood path. First to the cinema, and afterwards – what? He went back inside. He went back up to the room. He checked the incoming calls on Carla's mobile. She had deleted them. Why did she delete them? He poured himself another whisky. He took the glass out to the garden and threw himself down on a lounger. He drained the glass in one gulp. He went back inside to get the bottle. There was still enough for another three or four whiskies. He left it on the ground, close to him. And afterwards – what? It was half-past seven and she had not called him all day. She doesn't even care how I am, he thought. He shook the bottle over his glass; two drops fell out, then nothing. He went back into the house to fetch another bottle. He opened it. It was difficult opening it. He heard the noise of an engine in front of the house. He looked out of the window: it was someone using his drive for a manoeuvre. Someone. Not Carla. He remembered that Carla had been looking very pretty recently. Prettier than usual, tanned and toned from the gym. With the transparent cotton shirt. He went back out to the garden. He walked over to the swimming pool. A breeze moved on the water, but no more leaves had fallen in. He lay back down on the lounger. The telephone rang. He got up to answer it and, in his haste, knocked over the bottle. He ran to the house. "Shall we pick you up on the way to Ernesto's?" asked El Tano, at the other end.

"No, that's fine…"

"Seriously, are you all right?"

"Yes, don't worry."

"Are you going along later?"

"I don't know."

"What do you mean, you don't know?"

"I don't know, Tano, I don't know yet."

He went back up to the bedroom and into Carla's dressing room. He sat on the floor. He looked at her clothes, and now he suspected that the combination of colours and textures hanging from the rails concealed some message he must decipher. He spoke to them. Why is she doing this to me? He squeezed a dress with yellow flowers. He emptied his glass into his throat. I don't deserve this. He pulled open a black shirt, making all the buttons pop off. Then he lunged at the hangers, anyhow, grabbing two or three at a time, and hurling them at the end wall. Finally, the rails and the shelves were empty and he sat alone in the narrow dressing room, drunk and surrounded by colourful fabrics and hangers. He wept. On his knees, he wept, embracing the flowery dress. When no more tears came, he dried his face with the same dress. He kicked open the door of the dressing room, denting the wall, and went out. To walk in the grounds. The noise of the crickets in the night confused him. The sky, fuller of stars than he had ever seen it, weighed on his forehead. An engine rumbled in front of the house. But this time he did not go to see who it was; the effort of getting up from the lounger would take too long. The engine was switched off. There came the sound of a car door closing, and suddenly Carla appeared on the path that was made of strips of quebracho. Hurried. Pretty. Toned from the gym. Her hair tousled. Why was her hair tousled? She was walking on the wood to avoid the heels of her black shoes sinking into the recently watered lawn. First to the cinema, and afterwards – what? She wasn't wearing the cotton shirt. She had on a different one, in a bold colour, yellow or orange – in the dark it was hard to tell.

"Hello," she said. He stood next to the lounger and watched her come closer. "I'm running a bit late." He watched her come closer. "We've got the Andrades today, haven't we?" Gustavo walked towards her. Slowly, teetering a little. "I forgot my mobile." He stopped in front of her. Pretty. Tanned. Tousled. And afterwards? She made as if to kiss his cheek, but an instant before she could, Gustavo, his fist closed, landed a punch. An upper-cut, right on the jaw.

35

The Discipline Committee asks to see Mavi and Ronie. Not on their own account. On Juani's. Nobody mentions drugs. Or the list. Or the potheads. The file's heading is "Exhibitionism in Public Areas". He and two friends pulled down their trousers in front of the flag pole. It was in the early hours of Saturday morning, after a party. And there were girls present, according to the report. "Girls who were cheering," says Juani later, when Mavi and Ronie ask him to explain.

"Don't even think about saying that when they ask you about it," warns Ronie. The Committee is going to take a statement from the boys and, if they are found guilty, apply an appropriate sanction. "Guilty of hanging a moon? In front of our friends? Is this a wind-up or are you being serious?"

"It must not just have been your friends, because some-one's reported you."

"We were just farting around."

"Don't say that in your statement either."

"So what should I say?"

Their appointment is a week later. Their case is heard and evaluated. If the Committee finds them guilty, it has to settle on a suitable sanction and propose one of two options: option one – suspension; the offender may not take part in sporting activities or use the shared facilities for a set length of time. Option two – payment of a fine and continued free access to the social and sporting facilities "to prevent the culprit and his friends from roaming the vicinity, with all the problems that idleness brings". If the second option is chosen then the father pays the fine and the son avoids suspension.

Mavi and Ronie speak to Juani several times before the day of the hearing. They get their interrogation in first, to iron out any doubts or hesitations. They practise with him, giving him pointers. "It was a prank, you didn't know there were girls there, you didn't mean to upset anyone," Ronie recites.

"Had you been drinking? Had you been smoking?" asks Mavi. Ronie glares at her; Juani says nothing. She repeats the question regardless; she knows what they are going to ask.

"Beer," says Juani with irritation, "but I wasn't drunk." Mavi starts to cry.

"Mum, have you never had a beer?"

"I've never pulled my trousers down in front of anyone."

"I have," says Ronie and now it's her turn to glare at him.

"You'd been smoking," she says again, as if she hadn't heard any of what went before.

"Mum, it was for a laugh – can't anyone understand that?" And she does not understand it. Nor does she listen. Nor does she know what to think any more.

The Discipline Committee comprises three country club members. They deal with any infraction reported within the community. The talk is always of "infractions" rather than "crimes", because technically there are no crimes in Cascade Heights. Except for those that may be committed by servicemen, domestic staff or other workers, but in those cases, the matter proceeds along different lines. As regards members of The Cascade, if one of them, or their children, relations or friends commits a crime, no formal report is made to any authority outside the gates of the neighbourhood. We try to resolve everything behind closed doors. Behind the barriers. Theft, collisions, assault: all kinds of infractions come before the Discipline Committee. And solutions are always found, because there is a willingness to find them. If you get embroiled in a fight with some person in the street, in a bar or a cinema, and you hurt him, you may end up in prison. But if the fight is with your brother, in the garden of your own home, then of course it's different. No one would dream of taking such a dispute beyond the confines of that house and that family. The same is true of our community. Cascade Heights is like one big family with one big garden. And as such, the family itself must investigate the offence and choose the punishment. Through the auspices of the Discipline Committee. Federal law, as it applies to the world outside, the tribunals and law courts, almost never intervenes here. In private cases, if no charges are brought, there is no crime. And in a case for public action, the prosecutor either never finds out or turns a blind eye. No one in Cascade Heights would ever report something in a police station. Not only is it not the custom, but it's very much frowned upon. Everything is sorted out behind the bars. Complaints are brought to the country club's administration; the club makes a judgement; the club hands down a sanction or an absolution.

The real police never even set foot in here – neither the Buenos Aires force nor the federal police – only the private security guards paid for by members. There are some drawbacks to that arrangement: the youngsters take liberties and smoke marijuana in the youth club or on the further-flung tennis courts. They don't need to hide from anyone other than their parents – sometimes not even them. Like the adults, they know that whatever they do, the worst that can happen is that their infraction goes on record and they have to appear before the Discipline Committee. Just as Juani must now for exposing himself.

"Do I really have to go and make a statement?" he asks.

"Yes."

"What a bunch of hypocrites."

"This isn't about them, it's about you," says the mother, sobbing.

"It's about everyone," says the father.

"And what do they want me to tell them?" asks Juani, and immediately answers his own question: "I pulled my trousers down, OK, that much I can tell them, but there's nothing else I can say that those three windbags are going to understand."

Juani goes to make his statement. His friends go, too. Juani is suspended. Although nobody mentions it, in his file there is a copy of the Children at Risk file. Marcos's father prefers to pay the fine. Tobias gets away without a sanction or a fine after denying that he was in Cascade Heights that night and providing three witnesses to the effect. His father's a lawyer.

36

One Thursday, one of those Thursdays on which our husbands were due to gather in the evening to eat and play cards, El Tano telephoned. He asked to speak to me, not Ronie. I was invited, along with Carla Masotta and Lala Urovich, to join the men for dinner at the Scaglias' home. Teresa would be there too, obviously. The "Thursday Widows", as he had dubbed us, would be out in force.

In all these years, it was the first time that we were going to share our husbands' Thursday night fixture. I told Ronie and he was surprised – he hadn't known about it. "El Tano's been a bit weird recently," he said. I had not noticed anything untoward, but then, for a long time now all my attention had been focused on Juani, and the rest of the world had been reduced to ghostly apparitions passing by. Thanks to Ronie, my mood had progressed from one of unbridled rage to self-pity, which may not have been any better for Juani but was at least easier to conceal. However I could not yet control my compulsion to spy on him and keep going through his things. And I wasn't sure whether or not this was a good thing to do.

"Haven't you noticed that El Tano's growing a goatee?"

"What's that got to do with anything?"

"And he's taken up sunbathing."

"He must want to look good."

"That's what strange – he's always looked good," said my husband. I feared that the dinner might be intended as recompense for "the shame of not only having a drug-addict son but of us all knowing about it, too" as Teresa had sympathized when she turned up at the agency two or three days after that unforgettable phone call alerting me to my son's risky behaviour. If that were the case, I would prefer to cry off sick than end up making myself genuinely ill, so I called her. But it turned out that she had known nothing either; she was as surprised as the rest of us by El Tano's invitation. "He says there's something he wants to share with me and with all of you, but he won't say what it is." I felt a surge of relief: my woes were certainly not a matter for debating at a dinner in the company of friends (if that is what we were).

At nine on the dot we knocked on the door. Teresa greeted us, wearing a full-length black silk dress and the string of Spanish pearls that El Tano had given her for their last anniversary.

"I didn't know it was evening dress," I said with dismay; there I was wearing jeans and a linen twinset from two seasons back.

"Neither did I. El Tano chose my clothes and wouldn't let me change a thing. I'm starting to worry," she joked.

Ronie headed to the kitchen with the bottles of wine we had brought. Teresa and I followed a few steps behind. "Syrah," I heard him say as he handed the bottles to El Tano. "I'm wondering if he's about to announce a trip, or something like that," Teresa confided in a whisper.

"We've been talking about going to Maui, but I think this might be something much bigger, don't you?"

I answered "yes", but without much conviction. Usually I find it easy to get inside a person's head, to guess at what he might be thinking or feeling. It's a useful knack in my line of work. "Understanding what kind of house a client wants to buy, and that that house may not be what I would buy myself, saves on time-wasting and misunderstandings," I wrote in my red notebook after a difficult sale. But El Tano had always struck me as impenetrable – almost as much so as Juani – and although there were occasions when I felt I was beginning to understand him, almost immediately I would suspect that even this apparent empathy was a product of some deliberate ploy on his part.

In the kitchen, El Tano was preparing tandoori chicken for his guests. He had donned a white apron and chef's hat. Ronie was right – he seemed odd. But that wasn't on account of the goatee beard or the tan. It was because of his exaggerated body language. At times he seemed even to be counting his own steps. For all that he was resolute and powerful, El Tano had always been a measured fellow, very contained. If he wanted to make himself heard, he spoke quietly – he didn't need to shout. He had not needed to shout that day that he arrived at The Cascade and said, "I want that land." If he was happy, he shared a Pomery with his friends and, if he was depressed, he stood them up. Or he humiliated them. But he was not given to fits of laughter, or hugging people, or shedding tears. And that night he looked as though he might well be capable of doing any one of those three.

We waited until everyone had arrived before going through to the dining room. They'd given us champagne, and the alcohol in my empty stomach made me feel dizzy. I walked over to one of the big windows. A streak of lightning flashed across the sky and a few heavy raindrops broke the serenity of the water in the swimming pool. The wooden deck was splattered with wet stains. The smell of damp earth mingled with an aroma drifting from the kitchen. The maid had just finished bringing the first course to the table. Glasses containing spider crab and prawns with avocado, also prepared by El Tano. "Don't ask me for recipes – I never give them out," he said, and he made a sign to the maid that I did not understand but she clearly did, because she quickly scuttled out with her head bowed. Thursday was her day off, but El Tano had asked her to stay, because "the little widows are coming" – although I don't suppose she got the joke. Everyone in our neighbourhood knows about the "golf widows", whose husbands abandon them every weekend for at least four hours to play eighteen rounds on the course. Our nickname, inspired by them, was more private and might never have left our own circle had it not proved to be so prophetic.

As always, we women sat down together around one half of the table and left the other half for the men. El Tano's cherry-wood table is the biggest I've ever seen in my life. It easily seats twelve, and even sixteen can be squeezed in. "This time I want people to mix up," said El Tano. Ronie shot me a complicitous look. If El Tano was prepared to make conversation with one of us women, then things had changed indeed.

"Let's hear it for the *asador*," joked Gustavo when the second course was underway and El Tano had yet to make his announcement. "Is 'tandoori' the name of a species?" asked Lala. "You mean a 'spice'," Ronie corrected her quietly, but he did not answer her question. Neither did anyone else. Some of us because we didn't know and others because they had not heard her. El Tano, doubtless, because the question irritated him. Of all the women, the one he respected least was Lala. "How can so much idiocy fit into one person's brain?" El Tano had marvelled one night to Ronie, after she had tried to join in a group discussion on what priorities should govern the budget in the coming year and had insisted that a significant portion be dedicated to the eradication of the Tillandsia plant. "It must be a spice, no?" she answered herself. Carla barely said a word all night. She had been taking time off the agency. It was more than a week since she had last been in. She claimed that she had had a lethal dose of flu and that she still felt weak, but I didn't believe her. She seemed sad, subdued. "Tired," she had answered, when I asked her if she felt well. But the concealer she had used on her cheekbones did not altogether hide the purple skin underneath.

Before dessert, El Tano stood up at the head of the table and tapped his glass with a fork. "How disrespectful," he grumbled, "in movies, when someone does this, everyone falls silent."

"And do you believe in the movies, Tano?" asked Gustavo. "This is real life, Tanito, real life." El Tano laughed; all of us laughed without really knowing why.

"Friends," he said and, to Teresa, "my love, I want to share with you all a very important decision I've taken."

"You're quitting tennis…" quipped Ronie.

"That, never. I'm quitting Troost," he answered. And there was a silence. El Tano maintained his smile, and so did Teresa, but hers was empty, her eyes exaggeratedly wide open. I can't speak for the others, I was too preoccupied with my own reactions; I was finding it hard to understand – my neurons struggled against the champagne bubbles to establish what this Troost was that had suddenly left everyone dumbstruck, as though El Tano were a priest who had announced he was leaving Holy Orders.

"They've offered you something else…" Teresa managed to say, still smiling, presuming that her husband was about to take a new leap up the corporate ladder.

"No, no," he answered very calmly. "I'm sick of dependent relationships. So I'm joining the ranks of the unemployed," he laughed. Teresa appeared not to find the joke amusing.

"Watch your back, Gustavito, this business could be contagious," El Tano warned. Martín Urovich appeared to blush, but I don't know – perhaps it only looked that way to me; perhaps I thought he ought to have done, that, in his shoes, I would have blushed. Maybe I even did blush on his behalf. Or on Ronie's, since he was also unemployed, fooling himself that he lived on rental income, when those rents were far lower than the costs they entailed.

"No, please, I don't exist unless I'm inside a corporation. I need my Big Father," Gustavo answered finally. And Martín Urovich said: "We're considering moving to Miami."

"Don't give me that crap!" El Tano snapped.

"We're going to Miami," said Lala. Without looking at her, El Tano said to Martín: "Are you serious?" Martín shook his head. Lala's eyes filled with tears and she went to the bathroom.

"Does anyone want more tandoori?" asked Teresa.

"Are you happy?" I asked Martín, but El Tano answered me.

"Ecstatic," he said. "I've been planning this for a while. I'm sick of making money for other people; I want it all for myself."

"And what are you thinking of doing?" Ronie asked.

"I don't know yet. I've got a lot of projects in mind and luckily they gave me a very good severance deal, so, with money in the bank, I can take time to think about which one I get started on first."

"So everything was coldly calculated…" said Gustavo.

"Coldly calculated," El Tano replied.

"Before any new project, remember our trip to Maui," Teresa reminded him.

"That's going to be my very first project," said El Tano and he kissed her. It was the first time I had ever seen El Tano kiss his wife in public. She was also surprised, I'm sure. And then he proposed a toast. We raised our glasses and waited for El Tano to pronounce the name in whose honour we should clink glasses. This silent moment of anticipation, with our glasses still held aloft, seemed to go on too long.

"Let's drink… to freedom," he said, then immediately corrected himself: "no, even better, let's drink to 'real life'… that's it, to real life." And all the glasses met each other halfway across the table. Those same glasses that reappeared beside the swimming pool, that September night on which the Thursday Widows prophecy came true for three of our number. They were the glasses that El Tano only used on very special occasions. Such as that one.

214

37

In The Cascade, Romina feels like a misfit. Juani also feels like a misfit. That must be why they fit together so well. And they make plans to travel the world one day, when they have finished school. He doesn't like sport; he can spend hours holed up in his room listening to music, reading or doing God knows what. And for the adults of Cascade Heights, that counts as strange. Romina also spends a lot of time shut up in her room. But then she also has dark skin. It's pointless to deny it. Not even Mariana denies it – she mentions it to anyone who wants to listen. She's adopted. When she's out in the sun, Mariana makes her wear factor fifty. "Even if only on your knees – if they look like two lumps of coal at this time of year, imagine what they're going to be like in the summer."

Pedro is also dark, but less so than his sister. Sometimes Romina wonders if Mariana's given him something to whiten his skin. Once she found her washing his hair with camomile and since then she's been forbidden to enter the room while her brother's getting his bath. Pedro wears the clothes Mariana likes and speaks how she would like him to speak. And then Mariana behaves as though Pedro were the fruit of her body, as though she had never been told that her eggs were empty. And Romina hates her for it because that lie robs her of much more than a brother.

Romina and Juani meet every night. After having dinner, they go to their respective rooms, close the doors and climb out of the windows. Ever since Romina cut her leg with that beer bottle, she has to give too many explanations if she wants to go out with Juani at night. That's why she slips out without telling anyone. They meet halfway. Sometimes at the pedestrian crossing by the twelfth hole. Sometimes opposite the Araucaria tree on the roundabout. They go for a walk. Through the windows of their rooms, the quiet night, undisturbed by anyone out pacing the streets of Cascade Heights, looks too inviting. It's a shame to go to sleep. On nights when there is a full moon, the tops of the tallest trees are flecked with silver, as though painted. You would think the moon out-shone the city. The air feels less contaminated. And the silence. What Romina and Juani like best about their nocturnal escapades is the silence. The only sound to be heard is the song of the grasshoppers and frogs. The frogs, tiny and almost transparent, keep croaking all night. And both of them like summer. And jasmines. Romina more than Juani; it's her favourite flower and she taught him to how to pick out its perfume from the nocturnal melée.

They walk. They skate. They spy. Romina and Juani are on their night rounds. They carry torches, as they have since they were little; it's one of the few things that still amuse them at seventeen. They choose a house, a tree, a window. And they spy on it. They don't get as many surprises as they did at the start. Usually they are confirming what they already know. They know that Dorita Llambías's husband is sleeping with Nane Pérez Ayerra. They saw them on the night of the club's anniversary party. In her bed. All the adults were dancing in the function room, apart from them. After a while they got dressed and went off in their respective jeeps, doubtless to join the others. They know that Carla Masotta cries at night and that Gustavo throws glass bottles and plates against the wall when he's angry. They know that it is a lie that the youngest Elizondo boy broke his arm falling out of a tree. They were watching the night that – after crying and crying because his parents had locked him in his room – he opened his window, removed the netting and started to walk on the tiled roof. He took barely three steps before falling. They also see people who sleep peacefully. Family mealtimes that appear to be cordial. Children on the computer or watching television. But none of this detains them: it's not what they're looking for. Because they don't believe in these scenes. Or they believe in them, but they don't understand them. There are nights when it is enough to spy on one house alone, and others on which they go from tree to tree without finding what they are seeking. Romina and Juani don't know what they are looking for, but they do know that, at some given moment, as they watch from a branch through a window, the game ends: it's enough for one night and there is no need to see any more.

They walk. Music is coming from Willy Quevedo's house. He must be awake, too. His bedroom light is switched off, but the room is lit by a glow. Doubtless from his computer screen. He must be in a chat room. Romina wants to stay and watch him; she likes Willy and she still often thinks of him, in spite of what he did. He got off with Natalia Berardi while he was meant to be going out with her. But Juani takes her on somewhere else. They go round the first corner. They climb another tree. Malena Gómez's dad is putting hairpins in his hair before going to bed. Romina sees him through the window of his en-suite bathroom. And a hairnet. To start with, Juani doesn't believe his eyes. But they zoom in with the camera that Romina steals from her father on the nights when they "do the rounds". Malena's dad goes into the bathroom and has a pee, with the window open and the light switched on. Wearing hairpins and a hairnet.

In Cascade Heights no one worries about what the neighbours may see. The neighbours are very far away, in some distant place behind the trees. Who would ever imagine there was someone spying on them from behind the oak in their very own garden?

38

They took turns teeing off with their one woods at the ninth hole. A week earlier, Alfredo Insúa had invited El Tano to a round of golf. And El Tano had accepted. It was not a sport he liked much nor one in which he could shine, as he did at tennis – but Insúa was the kind of partner that no one who values good contacts would dare to snub. He had long ago recovered from that episode of the plate of shit left for him by his last wife and was happy to parade the new one around on weekends. "Just a quick nine holes, Tano," he had said, "because I have to be in the office by mid-morning." More than one person would have envied him this opportunity to spend a couple of hours chatting with the boss of a finance company. But El Tano was curious to know what Alfredo Insúa could need from him. They were not friends, merely acquaintances, although he had been at nearly all Alfredo's birthday parties, and vice versa. But it was a known fact that an invitation from Insúa always implied a return favour, even when the invited party had no idea of what he was giving in exchange. At any rate, they had already played eight holes and, apart from talking about the economy or finance in general, no subject had been raised from which either one could profit in any way.

El Tano's ball bounced off the top of a tree and came to rest halfway between the tee and Alfredo's ball. They had about a hundred yards to cover before it was El Tano's turn to play again. Each one grabbed his trolley and they walked on. This time they did talk about business. Perhaps Alfredo had been waiting for this precise moment: to be a stroke ahead.

"How are things at Troost, Tano?" El Tano was no longer bothered much by the question. A year had gone by since his dismissal, and he had worked on a serviceable reply.

"Fine, I suppose..."

"Why 'suppose'?"

"I'm outside the company now; I work with them but I'm not exclusive to them any more."

"Really? I had no idea..." He sounded surprised, but it was hard to believe that Alfredo Insúa knew nothing about his severance. The "market" is small and The Cascade even smaller. "But the company's doing OK? Or did you leave because the Dutch aren't managing the risk well?"

"No, I left because I was sick of it..." Alfredo stopped a moment to remove a stick that had got caught in the wheels of the trolley he used to transport his state-of-the-art Callaway graphite clubs.

"I completely understand. Do you know how often I ask myself what I'm doing, working twenty hours a day in the centre of town? Especially when you see this other world," he said and his gaze swept across the golf course in front of him.

219

They came to El Tano's ball. It wasn't an easy ball, positioned behind a line of trees. He would have to hit it right over them if he did not want to risk it getting stuck in the lower boughs. Chattering parrots emphasized the silence of the course. He selected a club, rehearsed his swing, lost his gaze among the distant tree tops, took up his stance once more, rehearsed again – and only then did he strike. The ball glided upwards, over the tops of the Eucalyptus trees, then fell two yards from Alfredo's ball, but behind it, so that it was his turn to hit again. "Nice shot, Tano," said Alfredo, walking towards the balls.

El Tano, following him, played down the shot: "It almost makes up for the last one."

"And what are you doing now?" asked Alfredo, when there was only one hole left to play.

"Things have worked out really well: I'm still linked to them and I lend a hand with consultancy. It's fine, relaxed, good money. I couldn't be playing golf on a Wednesday at this time of day if I was still working the way I used to."

"Whereas any minute now my mobile will ring and I'll have to dash off. Even if it means taking a pay cut, Tano, at our age quality of life is priceless…"

They came to El Tano's ball. They stopped – El Tano beside his ball, and Alfredo waited two yards behind. El Tano took his shot. Alfredo came forwards and played his ball. They both landed on the green but, at this distance, it was impossible to see which one was closer to the hole. Once more, they walked on together. Alfredo was wearing golf shoes with spikes that dug into the turf with every step. "How strange that they let you come out with spikes. I thought they were still banned on this course."

"They are. But, as my old man used to say, 'It's easier to ask forgiveness than to ask permission'. Although, if I'm honest, I don't much like asking for either of those things, Tanito." A hare ran in front of them, apparently in flight, then vanished somewhere beyond the lagoon. "Hey, but are the Troost people doing all right?" Alfredo pressed on.

"Very well, as always. Why are you so interested?"

"Because I'm doing something with them – strictly speaking not with them but with their policies. I'm viaticating life insurance."

"And what does that mean?"

"Buying insurance policies at a discount. You give people the money upfront and become the beneficiary of their policy. It's a very simple piece of paperwork. You can do it in a couple of minutes. We only do it with policies from reliable insurance companies and Troost has always been one of the best. But of course we've seen so many giants tumble that we're immune to shock, right Tanito?"

"And when do you get paid?" El Tano asked.

"Whenever any life insurance policy is cashed in – when the guy snuffs it."

Alfredo's phone rang; he stopped for a minute, gave two or three instructions and then rang off. "And the good thing about this system is that the person who takes out the policy gets to enjoy the money, not the relatives. It started with the whole AIDS business, with those guys whose treatment was hoovering up all their money… so, if they had a policy that predated their illness and it was clear that there was no ticket back – know what I mean? – you gave them the money, the guy could enjoy whatever time he had remaining and later you claimed the insurance."

"I never knew about this."

"And the financial markets are like that, things change quick as a flash, you have to be constantly looking out for new ways of doing stuff. When you know how to look, you can always find a new gap in the market."

"One door closes and another one opens."

"That's it, Tanito, you have to be alert and be the first to strike whenever possible. Viatication is one of those nice round business propositions: if it's properly evaluated, it's risk-free. Much better than discounting mortgages. You take on the policy at eighty per cent and start making money straight away. Just think that it often yields twenty per cent profit within the year, a bloody fantastic rate, and in dollars, Tano."

"Impressive."

"Pretty darn impressive."

"And do you only do this with people who have AIDS?"

"Far from it. That sector's gone off a bit now because of the new drugs which end up extending the lives of those guys. I mean, for what? The poor bastards are going to die anyway. But the time-span is lengthened and that makes it much harder to fix a profitable rate. It's a complicated market – you can mess up big time. These days, we're offering a better rate for other sorts of catastrophe."

"Such as?"

"Other illnesses... the kind that no one wants to mention... I don't know – lung cancer, acute liver failure, brain tumours... I'm not all that sure; that part of the business unnerves me a bit. We have medical assessors who study the case and write up a report... I'm better on numbers, Tanito..."

They arrived at the green. Alfredo crouched down to study the direction of the slope. He examined the drop from different angles. El Tano watched him, feeling no need to crouch down: he trusted his partner's judgement. Alfredo took out his putter and walked towards the ball. "Hey, Tano, do you happen to have a list of Troost clients? Because if you can bring us policies for discounting, I can arrange a percentage for you. In this business, the obstacle to growth is that it isn't possible to offer it on a massive scale, do you see? People are shocked to start with. It's the same with plots in private cemeteries – at the beginning it seemed creepy, and now everyone wants one…"

"I don't have a list, but I do have a good memory – and a plot in the Memorial Cemetery."

Alfredo laughed at the joke. "Well, just let me know, if you're interested. You could easily handle this product and, in any case, we'd give you a little training course; since it's a sensitive area, it's important to know which words to use when you're selling it, you know? We train with neurolinguistic professionals who can give you exactly the right words. Just let me know."

"I'll let you know."

Alfredo gave the ball a tap: the distance required no more. His ball passed alongside El Tano's and fell into the cup. A bogey: sufficient to make him feel better than average. Sufficient to see off El Tano's chances of beating him. He went up to the hole and took out his little ball. El Tano got out his putter and squared up to his own ball in the knowledge that he had already lost. He relaxed his knees, stretched his neck this way and that, lightly realigned himself. He was about to swing when suddenly he asked: "Hey, do you remember whose Troost policies you discounted?"

"No, but I wrote them down in my diary – I can tell you later." El Tano putted and his ball also went in, but it was not enough for him: he had dropped a shot among the tree tops. His rival had beaten him by one stroke.

They had a drink together in the bar before going home. Alfredo looked in his diary for the details of the Troost policies. "One of them was for a Margarita Lapisarreta... And the other Oliver Candileu."

"I know Oliver well, he's the ex-husband of a woman who works at Troost."

"This is confidential, mind Tano, remember the subject is... delicate."

"What's Oliver got?"

"A very good policy, underwritten in London, with a three-thousand-dollar premium, but with a very punitive early-withdrawal clause – they were taking almost half his cash." Alfredo put money to pay for both their drinks down on the table and stood up.

"But what's he got? What's he dying of?"

"I don't remember, but it must be something pretty devastating, because he went off with eighty-three per cent, if you can believe it... The highest discount we've given to date. Is this upsetting for you? Is he a friend?"

"No, not really a friend."

Alfredo lifted his golf bag onto his shoulder. "You'll let me know, then?"

"I'll let you know." He clapped him on the shoulder and went. El Tano stayed a little longer in the bar, gazing into the immaculate green of the golf course, wondering why they would have called it "viatication".

39

Ernesto wants Romina to study law. Next year, when she's finished secondary school. But she hasn't applied yet. If she can't make her mind up, he threatens to make it up for her. And Romina has made up her mind, but he doesn't want to listen. She does not want to study next year: she wants to take a year off. In spite of Romina having explained this, today Ernesto's secretary has sent her all the papers "with Doctor Andrade's instruction that they be completed by this afternoon at the latest, OK?"

"*Doctor?*"

"What?"

"Nothing."

"Time's running out, Romina, there's only one week left to register," he had said. And she imagined her father's Rolex chasing her through the streets of Cascade Heights, half-melted like those clocks she has seen in a Dalí painting they once had to copy at school. Ernesto said that he was not prepared to see her lose an entire year of her life. And at the time she wondered what the real loss was, knowing that so much of her life had been lost already. All those years she barely remembers. She had lost her name, Ramona. The father she never knew. The smells. The face of that other mother she no longer recalls. That brother who could have been different, but who was snatched away by Mariana.

The forms present her with two choices of private university: San Andrés or Di Tella. "I can't accept anything less. It's a question of excellence," he tells her. Excellence. But Romina does not aspire to be excellent. She would like to travel. For a year – not any longer

– she doesn't ask to spend her life travelling, just to satisfy that post-school impulse, to make a journey of discovery – to grab a rucksack and see what happens, with no fixed itinerary. Ernesto laughs at her; he says how can she set off to travel the world when she doesn't even know how to take the number 57 into town? He says it even though he doesn't know either: he wouldn't know how to use the ticket-vending machine. The last time he went on a bus you could still pay the driver with whatever note you had and the driver gave you change. It's true that she's never even been on a bus. But Juani knows what to do. He is one of the few boys of his age who do know. The others get around in minibuses and taxis, or their parents drive them. And they can't wait to get their licences when they're seventeen. It isn't unusual in this area to find young people of that age who know how to drive but not how to catch a bus. Where they live everything is far away: the cinema, the mall, school, friends' houses. You can't walk anywhere. She's thinking of going with Juani. If they can get enough money together for him. She already has hers. All these years, she's been saving it up. And when the moment comes, Ernesto will give her more. He always does: it gives him security, knowing that she has money on her, "in case anything happens". But she doesn't want to tell her father that she's thinking of going with Juani. She's afraid it will create more obstacles. So instead she tells him: "It can't be so difficult to take the number 57 or to use a ticket-vending machine. It's probably more or less like the one that dispenses condoms and tampons in the toilets at nightclubs." And Ernesto lifts his hand to give her a slap, but she stops him, catching his arm mid-air, and she says: "Don't ever do that again," fixing him with a look of fury before running up to her room, scared that she may not be strong enough to hold him back.

If only she could understand Ernesto. It puzzles her that, unlike Willy Quevedo's parents, he does not think of getting her to apply to a university in the United States. Even though he could afford to pay for an American college, he wants something else. Willy's parents were not sure of being able to meet the cost, so for years they've been paying into a saving plan to guarantee having the funds available to send him to study wherever they choose. Ernesto does not mention the United States. She doesn't know if he means deliberately to thwart her desire to travel, or if it is because he fears that, once abroad, she would not come back. No, it can't be that: she doesn't believe that he would even miss her. Or perhaps *he* would, but Mariana… Mariana would jump for joy. Perhaps he is choosing the local option because it offers more in the way of useful contacts for him. Or because he would not be able to go to her graduation if the injunction preventing him from leaving the country is not lifted. But it can't be that, because Ernesto's relaxed about it: one of his "friends at the Ministry" has told him that it's merely a formality, that the judge has agreed to lift it, that it's only a matter of days. Romina does not know why he can't leave the country, nor does she ask him, because she knows what the answer would be. "Because in this country, they don't bother putting the thieves in jail, they'd rather persecute people like us." She doesn't know who "people like us" are either, but she can imagine. All she knows is that "San Andres", or "Di Tella", are words calculated to soothe Ernesto. Certain words act like a balm on parents. The words alone, regardless of their meaning. Juani and she once compiled a list of proper nouns and common nouns that calm parents down. The names of certain universities. The names of certain banks. The names of certain "family" summer resorts. The names of a few scant friends. The names of certain schools that guarantee the best English grades in the area and offer IB – most parents don't know what "IB" means, but they still let it sort one school from another. Calming words. Sport. A boy who does plenty of sport is sure to be "healthy and steer clear of drugs". Any kind of sport, so long as it entails some kind of ball – be it green plush, number-five leather, Slazenger or Nike – and an implement with which to hit it (one's foot, a racket, a golf club, one's hand) and a goal to aim for (a net, a hole, a base line, a hoop).

Romina's sitting at her desk looking at the entry forms her father has sent. She draws little arses all over them. Inside each buttock, she draws another little arse, and inside that another, and more and more, to infinity. The picture within a picture. *Mise en abyme*. That's something else she's seen in art classes at school. The only thing she enjoys at school is art. *Mise en abyme*. Placed in the abyss. It frames them. In an hour an office boy is picking them up to take to the university.

40

Midway through 2001, the Uroviches announced officially that they were moving to Miami. "They're not the first and they won't be the last," I wrote in my red notebook, and made this the general heading of a new chapter. A little further down I wrote: "June 2001, the Uroviches leave Cascade Heights, thus baptizing the '** Effect'." I left blanks because I didn't know its name, or if it had one yet. But the preceding pages of my notebook had featured, one by one, the names of all the different economic effects of the last few years. Who gives them their names, I wondered. Hard to imagine some serious economist coming up with such creative labels. I awaited the new baptism as anxiously as someone in the Caribbean might listen out for the name of an approaching hurricane. I carefully reread the earlier pages in my notebook: "1994, Tequila Effect. Salaberry, Augueda and Tempone, all three of them owners of downtown financial companies, sell their houses. I don't know the names of their firms. Pablo Díaz Batán is also selling up; he's a retired empresario who had put all his money into Tempone's financial business." Díaz Batán had made his fortune on the back of an idea considered "brilliant" by many in The Cascade. Since the beginning of the 1990s, he had been registering in Argentina the brands of any number of American chains (that is, from the United States) which had yet to set foot on our soil. Ann Taylor, Starbuck's Café, Seven Eleven, Macy's – the sector was unimportant; all that counted was that the company not yet be installed or registered in our country and that there be a high chance that, in some prosperous moment, it would decide to come. And when that prosperous moment arrived, Díaz Batán presented his registered brand – their one, the one they wanted to register but which legally belonged to him. And even though it would be impossible for him to win a court case, these well-oiled companies balked at the slowness of Argentine justice, so they agreed a

229

settlement to speed up the process and, in the long run, save themselves money. "He's a very skilful man," said Andrade, when someone told him how Díaz Batán had made his fortune, during a dinner party at the Scaglias' house. "In my book, Housemann's what you'd call skilful," put in Ronie, and all I knew was that Housemann had been a football player for some club – but I understood perfectly what my husband meant by the allusion. Salaberry's house had gone for seventy per cent of its true value and Tempone's for eighty per cent. Augueda's turned out not to be his but his father-in-law's. And Díaz Batán's was sold at a judicial auction, in which he himself bought it back for less than half its worth, through a frontman.

I flicked on ten pages in my red notebook. "1997. Asian Crisis. Fall of Juan Manuel Martín and Julio Campinella." Campinella's house was bought by Ernesto Andrade, whose business really took off that year; he swapped his Ford Mondeo for an Alfa Romeo, bought Mariana a people-carrier and a golf buggy for the maid and the children. They say he clinched God knows what deal with God knows what bonds. Or that he was left with some bonds after a deal. Or that he went to court over some bonds. I don't really know – but he paid my commission in cash.

Five pages on: "1998, Vodka Effect". And two pages later: "1999, Caipirinha Effect". Clearly there was a drinking theme at work here. I turned back to the Uroviches' page and, in the blank space I'd left before "Effect", I wrote in "Yerba Maté", because I could not think of any alcoholic drink that was authentically ours. I don't know why I put "Yerba", but "Maté" on its own sounded insubstantial. I went back to the page with Caipirinha, the last effect to have warranted its own name. That was when the bank where Roberto Quevedo worked left the country and he lost his job. He still had not put his house on the market, but he was considering it. The fund that had bought the retail company where Lalo Richards was operations manager had already achieved a more than satisfactory return from the country and was leaving. The company was for sale, but so laden with debts that it was unlikely anyone would want to buy it. Lalo had had his house valued, fearing that the creditors would descend and he would be left with nothing. The case of Pepe Montes was similar to these others. And the Ledesmas, too. And the Trevisanis. The thing is, many of our neighbours made the mistake of thinking that they could keep spending as much as they earned for ever. And what they earned was a lot, and seemed eternal. But there comes a day when the taps are turned off, although nobody expects it until they find themselves in the bath tub, covered in soap, looking up at the shower head, from which not a single drop of water falls any more.

The vertiginous pace of the decade that was ending had shocked me. When I was a child, money took longer to change hands. There were families, people we knew, who were very wealthy and whose surnames were endlessly repeated in different double-barrelled combinations – usually they owned land. The land passed on to their children, who employed labourers, rather than work it themselves, but who could still make a good income, albeit one that was shared out among several siblings. But those siblings would also die one day, and then the land passed on to the grandchildren and there were more squabbles, more people to share the inheritance. Each person was allotted a parcel that was too small to work, and the land ended up neglected or sold in lots. But even so, and although no one can ever be sure of anything, two or three generations had to pass before the money that had been thought safe turned out not to be so. Whereas, in the last few years, money changed hands two or three times within the same generation, and no one had time to work out exactly what was going on.

I wrote: "2001, Yerba Maté Effect. The Uroviches leave, followed by…"

41

Lala surveyed the objects around her: the blue vase that Teresa Scaglia had given her; the imitation Tiffany lamp she had bought less than a year ago; the glass bell in the middle of the coffee table. To one side, Ariana was combing, almost obsessively, the hair of one of her Barbies. She thought back to when she was eight years old. At that time, Barbies didn't exist. She had had Piel Rose dolls. She would have liked to be eight years old now, and not to have to worry about anything except combing her doll's hair. She had filled in the form and sent it by post. That same afternoon they had called her: if it was urgent, they could organize everything for the following weekend. Lala wanted to do it as soon as possible. It was not the journey that was pressing – the tickets were for two months' time – but if they were going to leave, then she wanted the house emptied once and for all. The house had a hold on her, so long as her things remained in it. And she must not feel held back.

Every object around her had a story – looking at them was enough to spark a memory. And memory brought rage, hatred almost – she could not pinpoint it exactly, nor make sense of or find a reason for this feeling. Much less avoid it. All she knew was that she never wanted to see these things again. She wanted nothing that reminded her of the life she had lead in the last few years and that she could no longer keep leading. "Hold a garage sale," Teresa Scaglia suggested. "You'll get rid of the old stuff in a day and with that money you can buy everything you'll need over there." And she had given her the number of the company that Liliana Richards had used to clear the flat of her mother-in-law, a week after her death.

It was her father who had suggested they move to Miami. To start with, Lala didn't take the idea seriously. And Martín wouldn't hear of it. There was nothing for them in Miami: no relatives, no friends, no job offers. She did not even know how to speak English. "Why Miami?" Martín had asked.

"Because it's a city where you can do things; everything works well; there are all sorts of job opportunities flying around – you can feel it in the air. In Miami, with a bit of money you have a future. Here we soon won't have anything." Lala was repeating what her father had said. After eight years in a multinational company, Martín had lost his position as Planning Director after some internal restructuring failed to include him on the new organizational chart. His dismissal hit them hard – they hadn't seen it coming – but Martín had an excellent CV, an MBA from an American university and plenty of contacts. It was just a question of being a little more patient, Lala told herself, as time went by. However, for all that she tried to keep looking ahead and living as though nothing had happened, her husband's patience was directly proportional to the balance of their savings account and, month on month, their expenditure was eating away at both. One night, Martín sat her down opposite him at the desk and showed her a chart full of numbers. Why would her husband do something like that? She couldn't understand it. Lala was never any good at numbers. What was written on the paper looked jumbled up and rather hazy. Martín talked, explaining that eighty per cent of their savings were in government bonds and that the value of the bonds was falling. If they continued to live in Cascade Heights, sending Ariana to the same school, with Ariel starting university the following year, without cutting back on trips or new clothes, tennis, golf, painting classes and swimming, the nanny and other costs – what was left would be finished in exactly five months. Lala felt faint. She may not have followed all the details, but she understood the deadline. Five months was too soon. Five months was next summer. Five months was just short of Ariana's birthday. "And what will we do in five months' time?" she asked.

"I don't know," he answered. Lala cried. And in the midst of her tears she remembered her father, and dried her eyes.

"Let's sell the house and take that money with our savings to Miami and try something there – a business, anything. Over there money is a means to get more money, here it's just an invitation to get fleeced."

And the costs would not be so high. Ariana could go to a state school because "you can do that there – they're better than private ones here. And she's easygoing, she adapts well; the change won't be hard for her, quite the opposite, you can't imagine how much Ariana's going to learn there." They would rent a small place for a while; they would not have the expense of a nanny, or any other staff. They would cut back on outings, or even suspend them for a while. "And what if we made those same adjustments here?" Martín asked.

"Here? What is there here for us now? Staying would be our downfall, Martín, 'here' no longer exists for us. Can you see yourself living in a one-bedroom flat and sending Ariana to Bernasconi School in Parque Patricios?"

"I went to Bernasconi."

"But it isn't the future that we'd planned for our children."

"You can't speak English."

"You don't need to in Miami. Everyone speaks Spanish. It will be like here, but better. Things will be like they used to be, when everything was still OK." And suddenly she wasn't crying any more.

The auction-house people came the day before the date announced in the advertisements and organized everything. "Mark the things you want to take with you and we'll put a price ticket on everything else," said the man in charge of the garage sale, which was going to convert into hard cash the contents of what had been their home for the last eleven years. Ariel had stubbornly insisted that he was not going, that he would stay behind and live with his paternal grandparents. He and the golden retriever (for which Lala had never finished paying Carla Masotta). Ariana was envious: if she were old enough, she too would stay back with Ariel. But she was not old enough. "I'm taking my Barbies," she said.

"No one's taking anything," Lala replied.

"Why not?"

"Aren't you a bit big for Barbies?" Ariana didn't understand. She looked at her father.

"Why not, Daddy?" Martín did not answer her.

"Because you need to learn that nothing is for ever," said her mother.

The sale was going to take place in all the rooms in their house, although the advertisement alluded only to one: the garage. "Garage Sale. Family Moving Overseas: Battery Golf Buggy; Callaway Clubs, as new; Audio Equipment (Marantz, Sony); 2 Head Titanium Rackets; 2 Pentium PCs, Walkman, Discman, Minicomp, DVD, many more electrical items; Lamps, Ornaments, knickknacks." What would "knick-knacks" be, she wondered. "Automatic Washing Machine, front-loading; Curtains, Towels, Blankets, Clothes Male/Female, Medium Size; Children's Clothes; Treadmill; Perfumes; Soft Toys, Barbies; Sundries. Come and Have a Rummage."

Lala threw the newspaper down on the table. Nobody had told them they could put: "Come and Have a Rummage".

"It's a formality, Señora, we always put it," they had answered. It was eight o'clock on the Saturday morning. "For One Day Only, Saturday 12th, 9 a.m. – 5 p.m."

"Not my Barbies," wept Ariana, on discovering that a price tag had been affixed to the forehead of her Nurse Barbie. Lala sent her to play at Sofía Scaglia's house. Ariel had disappeared the day before with the announcement that he would not be back until late. Martín had gone off with El Tano; he had invited him to play tennis for the first time in years. "If I stay here I'll just be in the way." He had borrowed a racket, because

236

his own one was now stacked alongside the golf clubs, with a price tag stuck to the grip, which read US$100. But she did not want to go away. She wanted to see who bought what, the way they handled things, the way they walked through her house, how they discarded the things that did not interest them, how they haggled over prices or asked for discounts if they were buying several items.

She had finally gathered the strength to make her selection and now it was in the hands of the sale company. "I don't want to take anything; sell whatever can be sold and the rest you can throw away." For that reason – although she was surprised – she said nothing when she saw two piles of her old underwear on the bed, complete with price tags. By midday, the entire pile of Victoria's Secret knickers was sold. The Argentine knickers, meanwhile, were bought by Insúa's new wife, "for the girl who works in our house. If you saw the state of her underwear... I don't know how they get by."

A half-finished deodorant, a half-empty bottle of whisky, opened boxes of English tea, bottles of scent that had already been started: everything was carted off by friends, neighbours or strangers who had seen the advertisement. They left behind only a blanket bearing an iron-shaped burn mark and some clothes that were woefully out of season.

By nightfall all that remained were the beds, their toothbrushes, the clothes they had on, some bags containing purchases that, for various reasons, would be taken away the next day, and the two suitcases in which Lala had put the few items that would make the journey north with them. The four-by-four parked in front of the house was no longer theirs; they would have the use of it until they left and then it would serve to cancel a debt with Lala's parents. They were going to live like this for a few days, until they had to hand over the house, then for a time they would be at Martín's parents' house, and from there, once they had their visas, they would go north.

"Who took my Barbies?" Ariana asked her mother.

"They aren't your Barbies any more." Ariana pursed her lips and tried not to cry. "People have to grow up, Ariana."

"They could have left me one," she whimpered.

"It would have been worse," said her father.

They went to bed. In the middle of the night, Ariana woke up. Finding her brother's mattress empty, she made a tour of what was left of her house. Among the bags that were due to be picked up the next day she found one in which, through the plastic, she could make out the shape of her Barbies. The sealed bag was labelled with a piece of paper that said "Rita Mansilla". Ariana knew her: she was the grandmother of one of her friends who lived nearby. She imagined this friend brushing her dolls' hair. One by one, stroking their manes. Meanwhile she, in Miami, would be spending the grandmother's money on all those much more interesting things that her mother claimed were to be found there – things she could not imagine, let alone name. She opened the bag. There were ten of them: five blonde Barbies, three brunettes and two redheads. The Barbie nurse was blonde, the same as her. It was her favourite. When she grew up, Ariana wanted to be a nurse, if they had them in Miami. They must have them. If not, she would come back to The Cascade to be with

Ariel. Or rather, back to Ariel, but not to The Cascade, because he definitely wouldn't keep living here, she thought. The bag with the Barbies also contained a pair of boots and three white pairs of briefs belonging to her mother. She went to her bedroom to get some scissors from her school rucksack, then, returning to the opened bag, she sat on the floor and began to cut off the dolls' hair, one by one, until all were shorn. Blonde curls mingled with dark and red ones on the pine floor. Clumps of hair in artificial colours were strewn all around her. She cut a lock of her own hair, from the fringe, and mixed it with the dolls' hair. Then she gathered it all up in her hands and put the bundle of hair into her pyjama pocket. She looked at her dolls for the last time, returned them to the bag – trying to avoid their contact with the briefs – then tied the knot and went back to sleep.

42

After his meeting with Alfredo Insúa, and that business of the viatication, El Tano had started thinking more than ever about insurance. And about death. Death was somehow abroad in the atmosphere. Two aeroplanes had knocked down the Twin Towers as though they were a house of cards, and nobody could shake off their bewilderment. On the day of the attack, El Tano's children were at home; the towers' collapse coincided with National Teachers' Day, so there was no school – but they went to a birthday party before lunch.

"Make sure that they haven't cancelled it because of the Towers," El Tano had said to Teresa.

"What's that got to do with anything, if was in New York?" she countered, and then went out with the children to the party that awaited them. And El Tano had the house to himself again, to carry on thinking.

His life policy was with Troost. But his policy did not have an early-withdrawal clause. It was the same sort of policy they provided for the company's executives all over the world. And he had been fine with that: it never occurred to him that he might need the money sooner. He had thought that everything would carry on as before. Or better. Every time he had changed jobs, throughout his professional life, it had been in order to get a better salary and a job with more responsibility and challenges. It wasn't as if he had AIDS or some other illness that would lead to a certain death, such as the ones with which Alfredo Insúa negotiated discounts on life insurance. But all life leads to certain death, he thought. A death at some given moment, be it the right moment, or the wrong one, but certain, nonetheless.

He sat down in front of the computer. Through the window he saw Teresa arrive home and get to work, exchanging the dead shrubs in their garden for new plants, fresh from the shop. The plants were still in plastic bags from the Green Life nursery. He read the words "Green Life" through the window. His father called and asked how those new projects were coming along.

"Really well," he lied.

"I wouldn't expect anything less. You learned in a good school," said his father, then he invited him on a trip to Cariló in October, so that they could find summer houses to rent together in January. "You are going to Cariló this year, aren't you?"

"Of course," he lied again. He hung up. On the computer, he pulled up the page of his bank account, typed in his name and code. He looked at the totals, then tapped these figures into his calculator and totted them up. He added the money that he had in a foreign bank account. They were bonds and had lost much of their market value, thanks to the increased country risk. If he waited, they might rally, but he wasn't sure that he could wait. He looked on his computer for the Excel spreadsheet on which he kept a budget of the family's expenditure. He divided the grand total of his bank balances by that of his monthly outgoings. Fifteen months. If they continued this rate of spending, they would start to have problems in fifteen months. All of them. The children, Teresa and himself. That wasn't even taking into account the sum they would need to pay for the house they rented every summer in Cariló. And summer was getting closer. He studied each of the different columns of the budget in turn, trying to identify an expense that could be eliminated. He could stop paying the school fees, as Martín Urovich had finally done, at the start of the year. Or eliminate the nanny, like Ronie Guevara had. But he was neither Martín Urovich nor Ronie Guevara. If he stopped paying communal expenses, he would appear on the list of debtors. And if he continued living in Cascade Heights, it was inconceivable that his children might stop their sporting activities and drop their tennis lessons, or that Teresa might stop going to the gym or having a weekly massage. Cinema, clothes, music, wine: it was all necessary if they wanted to maintain their lifestyle. And El Tano could not picture himself living any other sort of life. Martín Urovich's exile struck him as one of the many stupid actions on which his friend based the organization of his life. Martín opted to get out of the system by choosing another country, on another continent, with another language. There he would have to send his children to state school and dispense with a nanny; he'd have to rent a much smaller house, stop going to the cinema and taking tennis lessons. But at least he would be in Miami, far enough away that no one would witness his disgrace. Even if he ended up living in the most godforsaken neighbourhood, it was still Miami. That was cowardice on his part, thought El Tano. The worst kind of cowardice. He could not allow his family to fall from grace, here or anywhere else in the world. The point was not that one should fall unobserved, but that one should not fall at all. There must be something else he could do. He made the calculation again: fifteen months. Perhaps less, if the bonds continued to fall and he did not dare sell them. Fifteen. With a five-hundred-thousand-dollar life insurance policy that couldn't be touched unless something nasty happened. He knew that he was not worth that much. But company politics dictated that all Troost Chief Generals, anywhere in the world, be insured at that level. And when El Tano had left, he had negotiated the continuation of that policy for another eighteen months. That deadline was about to be reached. In three months' time it would be a year and a half since his Dutch employers had dismissed him. A year and a half without working. A year and a half waiting for some head-hunter to call him, sending off CVs, waiting for answers. A year and a half. Fifteen months. Five hundred thousand dollars. And with no date fixed for a certain death.

43

After falling down the stairs, that night on which he had been so fixated by his friends swimming in El Tano Scaglia's pool, Ronie had to be admitted to hospital. They rushed him to an examination room and took X-rays. I called home to let Juani know that we were going to take longer than I had expected and that the hurried note I had scribbled in the midst of Ronie's screams – "Daddy and I have gone to do something, but we'll be back very soon. If you need me, call the mobile. Everything's fine. I hope you are too, love Mummy" – was no longer sufficient. At least not for me. I knew that Juani would not call me and I wanted to hear from him. I needed to hear from him if I was to stay calm enough to look after Ronie and his broken leg. The answering machine came on. I hung up. I wondered if he might still, at this time of night, be running around barefoot with Romina, as he had been when we passed them before leaving The Cascade. Or if they had put their skates on again. Where they might have been running. Why. Were they fleeing someone or something? Or were they the ones giving chase? Perhaps they were running for the hell of it, with no particular destination. I tried to put these thoughts out of my head. I looked for a cigarette in my bag then, not finding any, I set off to look for a kiosk. Three men in white were coming down the corridor towards me. I recognized the duty doctor, and later I found out that his companions were a traumatologist and the surgeon who was going to operate on Ronie. They stopped when they came to me. Facing them alone – these three strangers in white coats – I felt for the first time that everything going on around me was more than I could take in. And the feeling extended beyond my husband's broken leg. But at that time I never suspected how far. Wanting to be clear, the men explained what they were going to do calmly and in unnecessary detail. It was not simply a matter of putting a cast on the broken leg and stitching up the wound, they said. This was an exposed fracture; El Tano would need an operation, under general anaesthetic, to reset the bones and put in pins. My face crumpled, my legs felt as though they might give way. The surgeon kept talking, word upon word – tibia, fibula, compromised articulation – but the traumatologist realized that I was upset and tried to reassure me. "It's almost a routine intervention, very straightforward, don't worry."

I nodded, without giving a reason for my pained expression, which had nothing to do with the operation, nor with my husband's suffering, nor even with any surgical risks. It was the pins. It horrifies me to think of objects being inserted into the body and not decaying with the rest of it. It has always horrified me. Foreign bodies within us, that survive us. Pieces of metal, ceramic or rubber that will endure long after their function has become obsolete. When everything around them is wasted and decomposing.

The day my father died, my mother got it into her head to whip out his false teeth – much to my horror. "You can't take out Daddy's teeth," I said. She replied: "It isn't Daddy, it's Daddy's corpse." We had a terrible row. My father's sudden death almost seemed less important than what would happen to his false teeth. "Why do you want them?" I shouted at her. "To remember him by," she said, apparently surprised that I should not understand. "You're disgusting!" I yelled at her. "Not half

244

as disgusting as the sight of his false teeth lying beside his dusty bones the day they have to be exhumed," she said. And by way of a curse, she added: "I hope it falls to you to disinter them and not to me."

And so it was. One afternoon they called from the Avellaneda cemetery. They needed someone from our family to authorize the exhumation of my father's bones, so that they could be reassigned to a smaller plot, because of limited space at the cemetery. By then I lived in Cascade Heights, and Avellaneda seemed very far away in time and space. I had hardly been there since we moved to the new house – the one we bought from Antieri's widow and where we live now. A member of the family had to be present during the exhumation, so I went. My mother by this stage had herself been scattered as ashes, in accordance with her last wishes. My father reposed in the earth. Until that day. And the sight of those teeth still clinging to a metal plate, in spite of the best efforts of worms and the passing years, evoked my mother's ironic smile more than it did my father. Pins, like teeth, would endure. And there they would remain, waiting for whoever dared disinter them. Then again, neither Ronie nor I, nor any of our friends in Cascade Heights, would come to rest at the Avellaneda, or at any other municipal cemetery. In private cemeteries there is no need to compress bones in order to make more room for death. You can always buy another plot. You can always make another cemetery. You can invent a new solution. There is enough land in the area to divide into plenty more parcels. But if that were not the case, if one day the private cemeteries were also obliged to make more room for death, or if one day we could no longer meet our expenses and we lost our plot, if someone telephoned one day requesting the presence of a relative during the compression of what was left of Ronie, that person – whether myself, Juani or my grandchildren – would come face to face with the pins.

They are immortal intruders, I thought, as I waited outside the operating theatre. And I thought of other examples. I made myself think them up, so as not to think about Ronie's operation or Juani, who was still not answering the telephone. A stent, a pacemaker, some sophisticated prosthesis especially brought from the United States or Germany. An IUD. No, not an IUD, because an elderly woman would not have one fitted, and to think of a still-fertile woman inside a grave upset me so much that I had to reject the example. I wondered if valuable items such as a pacemaker or a stent might be removed from the deceased before burial. A kind of recycling. It surprised me that nobody in The Cascade had ever mentioned such things to me. I would not let them remove Ronie's pins. Then I thought of silicone implants, too. Silicone is another intruder able to outlive its host. Implants would survive burial, the body's wastage, the damp soil, the worms. In my grave someone will one day find two silicone globes. For what they were worth... They will find silicone globes in the graves of almost all my female neighbours, too. I imagined the private cemetery where they buried the women from Cascade Heights sown with silicone globes, orphaned now from the breasts that had owned them, six feet below that immaculate lawn. Bones, mud and silicone. And teeth. And pins.

I went out into the garden to smoke. I lit a cigarette. After that, another. Then another. I called Juani again. He didn't answer. He must be at home, though. He'll be sound asleep and can't hear the phone, I thought. I wanted to think that he was sound asleep. But it was also possible that he was out and about. Or lying unconscious somewhere. Or he had come home and was sleeping soundly but not as a result of fatigue. From alcohol. Or that other thing. I find it hard to name it. Marijuana. *Cannabis* is what it said in the *American Health and Human Service* report that Teresa Scaglia gave me soon after finding out about the "difficult time you're going through". No, not that; he had promised not to touch it and I "must believe in my son, because he can do it". That is what the specialists brought into Cascade Heights to support families with "children at risk" said – that we had to believe in our children. But what did they know? That wasn't the problem – the problem was believing in ourselves.

The operation was a success, so the surgeon informed me. He told me about it in that same corridor, with his gown still on, as he removed his latex gloves. I waited for them to bring Ronie back to the room and for him to come round from the anaesthetic. I rang the house and this time Juani answered. I told him everything. He sounded strange, very alert – it was obvious that he had not been sleeping.

"Is something wrong?" I asked.

"No, nothing. I've got a headache."

"What's up? Did you eat something that disagreed with you?..." He didn't answer. "Or did you drink something?... What time did you get back?"

"Stop it, Mum," he interrupted.

"Ring me whenever you want." He didn't ring.

What with the anaesthesia and the tranquillizers, Ronie slept for the rest of the morning. I dozed in an armchair beside him. Finally I went downstairs to get some lunch. I didn't ring anyone to let them know what had happened. Neither clients nor friends. My mobile rang a few times but, after checking that it wasn't Juani, I didn't answer. At one point I did think of telephoning the club's guard to let him know where we were, but straight away I realized that that would be a nonsense. Perhaps it was a premonition. Because, as I was finishing my lunch in the hospital cafe, in came Dorita Llambías, who had just been visiting a friend of hers. She approached my table, shaking her head.

"What a terrible thing to happen, Virginia! What can you tell me about it?" She reached for my hand on the table and gripped it tightly. I realized that she was not talking about Ronie's accident.

"What are you talking about, Dorita?"

"What, haven't you heard?" she said, and I noted in her voice an unmistakable excitement at being the bearer of news. She drew nearer, the better to break it to me.

"Last night there was an accident at the Scaglias' house – an electrical problem. El Tano, Gustavo Masotta and Martín Urovich were found drowned in the swimming pool. In reality they weren't drowned – they were electrocuted. It seems they were electrocuted by an extension cord."

I could not begin to make sense of her words: it was as if everything around us were moving about. I held on to my chair so as not to fall off it.

"Can you believe it – grown men messing around with cables and water?"

"Were all three of them electrocuted?"

"Yes, it seems that the cable fell into the water and they died instantly."

Scenes from the previous night flashed before me, like a film reeling forwards. The open fridge in front of me; Ronie coming into the house after abandoning the Thursday night fixture at El Tano's; the stairs; the terrace; the lounger beside the balustrade; my lounger beside his; the silence; the lights in the Scaglias' pool; the ice cubes falling to the floor and slipping away; the jazz permeating the poplars' lament; and especially his silence, my irritation, his anger; the fall on the stairs; his howl of pain.

"Poor Teresa and the children. Who's ever going to want to get back in that pool now?" said Dorita.

I thought of Ronie fleeing from that house that night, as though he foresaw the tragedy. Ronie, another death-defying survivor. The same as his pins. "When God is not present, he just isn't and there's nothing we can do about it. But what a stupid way to go and die, no?"

"Very stupid," I said, and I went to find my husband.

44

Within the same hour that Ronie was discharged from hospital, his friends' bodies were travelling in caravan along the Pan-American highway to a private cemetery. Virginia pushed her husband – his leg now plastered – in the wheelchair without any help along the hospital corridors. She had requested this: that no one go with them. The time spent negotiating the path through the hospital garden to the car would help her prepare for the task in hand, she thought. When they arrived at the car, she put the brakes on the chair, moved to face Ronie, then crouched down in front of him, grasping his hands.

"There's something I have to tell you."

Ronie listened without saying anything. "The night before last there was an accident at the Scaglias' house."

Ronie shook his head. "El Tano, Gustavo and Martín all died of electrocution."

"No," said Ronie.

"It was a dreadful accident."

"No, no it wasn't." Ronie tried to stand up, but immediately fell back into his chair.

"Keep calm, Ronie."

"No, it wasn't like that. I know it wasn't." He began to cry.

"The gardener found them yesterday morning at the bottom of the pool." Ronie tried again to stand up, but Virginia stopped him. "Ronie, you mustn't put weight on your leg because of the —"

He interrupted her: "Take me to the cemetery."

"It won't do you any good."

"Take me to the cemetery or I'll walk there myself." This time he did stand up and it was all Virginia could do to stop him from taking a step.

"Are you sure you want to go?"

"Quite sure."

"Well then, let's go together," she said. She helped her husband into the car, then put the wheelchair in the boot and sat down at the wheel beside her husband. She looked at him, stroked his face and started the engine, ready to do as he asked.

45

It was a sunny day. Spring had come to the tulip poplars which, still leafless, abounded in great violet flowers. Some of us parked on the verge. A full fifteen minutes before the ceremony was due to start, the underground parking was already full and security guards had been stationed along the side of the road, so that we could safely leave our cars there.

"I didn't recognize you. Have you changed your car?"

Everyone was there. It would be quicker to name the absentees than to run through the list of all those present. The Lauridos were travelling in Europe: "After what happened with the Twin Towers, people are so paranoid that now everything's on offer; hotel rooms are going for a song – you have to grab these chances while you can"; the Ayalas were staying with their son in Bariloche; Clarita Buzzette was recovering from pneumonia. The entire administrative staff from The Cascade were there; the tennis teachers, the golf Starter. Nothing like this had ever happened to us before. Never had there been so great a misfortune within our gates.

"It defies belief..."

"Poor Teresa..."

"It was an electric shock, wasn't it?"

We waited beside the chapel for the bodies to arrive, casting glances at each other, unsure what to say. And yet we all said something. "Haven't seen you for months."

"Let's hope next time we meet in happier circumstances."

Someone asked after Ronie and Virginia Guevara. Somebody else said that he had been discharged from hospital that morning. We speculated on the chances of

Ronie coming to the funeral. "No, I don't think so. It would be a very traumatic experience for him."

"Poor thing, he's already been through enough."

"Who's got your kids today?"

The police had handed over the bodies in the shortest possible time. Aguirre, the Chief of Security at Cascade Heights, had spoken personally to the superintendent. "On his private line – he's a friend." There was no need to heap more distress on the widows. Doctor Pérez Bran, a long-standing member of the community, offered to speak to the presiding judge.

"And why did a judge have to be involved?"

"It's standard: there were three deaths." Pérez Bran knew him: he was moving various cases through his court. The judge assured him that the matter would be expedited. The police carried out routine inspections. "Why Culpable Homicide? If no one was to blame?…" They should call it "Unintentional Homicide", the word "culpable" is too misleading.

"And why 'homicide'? They ought to put 'accident'."

"That definition doesn't exist in the Code."

"Which code?"

"The Penal Code."

"Well they should add it; if the thing's an accident, it's an accident. Why don't people call things by their name in this country?"

"Is that El Tano's mother?"

"No idea."

They had wanted to listen to music. They were listening to music. Diana Krall, apparently. But El Tano had wanted it closer: he had pulled the cable, the stereo had detached itself and the extension cord had fallen into the swimming pool. "Didn't the switch trip? You know those appliances have to be checked at least once a year."

"The thermal overload tripped, but they were already dead."

"What is the thermal overload?"

"I thought you knew all about circuit breakers..."

"You know, that must be the mother. She has a look of El Tano about the face."

"Do you want me to tell you what I think killed them?"

"What?"

"That monstrosity Carmen Insúa cooked up with the photos."

"Oh please! Just thinking about it makes my skin crawl."

At eleven o'clock on the dot, three coffins arrived: El Tano's, Gustavo's and Martín's. Apparently it was Teresa's idea to have them buried in a row. In death, as in life, she said. They had been together on their last night together, as they were every Thursday, without fail. Ronie Guevara had had a miraculous escape. He had gone home earlier – some say because he felt unwell, others that he argued with El Tano. For whatever reason, Fate had not chosen him to die that night with the others.

"Nobody dies before his time is up."[7]

"Where have I heard that before?"

"This is a case in point."

Teresa had taken charge of all the arrangements, before and during the ceremony. She must have been on something. She looked awful, yet serene. She seemed

---

7   This remark was famously made by President Carlos Menem after emergency surgery on a blocked artery in 1993.

to be coping reasonably well. They say that she paid for Martín Urovich's plot. Lala would not have been able to meet that expense. When the three coffins entered the chapel, there was a bit of whispering among some people who were not from The Cascade. Apparently they were Martín's relatives, from the Jewish branch, who objected to the choice of officiant to bless his journey to the next world. But nobody said anything. Not even his parents, who wept in each other's arms. The three widows sat together in the front pew. Teresa and Lala arm in arm, Carla a little apart. From the pew behind, a friend not known to the rest of us stroked her back. El Tano's children, and Martín's, were weeping, supported by friends and relatives. The priest spoke of the Lord's call, of how difficult it was to understand that He should call people so young and of how one must learn to accept His wisdom. He invited us to recite the Lord's Prayer. Those of us who could intoned the words. It wasn't very many, considering the number of people who were present. When it came to "Forgive us our sins…" many of us uttered the older form: "forgive us our trespasses". And in the murmured prayer, there was a commingling of trespasses and sins, trespassers and sinners. We made the sign of the cross. A mobile rang; various people fumbled in their handbags and pockets, but the ringing continued. "Hello, I'm at a funeral… I'll ring you back." May the Lord receive Martín, Gustavo and Alberto into his glory, said the priest. We all looked at each other. "Alberto" meant nothing to us. God must receive El Tano into his glory. El Tano Scaglia.

Afterwards the priest announced the times of mass in his chapel at the weekend. "Remember that the one on Saturday at 7 p.m. replaces Sunday's service." And he extended his sympathy to the bereaved widows, the relatives and friends. He was brief. They always are brief in those places. And monotone, lacking intonation, like a registrar performing the last marriage of the day in his office. It would have been unbearable to spend much more time in there. The chapels in cemeteries are very small. And inside this one there were three coffins, three widows, too many people who did not know the Lord's Prayer, the smell of flowers, weeping.

We walked in a group along the cobbled path. On either side, the freshly cut grass looked immaculately green. As we walked, our procession was joined by various latecomers. All of them silent. All of them wearing dark glasses. Our halting steps marked a beat for the coffin-bearers. A funeral march. Some cries were sharper than others. Some cries were younger: the cries of children. At the end of the path we came to the place where three graves had been dug. Beside them were green carpets. The cemetery workers stood beside the mechanism that would be used to lower the coffins into the graves. We grouped around the three pits. The administrative staff from Cascade Heights, the tennis teachers and the Starter kept a discreet distance. Alfredo Insúa said a few words: "I speak, not as the president of Cascade Heights, but as a friend." It was his first public speech since the elections which had named him president of the Council of Administration of our community. He stood next to Teresa as he spoke, firmly holding her hand. El Tano's mother cried out in the midst of her tears. And Urovich's bent down to embrace her son's coffin. Alfredo spoke of the pain that would linger in The Cascade, but also of "the pride in having known them, of having had them as neighbours and friends, of having shared games of tennis, conversations, country walks. The history of Cascade Heights is graven with their names." Someone automatically greeted this speech with applause and more clappers followed suit, but others joined in only tentatively, and there were some who wondered if it was even appropriate to clap at a funeral, so the applause was short-lived. Then the cemetery workers turned the handles and the three coffins descended together. El Tano's mother cried out once more. Carla walked forwards to throw some earth into her husband's grave. El Tano's children threw in some flowers that were passed to them by Insúa's new wife. Urovich's daughter hugged her mother's legs and would not look up while her father's coffin was being lowered down. Someone led El Tano's mother away. Now Lala kneeled down, embracing her daughter and weeping. The workers allowed a few more seconds' lamentation, then they pulled the green carpets over the open pits in the ground. Now each of us went up to kiss the widows. The bravest among us first. And then we hugged their children. We hugged one another. "I can't believe it," someone said. "I can't believe it either," people replied.

Finally, we drifted away from the graves and took the path back to the cars. Teresa and her children got into El Tano's Land Rover, but she was not driving – it was a brother or a brother-in-law, doubtless someone from the family, because we didn't recognize him. Carla left with a friend. And Lala with Martín's parents.

A few of us were left, still making our goodbyes in the car park, when Ronie arrived. In a wheelchair pushed by his wife. His leg was in plaster. He was dry-eyed. So was she. But their expressions would tear out the heart of anyone bold enough to look at them. Ronie's eyes were fixed straight ahead, as if willing people not to stop him, not to say anything. A futile hope. Dorita Llambías went straight up to him and squeezed his hand. "Be strong, Ronie." And Tere Saldívar placed her hand on Virginia's shoulder. "We're here whenever you need us." She nodded, but did not stop.

"They're beside the tub of fuschia Alpine violets," someone pointed out, but Mavi was already walking on as if she knew where to go, retracing our own footsteps on the path. Every so often the wheelchair got caught in the cobbles and she wrestled the chair back and forth to free the wheels, but she never stopped. We watched them as they went on. They did not pause until they reached the three open graves covered with the green carpet. Then Mavi positioned her husband's chair beside them and stepped back a few paces. Ronie, with his back to us, in line with the three graves, completed the quartet.

46

We got home at about lunchtime. Juani wasn't there, and that was something else to worry about. I made Ronie comfortable in the living room, positioning his wheelchair in front of the window that looks onto our grounds. "Would you like some tea?" He said that he would and I went to the kitchen to make it. I screwed up the courage to ring the Andrades' house. Juani was there, with Romina, and that made me feel a bit better. I poured two cups of tea and took them on a tray to the living room. The wheelchair was empty.

"Ronie!" I screamed. I searched frantically for him downstairs, then I went into the garden, as far as the street, looking in all directions. He could not have got very far with one leg in plaster. I went back into the house. I shouted his name again. I couldn't make sense of it – until I saw the staircase. Ronie was up on the terrace, clutching the balustrade, holding up his plastered leg and shaking from the effort of having hopped his way upstairs on the uninjured leg. He was looking at the Scaglias' swimming pool, behind the poplars. I approached him quietly, almost noiselessly. I put my arms around him. I couldn't remember how long it had been since I had last embraced my husband. He caught my hand and squeezed it hard. He began to sob, softly at first and then harder. Then he made an effort to calm down. He turned to face me, looked in my eyes and, still holding my hand, took me back to that night, the 27th of September 2001, when he was eating dinner with his friends at El Tano's house.

They had eaten pasta, home-made and cut into ribbons by El Tano himself. With tomato and basil. Afterwards they played *Truco*[8] – one game, two, three. And they drank, a lot. Ronie doesn't remember who was

---

8 *Truco*, a popular card game in Argentina and in several other Latin American countries, is usually played by two teams of two players. The game's appeal lies in the complicated bidding and in the devices used to trick one's opponent. Bids can be accepted (*quiero*), rejected (*no quiero*) or raised in a number ways. Players may also deliberately deceive their opponents, or make secret signs to their partners. To that end, the game is played in distracting and noisy conditions. Whereas poker players maintain a tense silence, *Truco* players continue to talk and make jokes while they play. Calls of '*truco*', '*envido*' and '*flor*' refer to different combinations of cards and alter the stakes accordingly. '*Retruco*' raises the value of the round being played. '*Vale cuatro*' increases it to the maximum. If the trick is a tie, '*parda*', it belongs to neither side. '*Voy callado*' means to play a card without calling anything. '*Maldón*' or 'misdeal' is a call for a new hand.

winning, but he does remember that Martín and Gustavo were playing against El Tano and himself. While they played, the subject of Martín's move to Miami came up. He doesn't remember the context, but it was El Tano who raised the subject. You have to stay, he said. What for? To die with dignity. I stopped feeling any dignity a long time ago. Because you're not going about things the right way. I've got the worst luck: just when I decide to go to Miami, they blow up the Twin Towers. Shall we play a trick? What are you going to Miami for? So that they can put anthrax in your water? *Truco.* To blow the few savings you have left? Pass me the wine. You're going to end up getting any job you can, while your wife cleans the house. *Quiero.* And if it comes to it, someone else's house too, for extra cash. I've got no choice. Yes you do. What? Stay here. You can't make a life here any more. Who said anything about life? Who wants more wine? If you can't live with dignity, die with dignity. Silence. Whose go is it? All four of us have the chance to make a grand exit. An exit? To get out of this. I don't understand you. I'm planning a grand exit and I'm giving you the chance to join me. Hey, I've still got a job, Gustavo laughs. And dignity? El Tano asks. *Envido. Envido.* Why do you say that? Twenty-nine. For no reason. What do you know? Me about you? What's important is what we all know about ourselves. *Voy callado.* And what each of us does when no one sees us. *Truco.* Or when we think that no one sees us. *Quiero retruco.* Why do you say that? I am going to die with dignity, tonight, alone or with you all. Tano, you're having a laugh, right? Me? Not at all, Ronie. *Parda.* No one here lacks a motive to do the same as me. Silence. It's in your hand, Tano. I have a five-hundred-thousand-dollar life insurance policy. That's a pretty dignified sum… *Truco*. If I die, my family can claim the premium and continue to live as they always have done, exactly as they always have done. *No quiero*. You're well prepared, Tano. You also have life insurance, Martín, worth less money, but still more than enough. You're wrong: I don't have life insurance. Yes you do, I pay for it along with your health insurance. *Maldón*. Silence. For how much did you take it out? Hey guys, can you stop this fucking around? *Envido*. I've never been more serious in my life. *Real envido. No queremos*. It's important that people don't suspect. Suspect what? That it was a suicide – otherwise they won't pay out. It has to look like an accident. Shall we go for a *truco*? No, we're folding. So have you forked out for life insurance for me, too? Gustavo asks. No, in your case it's better not to have a policy. Is this some sort of wind-up? Exactly what is my "case"? Hit your wife for real. Silence. Ronie takes a drink. The way you hit her at the moment is nothing; hit her hard, where it hurts: in her pocket. Gustavo throws his cards on the table. He gets up, walks around the table. He sits down again. Everyone in the club knows, Gustavo; your neighbours lodged a complaint in the duty room the last time, because of the shouting. Pick up the cards and deal, come on. I'll deal. Cut. I don't hit her. *Envido y truco. No quiero el primero, quiero el segundo. Quiero retruco*. I don't hit her. *Quiero*. There was one time, things got out of hand, but I don't hit her. *Quiero vale cuatro*. At least five off-the-record complaints have been lodged with Security. That's not me, it's not like that, she makes me do it… Have you got the ace, too? Shit. Pour me some wine. So how would it be? Come on boys, change the subject, Ronie insists. It's not me that wants to go to Miami – I'm doing it for them. Kill yourself for them, and leave them more money than you would ever make in the rest of your life, in Miami or anywhere else. Gustavo drinks: one glass, then another one. Let's make this good, says El Tano. I really don't appreciate this kind of wind-up. It's not a wind-up, Ronie. I don't believe you. So, how would it be? We die electrocuted, in the pool. First we go for a swim, we're drunk, we listen to music and when I want to pull the stereo closer, from the water, the extension lead falls out and slips into the water. Two hundred and twenty volts shoot through the water at the speed of lightning. We're killed outright. We all have to be touching the side, to be grounded. I've over-ridden the trip switch so that when the thermal overload jumps on the external circuit, we'll be home and dry. In the pool, but dry? Urovich laughs. You're all out of your minds. Don't make the wrong choice, Ronie. And you're the craziest of all. The craziest can also be the most clear-sighted, Ronie. Sometimes only a few of us see the reality: companies collapse, foreign capital leaves, more and more people fight over one managerial position – and you say I'm the madman? Have a drink. You should read up on oriental culture – the Chinese, the Japanese – they certainly know the value of ending one's life at the right moment. And since when have you been a fan of oriental culture, Tano? Ever since he started growing the goatee beard, jokes someone, not Ronie. Perhaps one day, one year, when this country is run by other people, things will change and we'll become a serious country. But by then it will be too late for us; we'll be too old to enjoy it. We can't save the house or the car, but we can save our families from falling. I'm not falling. You've already hit the ground, Gustavo. You're already broken into pieces. Shall I deal? I'm not playing any more. Don't leave us like this, Ronie. Go on, one more hand. Cut. And if the plan doesn't work? If they find out? *Flor.* About what? About the deception? Four victims of electrocution can't be suspected of suicide. Quite apart from being mad, you fancy yourself much more intelligent than everyone else, says Ronie. I don't know if intelligent is the right word, but this isn't Guyana and I'm not Jim Jones. No one will suspect. *Truco.* Are you in or not, Ronie? You're sick in the head, Tano. Is that it, or do you not want to confront your own reasons for suicide? I'm not as scared of falling as you are, Tano. True, I do believe that falling doesn't worry you, and that's why you don't want to face up to your own motive for killing yourself. It doesn't interest me: it would be your motive, not mine. It must at least interest you. You're unhinged. Do it for your son, Ronie. Don't get my son involved in this shit. Your son's already deep in shit. Ronie stands up and grabs him by his shirt collar. Martín and Gustavo separate them as best they can. They make them sit down. El Tano and Ronie watch each other. You're a failure, Ronie, and that's why your son takes drugs. Ronie moves to grab him again. You fucking son of a bitch. Let him go, Ronie. I'll beat the crap out of you. That's enough. Never mention my son again. He lets him go. How far do you plan to take this, Tano? There's no further to go – I'm already there. Don't get me wrong, Ronie. You've got no limit. No, that's true. You're a bastard. I'm not the one selling drugs to your son. Neither am I. But you're showing him the way to failure. And what is failure, Tano? Am I a failure? What about you? Is electrocuting yourself going to save you from being a fraud? He looks at the other two. And you, what kind of failures are you? My kind, or El Tano's? You should leave, Ronie, says

Martín. That would be best, Ronie, says Gustavo. Off you go, Ronie, they tell him. They've given you their answer. They've given me their answer. You're not equal to the circumstances. No, I'm not. What about you two? You can go home, Ronie, seriously, says Gustavo and he accompanies him to the door. Ronie goes. To his house, to his terrace. Ours. Convinced that they're mad, drunk, idiots but that – when it comes to it – they won't do it, that this will all have been hot air, that when the moment comes a jot of sanity will prevail and there will be no swimming, or music, there will be no cable, or electricity, or suicide. He's sure of it. They were right to ask him to leave; Gustavo and Martín will handle El Tano better than he could. Or perhaps the three of them have all conspired in this ruse and now they're laughing about it and pouring another drink. Ronie reaches his home and climbs the stairs. He sits down and waits, certain that events on the other side of the road will take a different course. However, upstairs on the terrace, while he drinks and the ice slides on the tiled floor, while Virginia talks to him and he fails to listen, while that sad, contemporary jazz plays and the poplars whisper in the heavy night air, what he sees through the trees shows him how wrong he was.

47

A week after the funeral, Ronie and Virginia invite the widows to their house. They needed this lapse of time to prepare themselves for the meeting. Carla and Teresa arrive punctually. Lala comes twenty minutes later. The first exchanges are difficult – impossibly painful – the first glances, the first words, the first silences. Virginia serves coffee. The women ask about Ronie's plaster cast. He tells them about the operation, the treatment, the rehabilitation. About his fall. He tells them about his fall without yet telling them why he fell. But it's enough to introduce the subject of that night. The moment has come, and he begins, once he has told them about the broken bone and the endless blood and how Virginia got him into the car and how they crossed paths with Teresa on the way out of the club. "I didn't think they were capable of it," he says, "I didn't think they would really do it." And they don't understand him. So Ronie tells them, as best he can, about El Tano's plan, about Martín Urovich's depression, of how El Tano had begun to tell a story, the story of his own death, to which Ronie had not given any credence. He does not mention the motives he used to convince Gustavo. There's no need. Carla weeps. Lala repeats "son of a bitch" several times, without clarifying whether she is referring to her own husband or to El Tano. Or to Ronie. Teresa cannot take it all in.

"But then, it wasn't an accident?"

"I don't think so."

"Did they commit suicide?"

"Yes, they committed suicide."

"That can't be, he never said anything to me," says Teresa.

"Son of a bitch," says Lala again.

"He must have thought that it would be best for you and the kids," says Virginia.

"He didn't think; El Tano's the one who does the thinking," says Lala, in the present tense, as though El Tano were still alive.

"I don't think any of us realized early enough how sick El Tano was," Ronie tries to explain.

"But he wasn't sick; we had projects – we were about to go on holiday," says Teresa, still without understanding.

"What about me?" Carla asks. Nobody answers. "How did El Tano persuade Gustavo?" she asks again.

"I don't know," says Ronie. "I thought that he had failed to persuade him."

"My God," she says, sobbing.

"I'm sorry. I would have preferred to spare you this distress, but you needed to know," says Ronie, as though justifying himself.

"Who says we needed to know?" asks Lala. Carla can't stop crying. Virginia goes over to her and takes her hand. They embrace. Lala leaves the room, slamming the door.

Teresa still cannot fit all the pieces together. "He wasn't ill. I swear he wasn't ill."

The four of them fall into a long silence that is interrupted only by Carla's sobbing. And then Teresa asks, "Are you sure of what you're saying?"

"Absolutely sure." Silence again and then El Tano's wife wants to know: "And does this change things somehow?"

"It is the truth," answers Ronie. "It doesn't change anything else but this: that now you know the truth."

Not two hours have gone by since the meeting in which Ronie told the widows about the events of that night, when Ernesto Andrade and Alfredo Insúa arrive at the house. They want to speak to him alone. They make this clear without actually saying it, so Virginia goes to the kitchen and takes longer than necessary to make coffee, hoping to avoid the disagreeable intimation that this conversation is "not for ladies". They begin by talking about something else.

"Does anyone know what level the country risk reached today?" Nobody knows.

"Things are getting sticky. If you've got money in the bank, take it out, Ronie – I've got it on good authority."

"All I've got in the bank is debts."

"I hope they're in pesos."

"Did you hear anything about safety deposit boxes?"

And so on, until finally they arrive at the subject they've come to discuss. "Does anyone else, other than you and Virginia, know about this business of the supposed suicide?" asks Andrade.

"Up until now I've only spoken about it to Lala, Carla and Teresa."

"Why do you say up until now?"

"I don't know – because that's the way it is, because that's what I've done up until now."

"Ronie, it can't have been a suicide."

"Yes, I know it's hard to understand."

"Never mind understanding, Ronie, it's just a fact: there simply was no suicide."

"But I was there, I heard them plan it – except that I didn't believe it, otherwise..."

"Then don't believe it now, either – that suicide helps no one," says Insúa. "Tell me: do you realize that if it was suicide, those women will be left with no roof over their heads?"

Ronie does not answer.

"You understand what I'm talking about, don't you?"

"How would I not understand when El Tano himself explained it to me?"

"Of course, you're right. We're giving the widows a hand sorting out all this mess they're landed in. Ernesto with the legal stuff and me with the insurance."

"Not with Carla, because she's been very distant and won't accept any help," Insúa clarifies.

"What it comes down to is this: if they can't cash in the insurance, they're completely screwed, Ronie," Andrade resumes. "If there's the slightest suspicion of suicide, however absurd, the company will start checking, the floodgates will open and those poor women will never see a penny, as long as they live."

"I never even thought about the insurance."

"That's understandable. You've been deeply affected by this business. It's no wonder you're not seeing the whole picture, but this requires a lot of clear thinking and luckily we're here for that."

Virginia brings in the coffee. The three men clam up. She passes each one his cup, exchanges a glance with her husband and goes back out with the empty tray. "So, do you see how things stand, Ronie?"

"I only wanted them to know the truth."

"Yes, we realize that, but the world is full of good intentions, Ronie, and, leaving aside the question of whether or not you did the right thing, because – what do I know if it's better for those women to think that their husbands were electrocuted accidentally or deliberately, right? But leaving that aside... leaving that... now I can't remember what I was going to say... It'll come back any minute."

"What's paramount is that the women get their hands on the insurance right away, Ronie."

"That's what I was going to say."

"I thought that they deserved to know the truth."

"Maybe they do – who knows? – I'm no expert on psychology. Maybe knowing that truth can help them turn the page on this incomprehensible tragedy and realize that their husbands were almost... well, heroes."

"What do you mean?" says Ronie, astonished.

"You've got to have balls to do what those boys did."

"They killed themselves to leave their families with something. Isn't there something heroic about that?"

Ronie listens as each one says more or less the same thing, repeating themselves. He says nothing. He stirs the sugar into his coffee and thinks. He thinks: I was not heroic – I was a coward; or rather – he corrects himself – they were cowards because, otherwise, what does that make me? Another kind of coward, or a failure, like El Tano said, someone clutching pathetically onto life. Or – what? All of those things; none of those things.

"We need to know we can rely on your silence," says Andrade firmly. Ronie looks up from his cup and catches sight of Juani, who is watching them from the landing. The men follow his gaze and see him too. "And on the silence of all your family."

"The widows are depending on it. We can't let them down."

"The worst thing would be for those men to have killed themselves for nothing."

Ronie stands up as best as his cast will allow. He looks at Juani and then at the men sitting opposite. "I've got the message; now I need to rest," he tells them.

"We can count on you, then." Ronie doesn't answer; the men don't move. Juani comes down a few more steps. "Is it fair to say we can leave it at that?"

Juani walks towards his father. Ronie tries to walk towards the door on his cast, hoping to steer his guests out. He stumbles and Juani catches him. The men still have not moved. "Didn't you hear my father? It's time to leave," says Juani.

Andrade and Insúa look at him and then at Ronie. "Think about it, Ronie. You don't gain anything by broadcasting the details."

"I'm not out to gain anything: that's what you don't seem able to understand."

"Think about it."

The men make their way to the door, unaccompanied. Juani does not move from his father's side. From the kitchen door, Virginia watches them leave.

48

I looked at my husband and son, standing together. "What are we going to do?" I asked.

"We've already done what we had to do," Ronie answered.

But Juani looked at us both: "And what if that weren't the truth?" We didn't understand. "Come upstairs – I want to show you something," he said.

We helped Ronie up the stairs. In Juani's room, sitting on the window frame waiting for us, was Romina. I hadn't known that she was there. She was holding her father's digital video camera. Juani asked us to sit on the bed. The television was on and a reporter was announcing an imminent attack on the part of the United States against the country thought to be responsible for the Twin Towers atrocity. "Our soldiers are ready and they will make us proud," announced their president, from the screen. Juani took the video camera over to the television. In a few seconds he plugged in some cables, unplugged others and replaced the image of the president with filmed material from the camera. Romina acted as assistant, handing him the necessary cables. At first I did not notice what it was he was showing us, so impressed was I by my son's technological dexterity. It would have taken me a whole day to sort out that connection, even supposing I could have done it at all. It was Ronie's expression and the way he clutched his head, his eyes fixed on the screen, that made me focus on the image before me. The picture was rather shadowy, but there was no doubting what it showed: the Scaglias' swimming pool.

It was filmed from above, as though the person holding the camera had climbed to his vantage point. "We go up trees," said Juani and now I realized that those obstructing shadows were leaves. Martín Urovich was already lying in the water in a starfish pose, while holding onto a float. He held onto the float with one hand and onto the side of the pool with the other. El Tano was positioning a hi-fi system close to the stairs, on top of the Travertilit tiles. "The stereo," said Ronie, and we both knew what he meant. The extension cable had been trailed across the ground from a socket over on the veranda. El Tano passed the long-handled net they used to remove leaves from the pool under the cable, then wound this around it, leaving the end of the handle close to the edge of the pool. Very close to him. Gustavo was sitting on the side, with his feet in the water. The distance was such that one could not be sure if he was crying, but the position of his body, its slight tremor and certain almost imperceptible spasms strongly suggested that to be the case.

When El Tano had finished arranging everything, he got into the water and drank from one of the three glasses that were lined up beside the pool. A branch moved, covering for an instant the camera's lens. Then El Tano appeared again, talking to Gustavo. We couldn't hear what he was saying, but Gustavo was shaking his head. El Tano's harangue became increasingly energetic and, faced with the other man's refusal, he grabbed his arm hard. Gustavo shook him off. Once again, he tried to grab him and, once again, Gustavo freed himself. El Tano scolded him as though he were a child – we couldn't hear his words, but the gestures were unmistakable. Gustavo broke down: he sobbed, with his elbows resting on his knees and his hands covering his face. Now his weeping was manifest. His shoulders heaved to the rhythm of his uneven breathing. El Tano grabbed him by the neck and pulled him into the pool and then immediately – almost as though this were part of the same movement – he used the cane to yank the extension cord out of the hi-fi. Urovich was still floating. Gustavo came up to the surface in spite of El Tano's efforts to hold his head under with his free hand. But Gustavo was stronger and younger than El Tano, and was able to shake him off once more as he tried to reach the edge of the pool. He grabbed the edge. It was too late: he couldn't get out. With his other hand – not the one that had pulled Gustavo in and held him under – El Tano submerged the bare end of the extension cable close to himself, so that electricity surged through the pool. The bodies went rigid, then sank. The water churned. And there was total darkness. All the outside lights went out and the music stopped. Then the camera started to register crazy images, very dark, scarcely visible: the leaves on the tree from which Romina and Juani were now descending; the ground beneath their feet as they ran. "What are we going to do?" Romina was heard saying on the tape. Then the dark ground again, the noise of running, of hurried breathing. A black background.

Ronie and I remained quiet, without finding words to say. Juani and Romina waited. "Could we have saved them?" asked Juani.

"He killed him," said Ronie, incredulous.

"Could we?" insisted my son. I glanced at Ronie. I knew what he was thinking and I quickly said: "Nobody could have."

Ronie turned to Romina. "Has your father seen this?"

"What for?" she said. "He would conceal it in the same way as he would a suicide – a murderer's widow can't claim insurance either."

We fell silent again; none of the four was bold enough to speak his or her mind. "What happens next, Dad?" my son finally asked. "Do we take this to the police?"

"They'll never forgive us," Ronie said quickly.

"Who?" Juani insisted.

"Our friends, the people we know," I answered.

"Is that so important?" my son asked.

"I'm scared of what could happen to us," his father replied.

"Whatever was going to happen to us has already happened, Dad," said Juani and his eyes filled with tears. Romina took a step forwards and put her arms around him, pressing all of her body against his. "So, what do we do then?" he asked again.

"I don't know," answered Ronie. Juani looked at me, waiting for me to say something. His damp eyes locked onto mine. I looked down. I felt helpless and alone. A widow in all but fact.

"I don't know," Ronie said again.

And Juani said, "You don't know? There are times when you have no choice but to know. You know even if you don't want to. You're on one side or the other. There's no alternative: pick your side."

Ronie was speechless, so I spoke for him. I asked Juani to help his father down the stairs. Romina followed us. The three of us got him into the jeep. Carefully I extended his plastered leg, then bent it again before shutting the door. I walked round to the other side and got in behind the wheel. I looked at Ronie: he was gazing ahead, at nothing in particular. Neither he nor I were sure of what we were about to do, but Juani was, and I was not prepared to let him do it alone.

I looked in the rear-view mirror: Juani had his camera around his neck and was holding Romina's hand. I turned the key and the engine started; I moved the gear stick and we rolled forwards, towards the exit barrier. Looking around gave me a strange sensation: it was already October in the first year of the new century, and spring felt out of kilter. The double bridal wreath spirea, which usually lasts until well into November, had already disappeared and some houses were splashed with the different whites of lilies and magnolias. That was strange – usually you don't see these flowers until much later in the summer. But there they were. As if Nature had intuited that December was already in the air.

When we arrived at the barrier, my hands were sweating. I felt as though I were in one of those films where the illegal immigrants have to cross a border.

Ronie was pale. The guard warned us: "Head straight to the highway without going through Santa María de los Tigrecitos; don't take that road, there's a security alert."

"What's happened?" I asked.

"Things are looking ugly."

"Have they closed the road?"

"I couldn't tell you, but even the people of Tigrecitos themselves are making barricades. They're frightened outsiders are going to come."

"Who?" I asked.

"The people from the shanty towns, I suppose. Apparently they've been looting places on the other side of the highway. But don't worry: we're prepared for it here. If they come, we'll be waiting for them." And he nodded towards two other guards who were standing to one side, next to a bed of azaleas, armed with rifles.

I looked ahead at the road leading to the highway: it was deserted. I swiped my card over the electronic reader and the barrier lifted. In the rear-view mirror the eyes of Juani and Romina watched me. Ronie tapped my thigh to get my attention. He looked terrified.

I asked him:

"Are you scared to go out?"

BACK TO THE COAST

Saskia Noort

Maria is a young singer with money problems, two children from failed relationships and a depressive ex-boyfriend. Faced with another pregnancy, she decides not to keep the baby, but after the abortion, threatening letters start to arrive. She flees from Amsterdam to her sister's house by the coast, a place redolent with memories of a childhood she does not want to revisit. But when the death threats follow her to her hiding place, Maria begins to fear not only for her life, but also for her sanity.

Saskia Noort is a bestselling author of literary thrillers. She has sold over a million copies of her first three novels.

PRAISE FOR SASKIA NOORT
AND *THE DINNER CLUB*

"A mystery writer of the heart as much as of the mind, a balance that marks her work with a flesh-and-blood humanity."
Andrew Pyper, author of *The Wildfire Season*

"Affairs, deceit, manipulation, tax dodges and murder – there's nothing Noort shies away from stirring into the mix, nicely showing off the sinister side of the suburbs." *Time Out*

"While there are echoes of Desperate Housewives here, this is closer to Mary Higgins Clark and is a good bet for her fans."
Library Journal Review

£8.99/$14.95/C$16.50
CRIME PAPERBACK ORIGINAL
ISBN 978-1-904738-37-4
www.bitterlemonpress.com

THE VAMPIRE OF ROPRAZ

Jacques Chessex

Jacques Chessex, winner of the prestigious Prix Goncourt, takes this true story and weaves it into a lyrical tale of fear and cruelty.

1903, Ropraz, a small village in the Jura Mountains of Switzerland. On a howling December day, a lone walker discovers a recently opened tomb, the body of a young woman violated, her left hand cut off, genitals mutilated and heart carved out. There is horror in the nearby villages: the return of atavistic superstitions and mutual suspicions. Then two more bodies are violated. A suspect must be found. Favez, a stableboy with blood-shot eyes, is arrested, convicted, placed into psychiatric care. In 1915, he vanishes.

PRAISE FOR JACQUES CHESSEX
AND *THE VAMPIRE OF ROPRAZ*

£6.99/$12.95/C$14.50
CRIME PAPERBACK ORIGINAL
ISBN 978-1-904738-33-6
www.bitterlemonpress.com

A NOT SO PERFECT CRIME

Teresa Solana

MURDER AND MAYHEM IN BARCELONA

Another day in Barcelona, another politician's wife is suspected of infidelity. A portrait of his wife in an exhibition leads Lluís Font to conclude he is being cuckolded by the artist. Concerned only about the potential political fallout, he hires twins Eduard and Borja, private detectives with a knack for helping the wealthy with their "dirty laundry". Their office is adorned with false doors leading to non-existent private rooms and a mysterious secretary who is always away. The case turns ugly when Font's wife is found poisoned by a marron glacé from a box of sweets delivered anonymously.

PRAISE FOR *A NOT SO PERFECT CRIME*

"The Catalan novelist Teresa Solana has come up with a delightful mystery set in Barcelona... Clever, funny and utterly unpretentious." *Sunday Times*

"Teresa Solana's book may be full of murder and mayhem, but it's also packed full of humour, acute observation, a complicated plot and downright ridiculousness... I cannot recommend it highly enough." *Oxford Times*

"Scathing satire of Spanish society, hilarious dialogue, all beautifully dressed up as a crime novel." *Krimi-Couch*

This deftly plotted, bitingly funny mystery novel and satire of Catalan politics won the 2007 Brigada 21 Prize.

£8.99/$14.95/C$16.50
CRIME PAPERBACK ORIGINAL
ISBN 978-1-904738-34-3
www.bitterlemonpress.com

DOG EATS DOG

Iain Levison

Philip Dixon is down on his luck. A hair-raising escape from a lucrative but botched bank robbery lands him gushing blood and on the verge of collapse in a quaint college town in New Hampshire. How can he find a place to hide out in this innocent setting? Peering into the window of the nearest house, he sees a glimmer of hope: a man in his mid-thirties, obviously some kind of academic, is rolling around on the living-room floor with an attractive high-school student... And so Professor Elias White is blackmailed into harbouring a dangerous fugitive, as Dixon – with a cool quarter-million in his bag and dreams of Canada in his head – gets ready for the last phase of his escape.

But the last phase is always the hardest... FBI agent Denise Lupo is on his trail, and she's better at her job than her superiors think. As for Elias White, his surprising transition from respected academic to willing accomplice poses a ruthless threat that Dixon would be foolish to underestimate...

PRAISE FOR IAIN LEVISON
author of *A Working Stiff's Manifesto* and *Since the Layoffs*

"The real deal... bracing, hilarious and dead on."
New York Times Book Review

"Witty, deft, well-conceived writing that combines sharp satire with real suspense." *Kirkus Reviews*

"There is naked, pitiless power in his work" *USA Today*

£8.99/$14.95/C$18.00
CRIME PAPERBACK ORIGINAL
ISBN 978-1-904738-31-2
www.bitterlemonpress.com